WHEN MERLE IN NO. 8 WON THE LOTTERY . . .

. . . A lot of people in the trailerpark suddenly needed money:

Bruce Severance, the long-haired kid who sold dope needed three hundred dollars fast, to get a very heavy dude off his back, he said. Noni Hubner, the college girl, was recuperating from her first nervous breakdown and wanted to do what her mother had so far refused to do—buy a proper gravestone for her father's grave; and Leon LaRoche, the bank teller, said he needed money to help pay his sick mother's hospital bills, but it came out (only as a rumor, however) that his mother was not ill and that he was spending money recklessly to support a young man supposedly going to college in Boston and whom Leon visited every weekend, practically. And then, finally, there was Marcelle Chagnon, the manager of the trailerpark, needing money to protect her job, because the Granite State Realty Development Corporation was billing her personally for the cost of replacing all the frozen pipes in trailer number 11, which Marcelle had neglected to drain last August. . . .

And then, well—then all the money was gone.

Also by Russell Banks

SEARCHING FOR SURVIVORS

FAMILY LIFE

HAMILTON STARK

THE NEW WORLD

THE BOOK OF JAMAICA

TRAILERPARK

CONTINENTAL DRIFT

TRAILERPARK

Russell Banks

BALLANTINE BOOKS · NEW YORK

Library of Congress Catalog Card Number: 81-7662

ISBN 0-345-33077-3

The following stories have appeared elsewhere: "The Right Way"
(*Boston Globe Magazine*), "Politics" (*Shenandoah*), "The Child
Screams and Looks Back at You" (*Fiction*), "Black Man and
White Woman in Dark Green Rowboat" (*Mississippi Review*), "The
Burden" (*Ploughshares*), "What Noni Hubner Did Not Tell the Police
About Jesus" (*Sun & Moon*), "Principles" (*Aspen Anthology*).

Manufactured in the United States of America

First Ballantine Books Edition: August 1986

for my mother

"A certain sense of tragedy, however attractive,
Is to be avoided.
Though there is no need to make a dogma of that . . ."
—*Bertolt Brecht*

Contents

The Guinea Pig Lady

THE STORY OF FLORA PEASE, HOW SHE GOT TO BE THE WAY she is now, isn't all that uncommon a story, except maybe in the particulars. You hear often in these small New Hampshire towns of a woman no one will deal with anymore, except to sell her something she wants or needs—food, clothing or shelter. In other words, you don't have a social relationship with a woman like Flora, you have an economic one, and that's it. But that's important, because it's what keeps women like Flora alive, and after all, no matter what you might think of her, you don't want to let her die, because if you're not related to her somehow, you're likely to have a friend who is, or your friend will have a friend who is, which is almost the same thing in a small town. And not only in a small town, either—these things are true for any group of people that knows its limits and plans to keep them.

1

When Flora Pease first came to the trailerpark and rented number 11, which is the second trailer on your left as you come in from Old Road, no one in the park thought much about her one way or the other. She was about forty or forty-five, kind of flat-faced and plain, a red-colored person, with short red hair and a reddish tint to her skin. Even her eyes, which happened to be pale blue, looked red, as if she smoked too much and slept too little, which, as it later turned out, happened to be true. Her body was a little strange, however, and people remarked on that. It was blocky and square-shaped, not exactly feminine and not exactly masculine, so that while she could almost pass for either man or woman, she was generally regarded as neither. She wore mostly men's clothing, a long, dark blue, wool overcoat or else overalls and workshirts and ankle-high workboots, which again, except for the overcoat, was not all that unusual among certain women who worked outside a lot and didn't do much socializing. But with Flora, because of the shape of her body, or rather, its shapelessness, her clothing only contributed to what you might call the vagueness of her sexual identity. Privately, there was probably no vagueness at all, but publicly there was. People elbowed one another and winked and made not quite kindly remarks about her when she passed by them on the streets of Catamount or when she passed along the trailerpark road on her way to or from town. The story, which came from Marcelle Chagnon, who rented her the trailer and who therefore ought to know, was that Flora was retired military and lived off a small pension, and that made sense in one way, given people's prejudices about women in the military, and in another way too, because at that time Captain Dewey Knox (U.S. Army, ret.) was already living at number 6 and so people at the park had got used to the idea of someone living off a military pension instead of working for a living.

What didn't make sense was how someone who seemed slightly cracked, as Flora came quickly to seem, could have stayed in the military long enough to end up collecting a pension for it. Here's how she first came to seem cracked. She sang out loud, in public. That's the first thing. She supposedly was raised here in Catamount, and though she had moved away when she was a girl, she still knew a lot of the old-timers in town, and she would walk into town every day or two for groceries and beer, singing in a loud voice all the way, as if she were the only person who could hear her. But by the time she had got out to Old Road, she naturally would have passed someone in the park who knew her, so she had to be aware that she wasn't the only person who could hear her. Regardless, she'd just go right on singing in a huge voice, singing songs from old Broadway musicals, mostly. She knew all the songs from *Oklahoma* and *West Side Story* and a few others as well, and she sang them, one after the other, all the way into town, then up and down the streets of town as she stopped off at the A & P, Brown's Drug Store, maybe Hayward's Hardware, finally ending up at the Hawthorne House for a beer before she headed back to the trailerpark. Everywhere she went, she sang those songs in a loud voice that was puffed up with feeling if it was a happy song or thick with melancholy if it was a sad song. You don't mind a person whistling or humming or maybe even singing to him- or herself under his or her breath while he or she does something else, sort of singing absentmindedly. But you do have to wonder about someone who forces you to listen to him or her the way Flora Pease forced everyone within hearing range to listen to her. Her voice wasn't half-bad, actually, and if she had been singing for the annual talent show at the high school, say, and you were sitting in the audience, you might have been pleased to listen, but at midday in June on Main Street, when you're coming out of the bank and about to step into your car, it can be a slightly jarring experience to see and hear a person who looks like Flora Pease come striding down the sidewalk singing in full voice about how the corn's as high as an elephant's eye. It can unsettle your entire day if you let it. And of course most people can't help but let it.

The second thing that made Flora seem cracked early on was the way she never greeted you the same way twice, or at least twice in a row, so you could never work out exactly how to act toward her. You'd see her stepping out of her trailer early on a summer day—it was summer when she first moved into the park, so everyone's first impressions naturally put her into summertime scenes—and you'd give a friendly nod, the kind of nod you offer people you live among but aren't exactly friends with, just a quick, downward tip of the face, followed by a long, upsweeping lift of the whole head, with the eyes closed for a second as the head reaches its farthest point back. Then, resuming your earlier expression and posture, you'd continue walking on, wholly under the impression that when your eyes were closed and your head tilted back Flora had given you the appropriate answering nod. But no, or apparently no, because she'd call out, as you walked off, "Good *morn*-ing!" and she'd wave her hands at you as if brushing cobwebs away. "*Wonderful* morning for a walk!" she'd bellow (her voice was a loud one), and caught off guard like that, you'd agree and hurry away. The next time you saw her, however, the next morning, for instance, when once again you walked out to Old Road to the row of mailboxes for your mail and passed her as, mail in hand, she headed back in from Old Road, you'd recall her greeting of the day before and how it had caught you off guard, and you'd say, "Morning," to her and maybe smile a bit and give her a friendly and more or less direct gaze. But this time what you'd get back would be a glare, a harsh, silent stare, as if you'd just made an improper advance on her. So you'd naturally say to yourself, "The hell with it," and that would be fine until the following morning, when you'd try to ignore her and she wouldn't let you. She'd holler the second she saw you, "Hey! A scorcher! Right? Goin' to be a scorcher today, eh?" It was the sort of thing you had to answer, even if only with a word, "Yup," which you did, wondering as you said it what the hell was going on with that woman?

YOU WOULDN'T BE ALONE IN WONDERING. EVERYONE IN THE park that summer was scratching his or her head and asking one another what the hell was going on with the woman in number 11. Doreen Tiede, who lived with her five-year-old daughter Maureen in number 4, which was diagonally across the park road from Flora Pease's trailer, put Marcelle on the spot, so to speak, something Doreen could get away with more easily than most of the other residents of the park. Marcelle Chagnon intimidated most people. She was a large, hawk-faced woman, and that helped, and she was French Canadian, which also helped, because it meant that she could talk fast and loud without seeming to think about it first and most people who were not French Canadians could not, so most people tended to remain silent and let Marcelle have her way. In a sense she was a little like Flora Pease—she was sudden and unpredictable and she said what she wanted to, or so it seemed, regardless of what you might have said first. She didn't exactly ignore you, but she made it clear that it didn't matter to her what you thought of her or anything else. She always had business to take care of. She was the resident manager of the Granite State Trailerpark, which was owned by the Granite State Realty Development Corporation down in Nashua, and she had certain responsibilities toward the park and the people who lived there that no one else had. Beyond collecting everyone's monthly rent on time, she had to be sure no one in the park caused any trouble that would hurt the reputation of the park, she had to keep people from infringing on other people's rights, which wasn't all that simple, since in a trailerpark people live within ten or fifteen feet of each other and yet still feel they have their own private dwelling place and thus have control over their own destiny, and she also had to assert the rights of the people in the park whenever those rights got stepped on by outsiders, by Catamount police without a warrant, say, or by strangers who wanted to put their boats into the lake from the trailerpark dock, or by ex-husbands who might want to hassle ex-wives and make their kids cry. These things happened, and Marcelle was always able to handle them efficiently, with force and intelligence, and with no sentimentality, which, in the end, is probably the real reason she intimidated most people. She seemed to be without sentimentality.

Except when dealing with Doreen Tiede, that is. Which is why Doreen was the one who was able to put Marcelle on the spot and say to her late one afternoon in Marcelle's trailer at number 1, "What's with that woman, Flora Pease? Is she a fruitcake, or what? And if she is, how come you let her move in? And if she isn't a fruitcake, how come she looks the way she does and acts the way she does?" There were in the park, besides Doreen, Marcelle and Flora, three additional women, but none of them could make Marcelle look at herself and give a straight answer to a direct question. None of them could make her forget her work and stop, even for a second, protecting it. Only Doreen could get away with embarrassing Marcelle, or at least with demanding a straight answer from her, and getting it, too, probably because both Doreen and Marcelle looked tired in the same way, and each woman understood the nature of the fatigue and respected it in the other. They didn't feel sorry for it in each other; they respected it. There were twenty or more years between them, and Marcelle's children had long ago gone off and left her—one was a computer programmer in Billerica, Massachusetts, another was in the Navy and making a career of it, a third was running a McDonald's in Seattle, Washington, and a fourth had died. Because she had raised them herself, while at the same time fending off the attacks of the man who had fathered them on her, she thought of her life as work and her work as feeding, housing and clothing her three surviving children and teaching them to be kindly, strong people despite the fact that their father happened to have been a cruel, weak person. A life like that, or rather, twenty-five years of it, can permanently mark your face and make it instantly recognizable to anyone who happens to be engaged in similar work. Magicians, wise men and fools are supposed to be able to recognize each other instantly, but so too are poor women who raise children alone.

They were sitting in Marcelle's trailer, having a beer. It was five-thirty, Doreen was on her way home from her job at the tannery, where she was a bookkeeper in the office. Her daughter Maureen was with her, having spent the afternoon with a babysitter in town next door to the kindergarten she attended in the mornings, and was whining for her supper. Doreen had stopped in to pay her June rent, a week late, and Marcelle had accepted her apology for the lateness and had offered her a beer. Because of the lateness of the payment and Marcelle's graciousness, Doreen felt obliged to accept it, even though she preferred to get home and start supper so Maureen would stop whining.

Flora's name had come up when Maureen had stopped whining and had suddenly said, "Look, Momma, at the funny lady!" and had pointed out the window at Flora, wearing a heavy, ankle-length coat in the heat, sweeping her yard with a broom. She was working her way across the packed dirt yard toward the road that ran through the center of the park, raising a cloud of dust as she swept, singing in a loud voice something from *Fiddler on the Roof*—"If I were a rich man . . ."—and the two women and the child watched her, amazed. That's when Doreen had demanded to know what Marcelle had been thinking when she agreed to rent a trailer to Flora Pease.

Marcelle sighed, sat heavily back down at the kitchen table and said, "Naw, I knew she was a little crazy, you know, but not like this." She lit a cigarette and took a quick drag. "I guess I felt sorry for her, and I'll be honest, I needed the money. We got two vacancies now out of twelve trailers, and I get paid by how many trailers got tenants, you know. When Flora come by that day, we got three vacancies, and I'm broke and need the money, so I look the other way a little and I say, sure, you can have number eleven, which is always the hardest to rent anyhow, because it's on the backside away from the lake and it's got number twelve and number ten tight next to it and the swamp behind. Number five I'll rent easy, it's on the lake, and nine should be easy too, soon's people forget about the suicide. It's the end of the row and has a nice yard on one side plus the tool shed in back. But eleven has always been a bitch to rent. So here's this lady, if you want to call her that, and she's got a regular income from the Air Force, and she seems friendly enough, lives alone, she says, has relations around here, she says, so what the hell, even though I can already see she's a little off, you know what I mean? Not quite right. I figure it was because of her being, you know, not interested in men, one of them kind of women, and I figure, what the hell, that's her business, not mine, I don't give a damn what she does or who she does it with, so long as she keeps it to herself, so I say, sure, take number eleven, thinking maybe she won't. But she did.''

Marcelle sipped at her can of beer, and Doreen went for hers. The radio was tuned quietly in the background to the country and western station from Dover. Doreen reached across the counter to the radio and turned up the volume, saying to no one in particular, ''I like this song.''

''That's 'cause you're not thirty yet, honey,'' Marcelle told her. ''You'll get to be thirty, and then you'll like a different kind of song. Wait.''

Doreen smiled from somewhere behind the veil of fatigue that covered her face. It was a veil she had taken several years ago, and she'd probably wear it until she either died or lost her memory, whichever came first. Anyone who wished to could see it, but only someone who wore it herself knew what it signified. She looked at her red-painted fingernails. ''What happens when you're forty and then fifty? You like a different kind of song then too?''

''Can't say for fifty yet, but yes, for forty. Thirty, then forty, and probably then fifty, too. Sixty, now, that's the question. That's probably when you decide you don't like any of the songs they play and so you go and sit in front of the TV and watch them game shows,'' she laughed.

''Well, I'll tell you,'' Doreen said, finishing her beer off and standing up to leave, ''that Flora Pease over there, let me warn you, she's going to be trouble, Marcelle. You made a big mistake letting her in the park. Mark my words.''

"Naw. She's harmless. A little fruity, that's all. We're all a little fruity, if you want to think about it," she said. "Some are just more able to cover it up than others, that's all."

Doreen shook her head and hurried her daughter out the screened door and along the road to number 4. When she had left, Marcelle stood up and from the window over the sink watched Flora, who swept and sang her way back from the road across her dirt yard to the door, then stepped daintily up the cinderblocks and entered her home.

THEN, IN AUGUST THAT SUMMER, A QUARREL BETWEEN Terry Constant and his older sister Carol, who were black and lived in number 10 next door to Flora, caused young Terry to fly out the door one night around midnight and bang fiercely against the metal wall of their trailer. It was the outer wall of the bedroom where his sister slept, and he was doubtlessly pounding that particular wall to impress his sister with his anger. No one in the park knew what the quarrel was about, and at that hour no one much cared, but when Terry commenced his banging on the wall of the trailer, several people were obliged to involve themselves with the fight. Lights went on across the road at number 6, where Captain Knox lived alone, and 7, where Noni Hubner and her mother Nancy lived. It wasn't unusual for Terry to be making a lot of noise late at night, but it was unusual for him to be making it this late and outside the privacy of his own home.

It was easy to be frightened of Terry if you didn't know him—he was about twenty-five, tall and muscular and very dark, and he had an expressive face and a loud voice—but if you knew him, he was, at worst, irritating. To his sister Carol, though, he must often have been a pure burden, and that was why they quarreled. A few years ago she had come up from Boston to work as a nurse for a dying real estate man who had died shortly after, leaving her sort of stuck in this white world, insofar as she was immediately offered a good job in town as Doctor Wickshaw's nurse and had no other job to go to anywhere else and no money to live on while she looked. Then her mother down in Boston had died, and Terry had come with his sister for a spell and had stayed on, working here and there and now and then for what he called "monkey-money" as a carpenter's helper or stacking hides in the tannery. Sometimes he and Carol would have an argument, caused, everyone was sure, by Terry, since he was so loud and insecure and she was so quiet and sure of herself, and then Terry would be gone for a month or so, only to return one night all smiles and compliments. He was skillful with tools and usually free to fix broken appliances or plumbing in the trailerpark, so Marcelle never objected to Carol's taking him back in—not that Marcelle actually had a right to object, but if she had fussed about it, Carol would have sent Terry packing. People liked Carol Constant, and because she put up with Terry, they put up with him too. Besides, he was good-humored and often full of compliments and, when he wasn't angry, good to look at.

Captain Knox was the first to leave his trailer and try to quiet Terry. In his fatherly way, embellished somewhat by his tousled white hair and plaid bathrobe and bedroom slippers, he informed Terry that he was waking up working people. He stood across the road in the light from his window, tall and straight, arms crossed over his chest, one bushy black eyebrow raised in disapproval, and said, "Not everybody in this place can sleep till noon, young man."

Terry stopped banging for a second, peered over his

shoulder at the man, and said, "Fuck you, honkey!" and went back to banging on the tin wall, as if he were hammering nails with his bare fists. Captain Knox turned and marched back inside his trailer, and after a few seconds, his lights went out.

Then the girl, Noni Hubner, in her nightgown, appeared at the open door of number 7. Her long, silky blond hair hung loosely over her shoulders, circling her like a halo lit from behind. A woman's voice, her mother's, called from inside the trailer, "Noni, *don't!* Don't go out there!"

The girl waved the voice away and stepped out to the landing, barefoot, delicately exposing the silhouette of her body against the light of the living room behind her.

Now the mother shrieked. "Noni! Come back! He may be on drugs!"

Terry had ceased hammering and had turned to stare at the girl across the road. He was wearing a tee shirt and khaki work-pants and blue tennis shoes, and his arms hung loosely at his sides, his chest heaving from the exertion of his noise-making and his anger, and he smiled over at the girl and said, "Hey, honey, you want to come beat on my drum?"

"You're waking everyone up," she said politely.

"Please come back inside, Noni! *Please!*"

The black man took a step toward the girl, and suddenly she whirled and disappeared inside, slamming the door and locking it, switching off the lights and dumping the trailer back into darkness.

Terry stood by the side of the road looking after her. "Fuck," he said, and then he noticed Flora Pease standing next to him, a blocky figure in a long overcoat, barefoot, and carrying in her arms, as if it were a baby, a small, furry animal.

"What you got there?" Terry demanded.

"Elbourne." Flora smiled down at the chocolate-colored animal and made a quiet, clucking noise with her mouth.

"What the hell's an Elbourne?"

"Guinea pig."

"Why'd you name him Elbourne?"

"After my grandfather. How come you're making such a racket out here?"

Terry took a step closer, trying to see the guinea pig more clearly, and Flora wrapped the animal in her coat sleeve, as if to protect it from his gaze.

"Listen, I won't hurt ol' Elbourne. I just want to see him. I ain't ever seen a guinea pig before," the man said.

"He's a lot quieter than you are, mister, I'll tell you that much. Now, how come you're making such a racket out here banging on the side of your house?"

"That ain't my house. That's my *sister's* house!" he said, sneering.

"Oh," Flora said, as if she now understood everything, and she extended the animal toward Terry so he could see it entirely. It was a long-haired animal shaped like a football with circular, dark eyes on the sides of its head and small ears and almost invisibly tiny legs tucked beneath its body. It seemed terrified and trembled in Flora's outstretched hands.

Terry took the animal and held it up to examine its paws and involuted tail, then brought it close to his chest, and holding it in one large hand, tickled it under the chin with his forefinger. The animal made a tiny cluttering noise that gradually subsided to a light drr-r-r, and Terry chuckled. "Nice little thing," he said. "How many you got, or is this the only one?"

"Lots."

"Lots? You got a bunch of these guinea pigs in there?"

Flora looked at him suspiciously, the way you'd look

at someone accusing you of deliberately withholding information. "I said so, didn't I?"

"Suppose you did."

"Here," she said brusquely, "give him back," and she reached out for the animal.

Terry placed Elbourne into Flora's hands, and she turned and walked swiftly on her short legs back around the front of her trailer. After a few seconds, her door slammed shut, and then the lights went out, and Terry was once again standing alone in darkness in the middle of the trailerpark. Tiptoeing across the narrow belt of knee-high weeds and grass that ran between the trailers, he came up close to Flora's bedroom window. "No pets allowed in the trailerpark, honey!" he called out, and then he turned and strolled off to get some sleep so he could leave this place behind him again early in the morning.

EITHER TERRY DIDN'T FIND THE OPPORTUNITY TO TELL anyone about Flora Pease having "lots" of guinea pigs in her trailer or he simply chose not to mention it, because it wasn't until after he had returned to the trailerpark, two months later, in early October, that anyone other than he had a clue to the fact that, indeed, there were living in number 11, besides Flora, a total of seventeen guinea pigs, five of which were male. Of the twelve females, eight were pregnant, and since guinea pigs produce an average of 2.5 piglets per litter, in a matter of days there would be an additional twenty guinea pigs in Flora's trailer, making a total of thirty-seven. About two months after birth, these newcomers would be sexually mature, with a two-month gestation period, so that if half the newborns were females, and if the either mothers continued to be fertile, along with the four other original females, then sometime late in De-

cember there would be approximately one hundred fifteen guinea pigs residing in Flora's trailer, of which
fifty-four would be male and sixty-one female. These
calculations were made by Leon LaRoche, who lived at
number 2, the second trailer on your right as you entered the park. Leon worked as a teller for the Catamount Savings and Loan, so calculations of this sort
came more or less naturally to him.

"That's a *minimum!*" he told Marcelle. "One hundred fifteen guinea pigs, fifty-four males and sixty-one
females. Minimum. And you don't have to be a genius
to calculate how many of those filthy little animals will
be living in her trailer with her by March. Want me to
compute it for you?" he asked, drawing his calculator
from his jacket pocket again.

"No, I get the picture," Marcelle scowled. It was a
bright, sunny, Sunday morning in early October, and the
two were standing in Marcelle's kitchen, Marcelle, in
flannel shirt and jeans, taller by half a hand than Leon,
who, in sport coat, slacks, shirt and tie, was dressed for
mass, which he regularly attended at St. Joseph's Catholic Church in Catamount. It was a conversation last
night with Captain Knox that had led young Leon to
bring his figures to the attention of the manager, for it
was he, the Captain, who had made the discovery that
there were precisely seventeen guinea pigs in Flora's
trailer, rather than merely "lots," as Terry had discovered, and the Captain was alarmed.

It hadn't taken much imagination for the Captain to
conclude that something funny was going on in number
11. When you are one of the three or four people who
happen to be around the park all day because you are
either retired or unemployed, and when you live across
the road from a woman who announces her comings and
goings with loud singing, which in turn draws your attention to her numerous expeditions to town for more

food than one person can consume, and when you notice her carting into her trailer an entire bale of hay and
daily emptying buckets of what appears to be animal
feces, tiny pellets rapidly becoming a conical heap behind her trailer, then before long you can conclude that
the woman is doing something that requires an explana-
tion. And when you are a retired captain of the United
States Army, you feel entitled to require that explana-
tion, which is precisely what Captain Dewey Knox did.

He waited by his window until he saw Flora one
morning carrying out the daily bucket of droppings, and
he strode purposefully out his door, crossed the road
and passed her trailer to the back, where he stood silently behind her, hands clasped behind his back, briar
pipe stuck between healthy teeth, one dark bushy eyebrow raised, so that when the woman turned with her
empty bucket, she met him face to face.

Switching the bucket from her right hand to her left,
she saluted smartly. "Captain," she said. "Good morning, sir."

The Captain casually returned the salute, as befitted
his rank. "What was your rank at retirement, Pease?"

"Airman Third Class, sir." She stood not exactly at
attention, but not exactly at ease, either. It's difficult
when retired military personnel meet each other as civil-
ians: their bodies have enormous resistance to accepting
the new modes of acknowledging each other, with the
result that they don't work quite either as military or
civilian bodies but as something uncomfortably neither.

"Airman Third, eh?" The Captain scratched his cleanly
shaved chin. "I would have thought after twenty years
you'd have risen a little higher."

"No reason to, sir. I was a steward in the officers'
clubs, sir, mostly in Lackland, and for a while, because
of my name, I guess," she said, smiling broadly, "at

Pease down in Portsmouth. Pease Air Force Base,'' she added.

"I know that. You were happy being a steward, then?"

"Yes, sir. Very happy. That's good duty, people treat you right, especially officers. I once kept house for General Curtis LeMay, a very fine man who could have been vice president of the United States. Once I was watching a quiz show on TV and that question came up, 'Who was George Wallace's running mate?' and I knew the answer. But that was after General LeMay had retired . . ."

"Yes, yes, I know," the Captain interrupted. "I thought the Air Force used male stewards in the officers' clubs."

"Not always, sir. Some of us like that duty and some don't, so if you like it you have an advantage, if you know what I mean, and most of the men don't much like it, especially when it comes to the housekeeping, though the men don't mind being waiters and so forth . . ."

The Captain turned aside to let Flora pass and walked along beside her toward the door of her trailer. At the door they paused, unsure of how to depart from one another, and the Captain glanced back at the pyramid of pellets and straw. "I've been meaning to ask you about that, Pease," he said, pointing with his pipe stem.

"Sir?"

"What is it?"

"Shit, sir."

"I surmised that. I mean, what kind of shit?"

"Guinea pig shit."

"And that implies you are keeping guinea pigs," he said.

Flora smiled tolerantly. "Yes, sir. It does."

"You know the rule about pets in the trailerpark, don't you, Pease?"

"Oh, sure I do."

"Well, then," he said, "what do you call guinea pigs?"

"I don't call them pets. Dogs and cats I call pets. But not guinea pigs. I just call them guinea pigs. They're sort of like plants, sir," she explained patiently. "You don't call plants pets, do you?"

"But guinea pigs are alive, for heaven's sake!"

"There's some who would say plants are alive, too, if you don't mind my saying so, sir."

"Yes, but that's different! These are animals!" The Captain sucked on his cold pipe, drew ash and spit into his mouth and coughed.

"Animals, vegetables, minerals, all that matters is that they're not like dogs and cats, which are pets because they can cause trouble for people. They're more like babies. That's why they have rules against pets in places like this, sir," she explained.

"How many guinea pigs have you?" the Captain coldly inquired.

"Seventeen."

"Males and females as well, I suppose."

"Yes, sir," she said, smiling broadly. "Twelve females, and eight of them is pregnant at this very moment. If you take good care of them, they thrive," she said with pride. "Like plants," she added, suddenly growing serious.

"But they're not plants! They're animals, and they produce . . . waste materials," he said, again pointing with the stem of his pipe at the pile behind the trailer. "And they're dirty."

Flora stepped onto her cinderblock stairs, bringing herself to the same height as the Captain. "Sir, guinea pigs are not dirty, they're cleaner than most people I know, and I know how most people can be. Don't forget, I was a steward for twenty years almost. And as for producing 'waste materials,' well, even plants produce waste materials. It's called oxygen, sir, which we human people find pretty useful, if you don't mind my saying so, sir, and as a matter of fact, come next spring you might want me to let you take some of that pile of waste material I got going out back for that little vegetable garden you got going out in back of your place.'' She shoved her chin in the general direction of Captain Knox's trailer, where indeed there was a now-dormant ten-foot by ten-foot garden plot on the slope facing the lake. Then she turned and abruptly entered her home.

That same evening, the Captain, in number 6, telephoned Leon LaRoche, in number 2, to explain the situation. "I'd take it to her myself," he said, meaning to Marcelle Chagnon, "but she's got it into her head that I'm trying to take over her job of running this place, so every time I ask her to do something, she does the opposite."

LaRoche understood. "I'll put a little data together first," he said. "To impress her. Guinea pigs are like rats, aren't they?"

"Very much," the Captain said.

LaRoche was eager to please the older man, as he admired and even envied him a little. He had once confessed to Doreen, after her ex-husband had made one of his brutal, unexpected visits and had been hauled away by the Catamount Police Department, that while he was open to the idea of marriage, if it turned out that he remained a bachelor all his life, he hoped he would be able to achieve the dignity and force, by the time he reached sixty or sixty-five, of a Captain Dewey Knox, say.

That night he researched guinea pigs in volume seven of his complete *Cooper's World Encyclopedia*, which he had obtained, volume by volume, by shopping every week at the A & P, and in that way he learned that guinea pigs, or cavies (*Rodentia caviidae*), a descendant of the Peruvian *Cavia aperea porcellus*, which were kept by the Indians for food and even today are sold as a

delicacy in many South American marketplaces, have a
life expectancy of eight years maximum, an average
litter size of 2.5, a gestation period of sixty-three days
and reach reproductive maturity in five to six weeks.
Furthermore, he learned (to his slightly prurient interest)
that the female goes through estrus every sixteen days
for fifty hours, during which time the female will accept
the male continuously but only between the hours of
5:00 PM and 5:00 AM. He also discovered that 8 percent
of all guinea pig pregnancies end in abortion, a variable
that made his calculations somewhat complicated but
also somewhat more interesting to perform. He learned
many other things about guinea pigs that night, but it
was the numbers that he decided to present to Marcelle.
He thought of telling her that guinea pigs are coprophagites,
eaters of feces, a habit necessitated by their innate difficulty in digesting cellulose tissue, creating thereby a
need for bacteria as an aid to digestion, but he thought
better of it. The numbers, he decided, would be suffi-
cient to make her aware of the gravity of the situation.

The next morning, a crisp, early fall day, with the
birches near the lake already gone to gold and shimmering in the clear air, LaRoche walked next door to
Marcelle's trailer fifteen minutes before his usual departure time for Sunday mass and presented her with the
evidence and the mathematical implications of the evidence. Captain Dewey Knox's testimony was unimpeach-
able, and Leon LaRoche's logic and calculations were
irrefutable. Marcelle's course of action, therefore, was
inescapable. The guinea pigs would have to go, or Flora
Pease would have to go.

"Boy, I need this like I need a hole in the head,"
Marcelle griped, when LaRoche had left her alone with
her cup of coffee and cigarette. Winter was coming on
fast, and she had to be sure all the trailers were winter-
ized, storm windows repaired and in place, exposed

water pipes insulated, heating units all cleaned and operating at maximum efficiency to avoid unnecessary break-
downs and expensive service calls, contracts for fuel oil
and snowplowing made with local contractors and approved by the Granite State Realty Development Corporation, leaky roofs patched, picnic tables and waterfront
equipment and docks stored away until spring, and on
and on—a long list of things to do before the first snow-
fall in November. Not only that, she had to collect
rents, not always a simple job, and sometime this month
she had to testify in court in the case involving Doreen's
ex-husband, since she had been the one to control him
with her shotgun while Doreen called the police, and
Terry Constant had taken off again for parts unknown,
so she had no one to help her, no one (since Terry had a
deal with his sister whereby his work for Marcelle helped
pay her rent) she could afford. And now in the middle of
all this she has to deal with a fruitcake who has a
passion for raising guinea pigs and doesn't seem to realize that they're going to breed her out of her own home
right into the street. Well, no sense treating the woman
like a child. Rules were rules, and it wasn't up to Flora
Pease to say whether or not her guinea pigs were pets, it
was up to management, and Marcelle was management.
The pigs would have to go, or else the woman would
have to go. LaRoche was right.

DAYS WENT BY, HOWEVER, AND FOR ONE REASON OR ANOTHER,
Marcelle left Flora alone, let her come and go as usual
without bothering to stop her and inform her that guinea
pigs were pets and pets were not allowed in the trailerpark.
Terry came back, evidently from New York, where he'd
gone to hear some music, and she put him to work
winterizing the trailers, which, for another week, as she
laid out Terry's work and checked after him to be sure

he actually did it, allowed Marcelle to continue to ignore the problem. Leon LaRoche thought better of the idea of bringing up the topic again and generally avoided her, although he did get together several times with Captain Knox to discuss Marcelle's obvious unwillingness to deal forthrightly with what would very soon turn into a sanitation problem, something for the health department, Captain Knox pointed out.

Finally, one morning late in the month, Marcelle went looking for Terry. It was a Saturday, and ordinarily she didn't hire him on Saturdays because it brought forward speeches about exploitation of the minorities and complaints about not getting paid time-and-a-half, which is what anyone else would have to pay a man to work on Saturdays, unless of course that man happens to be a black man in a white world. Marcelle more or less accepted the truth of Terry's argument, but that didn't make it any easier for her to hire him on Saturdays, since she couldn't afford to pay him the six dollars an hour it would have required. On this day, however, she had no choice in the matter—the weather prediction was for a heavy freeze that night and Sunday, and half the trailers had water pipes that would surely burst if Terry didn't spend the day nailing homosote skirting to the undersides.

He wasn't home, and his sister Carol didn't know where he'd gone, unless it was next door to visit that woman Flora Pease, where he seemed to spend a considerable amount of his spare time lately, Carol observed cautiously. Yes, well, Marcelle didn't know anything about that, nor did she much care where Terry spent his spare time so long as he stayed out of her hair (Carol said she could certainly understand that), but right now she needed him to help her finish winterizing the trailerpark by nightfall or they would have to spend the next two weeks finding and fixing water pipe leaks.

Carol excused herself, as she had to get dressed for work, and Marcelle left in a hurry for Flora's trailer.

At first when she knocked on the door there was no answer. A single crow called from the sedgy swamp out back, a leafless and desolate-looking place, with a skin of ice over the reedy water. The boney low trees and bushes clattered lightly in the breeze, and Marcelle pulled the collar of her denim jacket tightly against her face. The swamp, which was more of a muskeg than an actual swamp, lay at the southern end of about three thousand acres of state forest—most of the land between the northwest shore of Skitter Lake and the Turnpike, Route 28, which ran from the White Mountains, fifty miles to the north, to Boston, ninety miles to the south. The trailerpark had been placed there as a temporary measure (before local zoning restrictions could be voted into action) to hold and initiate development on the only large plot of land available between the town of Catamount and the Skitter Lake State Forest. That was right after the Korean War, when the Granite State Realty Development Corporation, anticipating a coming statewide need for low-income housing, had gone all over the state purchasing large tracts of land that also happened to lie close to cities and towns where low-income people were employed, usually mill towns like Catamount, whose tannery kept between seventy and eighty families in the area of the marginally poor. As it turned out, the trailerpark was all the Granite State Realty Development Corporation could finance in Catamount, for it soon became apparent that no one in the area would be able to purchase houses if the Corporation built single-family dwellings, or pay high enough rents to justify the expense of constructing a town house apartment complex. Soon it became clear that the best use the Corporation could make of the land and trailers was as collateral for financing projects elsewhere in the state, in the larger towns and cities where there were people who could afford to buy single-family dwellings or rent duplex apartments. In the meantime, the Corporation maintained the twelve trailers just adequately, paid the relatively low taxes, and came close to breaking even on its investment. Marcelle had been the first tenant in the trailerpark, moving out of a shabby woodframe tenement building in town because of her kids, who she believed needed more space, and she had immediately become the manager—when the company representative recognized her tough-mindedness, made evident, as soon as there were no more vacancies, by her ability to organize a rent strike to protest the open sewage and contaminated water. They had installed septic tanks and leach fields, and she had continued as resident manager ever since.

Flora's door opened a dark inch, and Marcelle saw a bit of cheek, blond hair and eye looking through the inch. She shoved against the door with the flat of one hand, pushing it back against the face behind it, and stepped up the cinderblocks and in, where she discovered the owner of the cheek, blond hair and eye—Bruce Severance, the college kid who lived in number 3, between LaRoche and Doreen.

"Hold it a minute, man," he said uselessly, rubbing his nose from the blow it had received from the door and stepping back into the room to make space for the large, gray-haired woman. The room, though dark from the venetian blinds being drawn, was filled with at least two other people than Bruce and Marcelle, batches of oddly arranged furniture, and what looked like merchandise counters from a department store.

"Don't you have any lights in here, for Christ's sake?" Marcelle demanded. She stood inside the room in front of the open door, blinking as she tried to accustom herself to the gloom and see who else was there. "Why are all the blinds drawn? What the hell you doing here,

Severance?'' Then she smelled it. "Grass? You smoking
your goddamned hippy pot in here with Flora?''

"Hey, man, it's cool.''

"Don't 'man' me. And it isn't cool. You know I don't
let nothing illegal go on here. Something illegal goes on
and I happen to find out about it, I call in the goddamned cops. Let them sort out the problems. I don't
need problems, I got enough of them already to keep me
busy.''

"That's right, baby, you don't want no more problems,'' came a soft voice from a particularly dark corner.

"Terry! What the hell you doing here?'' She could
make out a lumpy shape next to him on what appeared
to be a mattress on the floor. "Is that Flora over there?''
Marcelle asked, her voice suddenly a bit shaky. Things
were changing a little too fast for her to keep track of.
You don't mind the long-haired hippy kid smoking a
little grass and maybe yakking stupidly the way they do
when they're stoned with probably the only person in
the trailerpark who didn't need to get stoned herself in
order to understand him. You don't really mind that. A
kid like Bruce Severance, you knew he smoked marijuana, but it was harmless, because he did it for ideolog-
ical reasons, the same reasons behind his diet, pure
vegetarianism, and his exercise, T'ai Chi, and his way of
getting a little rest, transcendental meditation—he did all
these things not because they were fun but because he
believed they were good for him, and good for you, too,
if only you were able to come up with the wisdom,
self-discipline and money so that you, too, could smoke
marijuana instead of drink beer and rye whiskey, eat
organic vegetables instead of supermarket junk, study
and practice exotic, ancient Oriental forms of exercise
instead of sit around at night watching TV, learn how to
spend a half-hour in the morning and a half-hour in the
evening meditating instead of sleeping to the last minute

before you have to get up and make breakfast for your-self and the kid and rush off to work and in the evening drag yourself home just in time to make supper for the kid—if you could accomplish these things, you would be like Bruce Severance, a much improved person. That was one of his favorite phrases, "much improved per-son," and he believed that it ought to be a universal goal and that only ignorance (fostered by the military-industrial complex), sheer laziness, and/or purely malicious ideo-logical opposition (that is to say, a "fascist mentality") kept the people he lived among from participating with him in his several rites. So, unless you happened to share his ideology, you could easily view his several rites as harmless, mainly because you could also trust the good sense of the poor people he lived among, and also their self-discipline and the day-to-day realities they were forced to struggle against. A fool surrounded by sensible poor people remains a fool and is therefore seldom troublesome. But when it starts to occur to you that some of the poor people are not so sensible—which is what occurred to Marcelle when she peered into the dingy, dim clutter of the trailer and saw Terry sprawled out on a mattress on the floor with Flora Pease clumped next to him, both with marijuana cigarettes dangling from their lips—that's when you start to view the fool as troublesome.

"Listen, Bruce," she said, wagging a finger at the boy, "I don't give a damn about you wearing all them signs about legalizing pot and plastering bumper stickers against nuclear energy and so on all over your trailer, just so long as you take 'em down and clean the place up the way you found it when you leave here, and I don't mind you putting that kind of stuff on your clothes," she said, pointing with her forefinger at the image of a can-nabis plant on the chest of Bruce's tie-dyed tee shirt. "Because what you do behind your own closed door and how you decorate your trailer or your van or your clothes is all your own private business. But when you start mixing all this stuff up together like this," she said, waving a hand contemptuously in the direction of Terry and Flora, "well, that's a little different."

"Like what, man?" Bruce asked. "C'mon in, will you, and hey, calm down a little, man. No big thing. We're just havin' us a little morning toke, then I'm headin' out of here. No big thing."

"Yeah, it's cool," Terry said lightly from the corner.

Marcelle shot a scowl in his direction. "I don't want no dope dens in this park. I got my job to look out for, and you do anything to make my job risky for me, I'll come down on you," she said to Terry. "And you, too," she said to Bruce. "And you, too, sister," she said to Flora. "Like a goddamned ton of bricks!"

"No big thing, man," Bruce said, closing the door behind her, wrapping them all in the gray light of the room. Now Marcelle noticed the sharp, acidic smell of animal life, not human animals, but small, furred animals—urine and fecal matter and straw and warm fur. It was the smell of a nest. It was both irritating and at the same time comforting, that smell, because she was both un-used to the smell and immediately familiar with it. Then she heard it, a chattering, sometimes clucking noise that rose and ran off to a purr, then rose again like a shud-der, diminishing after a few seconds to a quiet, sustained hum. She looked closely at what she had thought at first were counters and saw that they were cages, large, waist-high cages, a half-dozen of them, placed in no clear order around the shabby furniture of the room, a mattress on the floor, a rocker, a pole lamp, a Formica-topped kitchen table and, without the easy chair, a has-sock. Beyond the living room, she could make out the kitchen area, where she could see two more of the large cages.

"You want a hit, man?" Terry asked, holding his breath as he talked so that his words came out in high-pitched, breathless clicks. He extended the joint toward her, a relaxed smile on his thick lips. Next to him, Flora, who lay slumped against his muscular frame like a sack of grain dropped from several feet above, seemed to be dozing.

"A hit. That's what *she* looks like, like she got hit."

"Ah, no, Flora's happy. Ain't you, Flora honey?" Terry asked, chucking her under the chin.

She rolled her head and came gradually to attention, saw Marcelle and grinned. "Hi, Mrs. Chagnon!" she cried, just this side of panic. "Have you ever smoked marijuana?"

"No."

"Well, I have. I love to smoke marijuana!"

"That right?"

"Yep. I can't drink, it makes me crazy and I start to cry and hit people and everything . . ."

"Right on," Bruce said.

". . . so I drink marijuana, I mean, I smoke marijuana, and then I feel real fine and everything's a joke, just the way it's s'posed to be. The trouble is, I can't get the knack of rolling these little cigarettes, so I need to have someone roll them for me, which is why I asked these boys here to come in and help me out this morning. You want a seat, why don't you sit down, Mrs. Chagnon? I been meaning to ask you over to visit sometime, but I been so busy, you know?" She waved toward the hassock for Marcelle to sit down.

"You sure you don't want a hit, Marcelle baby?" Terry offered again. "This's some dynamite shit. Flora's got herself some dynamite grass, right, man?" he said to Bruce.

"Oh, wow, man. Dynamite shit. Really dynamite shit."

"No, thanks." Marcelle sat down gingerly on the

hassock in the middle of the room. Bruce strolled loosely over and dropped himself onto the mattress, plucked the joint from Terry's hand and sucked noisily on it. "So *you're* the one who smokes the marijuana," Marcelle said to Flora. "I mean, these boys didn't . . ."

"Corrupt her?" Bruce interrupted. "Oh, wow, man, no way! She corrupted us!" he said, laughing and rolling back on the mattress. "Dynamite shit, man! What fucking dynamite grass!"

"He's just being silly," Flora explained. "It makes you a little silly sometimes, Mrs. Chagnon. Nothing to worry about."

"But it's illegal!"

"These days, Mrs. Chagnon, what isn't? I mean, honestly. I'm really not surprised."

"Yeah, well, I suppose it's okay, so long as you do it in the privacy of your own home, I mean."

"Really, Mrs. Chagnon! I would never be so foolish as to risk being arrested by the police!" Flora was now sitting pertly, her legs crossed at the ankles, gesturing limp-wristedly as she talked and manifesting a somewhat over-intensified effect.

"Well, I'll tell you," Marcelle said, and she sighed heavily, "I came over here looking for Terry to help me finish winterizing because we got a cold snap coming, but I can see he won't be any good today, all doped up like he is . . ."

"Hey, man!" Terry said and sat up straight, his feelings hurt. "You paying time-and-a-half, you got yourself a man. In fact, you pay time-and-a-half, you might getcha self two men," he said, waving toward Bruce. "You need a few bucks, man?"

"No, no, not today. I gotta study for a quiz on Monday, and I haven't even looked at the stuff . . ."

"Right, right," Terry said. "I forgot, you college boys, you gotta study for quizzes and stuff. But that's okay.

More for me, as I always say." His voice was crisp and loud again, which to Marcelle was cheering, for she had been made anxious by his slurred, quiet voice. It had made her nervous, as if his voice had an edge she couldn't see—if he was going to say things that cut, she wanted to be able to see them coming, and usually, with Terry, she could do precisely that, so she was relieved to hear him yammering away again, snapping and slashing with his sarcasm and bravado.

"Hey, Flora," Terry suddenly said, "now that you got the boss lady over here, whyn't you show her all your little furry friends! C'mon, baby, show the boss lady all your furry little friends!" He jumped up and urged Marcelle to follow. "C'mere and take a peek at these little beasties. She's got a whole heap of 'em."

"Not so many," Flora said shyly from the mattress.

"I gotta go," Bruce said. "I gotta study," he added, and he quickly let himself out the door.

Marcelle said not now and told Terry that he could start work by putting the winter skirting around Merle Ring's trailer, which was the most exposed in the park, located as it was out there on the point facing the lake. She reminded him where the sheets of homosote were stored, and he took off, not before, as usual, synchronizing watches with her, so that, as he put it, she wouldn't be able later on to say he didn't work as long as he did. "I've been screwed that way too many times," he always reminded her.

Then he was gone, and Marcelle was alone in the trailer with Flora—alone with Flora and her animals, which to Marcelle seemed to number in the hundreds. Their scurrying and rustling in the cages and the chittering noises they made filled the silence, and the smell of the animals thickened the air. Then Flora was moving about the room with a grace and lightness Marcelle had never seen in her before. She seemed almost to be dancing, and Marcelle wondered if it was the effect of the marijuana, an effect caused by inhaling the smoke-filled air, because after all, she knew Flora was a heavy, awkward woman who moved slowly and deliberately, not in this floating, delicate, improvisational way, almost as if she were underwater.

Marcelle Chagnon, the resident manager of the trailer-park, called across to Flora as she drifted by on her way to the kitchen area. "Flora! You can't keep these animals in here anymore!"

Flora ignored the words and waved for Marcelle to follow into the kitchen area, where, she explained, the babies were. "The babies and the new mommies, actually," she went on with obvious pride. As soon as they were weaned, she would place the mommies back with the daddies in the living room. Soon, she pointed out, she was going to have to build some more cages, because these babies would soon need to be moved to make room for more babies. She repeated what she had told Captain Knox: "When you take care of them, they thrive. Just like plants."

Marcelle Chagnon said it again, this time almost pleading. "You can't keep these animals in here anymore!"

Flora stopped fluttering. "It's getting colder, winter's coming. I must keep them inside, or they'll freeze to death. Just like plants."

Marcelle Chagnon crossed her arms over her chest and for the third time informed Flora that she would not be able to keep her guinea pigs inside her trailer.

This time the words seemed to have been understood. Flora stood still, hands extended as if for alms, and cried, "What will I do with them, then? I can't put them outside, they'll freeze to death, if they don't starve first. They're weak little animals, not made for this climate. You want me to *kill* them? Is that what you're telling me? That I have to *kill* my babies?"

"I don't know what the hell you're going to do with them!" Marcelle was angry now. Her head had cleared somewhat, and she knew again that this was Flora's problem, not hers. "It's your problem, not mine. I'm not God. What you do with the damned things is your business . . ."

"But I'm not God, either!" Flora cried. "All I can do is take care of them and try to keep them from dying unnaturally," she explained. That was all anyone could do and, therefore, it was what one had to do. "You do what you can. When you can take care of things, you do it. Because when you take care of things, they thrive." She said it as if it were a motto.

"Then I'll just have to call the health board and have them come in here and take the guinea pigs out. I don't want the scandal, it'll make it hard to rent, and it's hard enough already, but if I can't get you to take care of these animals by getting rid of them, I'll have someone else do it."

"You wouldn't do that," Flora said, shocked.

"Yes."

"Then you'll have to get rid of me first," she said. "You'll have to toss *me* out into the cold first, let me freeze or starve to death first, before I'll let you do that to my babies." She pushed her square chin out defiantly and glared at Marcelle.

"Oh, Jesus, what did I do to deserve this?"

Quickly, as if she knew she had won, Flora started reassuring Marcelle, telling her not to worry, no one would be bothered by the animals, their shit was almost odorless and would make good fertilizer for the several vegetable and flower gardens in the park, and she, Flora, took good care of them and kept their cages clean, so there was no possible health hazard, and except for their relatively quiet chitchat, the animals made no noise that would bother anyone. "People just don't like the *idea* of my having guinea pigs, that's all," she explained. "The *reality* of it don't bother anyone, not even Captain Knox. If people were willing to change their ideas, then everyone could be happy together," she said brightly.

In a final attempt to convince her to give up the guinea pigs, Marcelle tried using some of Leon LaRoche's calculations. She couldn't remember any of the specific numbers, but she understood the principle behind them. "You know you'll have twice as many of these things by spring. And how many have you got now, seventy-five or a hundred, right?"

Flora told her not to worry herself over it, she already had plenty to worry about with the trailerpark and winter coming and all. She should forget all about the guinea pigs, Flora told her with sympathy, and look after the people in the trailerpark, just as she always had. "Life is hard enough, Mrs. Chagnon, without us going around worrying about things we can't do anything about. You let me worry about taking care of the guinea pigs. That's something I can do something about, and you can't, so therefore it's something I *should* do something about, and you shouldn't even try." Her voice had a consoling, almost motherly tone, and for a second Marcelle wanted to thank her.

"All right," she said brusquely, gathering herself up to her full height. "Just make sure these bastards don't cause any trouble around here, and make sure there ain't any health hazard from . . . whatever, bugs, garbage, I don't know, anything . . . and you can keep them here. Till the weather gets warm, though. Only till spring."

Marcelle moved toward the door, and Flora smiled broadly. She modestly thanked Marcelle, who answered that if Flora was going to smoke pot here, she'd better do it alone and not with those two big-mouthed jerks, Terry and Bruce. "Let me warn you, those jerks, one or

the other of 'em, will get you in trouble. Smoke it alone,
if you have to smoke it."

"But I don't know how to make those little cigarettes.
My fingers are too fat and I spill it all over."

"Buy yourself a corncob pipe," Marcelle advised.
"Where do you buy the stuff from, anyway," she suddenly asked, as she opened the door to leave and felt the
raw chill from outside.

"Oh, I don't *buy* it!" Flora exclaimed. "It grows wild
all over the place, especially along the side of Old Road
where there used to be a farm, between the river and the
state forest." There were, as part of the land owned by
the Corporation, ten or fifteen acres of old, unused
farmland now grown over with brush and weeds. "They
used to grow hemp all over this area when I was a little
girl," Flora told her. "For rope during the war. But
after the war, when they had to compete with the Filipi-
nos and all, they couldn't make any money at it anymore, so it just kind of went wild."

"That sure is interesting," Marcelle said, shaking her
head. "And I don't believe you. But that's okay, I don't
need to know who you buy your pot from. I don't *want*
to know. I already know too much," she said, and she
stepped out and closed the door quickly behind her.

THE TRAILERPARK WAS LOCATED A MILE AND A HALF NORTH-
west of the center of the town of Catamount, a mill town
of about 5000 people situated and more or less organized
around a dam and mill pond first established on the
Catamount River some two hundred years ago. The mill
had originally been set up as a gristmill, then a lumber
mill, then a shoe factory, and in modern times, a tannery
that processed hides from New Zealand cattle and sent
the leather to Colombia for the manufacture of shoes.

To get to the trailerpark from the town, you drove

north out of town past the Hawthorne House (named after the author, Nathaniel Hawthorne, who stopped there overnight in May of 1864 with the then ex-president Franklin Pierce on the way to the White Mountains for a holiday; though the author died the next night in a rooming house and tavern not unlike the present Hawthorne House but located in Plymouth, New Hampshire, the legend had grown up int he region that he had died in his bed in Catamount), then along Main Street, past the half-dozen or so blocks of local businesses and the large white Victorian houses that once were the residences of the gentry and the owners of the mill or shoe factory or tannery, whichever it happened to be at that time, and that were now the residences and offices of the local physician (for whom Carol Constant worked), dentist, lawyer, certified public accountant, and mortician. A ways beyond the town, you came to an intersection, or you might more properly say Main Street came to an end. To your right Mountain Road ran crookedly uphill toward the mountain, the hill, actually, that gave the town its name, Catamount Mountain, so named by the dark presence in colonial times of mountain lions at the rocky top of the hill. Turning left, however, you would drive along Old Road, called that only recently and for the purpose of distinguishing between it and New Road, or the Turnpike, that ran north and south between the White Mountains and Boston. When, a mile and a half from town, you had crossed the Catamount River, you would turn right at the tipped, flaking sign, GRANITE STATE TRAILERPARK, posted off the road behind a bank of mailboxes standing like sentries at the intersection. Passing through some old, brush-filled fields and then some pine woods that grew on both sides of the narrow, paved lane, you would emerge into a clearing, with a sedge-thickened swamp on your left, the Catamount River on your right, and beyond, a cluster of somewhat battered and aging housetrailers. Some were in better repair than others, and some, situated in obviously more attractive locations than others, were alongside the lake where they exhibited small lawns and flower gardens and other signs of domestic tidiness and care. The lake itself lay stretched out beyond the trailerpark, four and a half miles long and in the approximate shape of the silhouette of a turkey. For that reason, it was called Turkey Pond for over a hundred years, until Ephraim Skitter, who owned the shoe factory, left the town a large endowment for its library and a bandstand, and in gratitude the town fathers changed the name of the lake. That in turn gave the name Skitter to the large parcel of land that bordered the north and west sides of the lake, becoming by 1950, when the Turnpike was built, the Skitter Lake State Forest. All in all, it was a pretty piece of land and water. If you stood out on the point of land where the trailerpark was situated, with the swamp and pine woods behind you, you could see, way out beyond the deep blue water of the lake, spruce-covered hills that humped their way northward all the way to the mauve-colored wedges at the horizon that were the White Mountains.

In the trailerpark itself, there were an even dozen trailers, pastel-colored blocks, some with slightly canted roofs, some with low eaves, but most of them simply rectangular cubes sitting on cinderblocks, with dirt or gravel driveways beside them, usually an old car or pickup truck parked there, with some pathetic, feeble attempt at a lawn or garden evident, but evident mainly in a failure to succeed as such. Some of the trailers, Leon LaRoche's, for example, looked to be in better repair than others, and a few even indicated that the tenants were practically affluent and could afford embellishments such as glassed-in porches, wrought-iron railings at the doorstep, tool sheds, picnic tables and lawn furniture by the shoreside yard and a new or nearly new car in the driveway. The trailer rented to Noni Hubner's mother Nancy was one of these—Nancy Hubner was a widow whose late husband had owned the Catamount Insurance Company and was rumored to have had a small interest in the tannery—and Captain Dewey Knox's was another. Captain Knox, like Nancy Hubner, was from an old and relatively well off family in town, as suggested by the name of Knox Island, located out at the northern end of Skitter Lake where the turkey's eye was. Captain Knox enjoyed recalling childhood summer picnics on "the family island" with his mother and his father, a man who had been one of the successful hemp growers before and during the war, or "War Two," as Captain Knox called it. His father prior to that had been a dairy farmer, but after the war decided to sell his land and moved to Florida, where he died within six months and where Captain Knox's mother, a woman in her eighties, still lived. Captain Knox's return to Catamount after his retirement, he said, had been an act of love "for this region, this climate, this people, and the principles and values that have prospered here." He talked that way sometimes.

Two of the twelve trailers, numbers five and nine, were vacant at this time, number nine having been vacated only last February as the result of the suicide of a man who had lived in the park almost as long as Marcelle Chagnon and who had been extremely popular among his neighbors. Tom Smith was his name, and he had raised his son alone in the park, and when his son, at the age of twenty-one or so, had gone away, Tom had withdrawn into himself and one gray afternoon in February shot himself in the mouth. He had been a nice man, everyone insisted, though no one had known him very well. In fact, people seemed to think he was a nice man mainly because his son Buddy had been so troublesome, always drunk and fighting at the Hawthorne House and, according to the people in the park, guilty of stealing and selling in Boston their TV sets, stereos, radios, jewelry, and so forth. Tom Smith's trailer, number 9, wasn't a particularly fancy one, but it was well located at the end of the landside of the park, right next to Terry and Carol Constant and with a view of the lake, but even so, Marcelle hadn't yet been able to rent it, possibly because of the association with Tom's suicide, but also possibly because of there being black people living next door, which irritated Marcelle whenever it came up, bringing her to announce right to the prospective tenant's face, "Good, I'm glad you don't want to rent that trailer, because we don't want people like you living around here." That would be the end of the tour, and even though Marcelle felt just fine about losing that particular kind of tenant, her attitude certainly did not help her fill number 9, which cost her money. But you had to admire Marcelle Chagnon—she was like an old Indian chief, the way she came forward to protect her people, even with nothing but her pride, if that was all she had to put up, and even at her own expense.

Number 5, the other vacancy, was located between Doreen Tiede, the divorcée who lived with her little girl, and Captain Knox, and was on the lake side of the park, facing the stones and sticks where the lake flowed into the Catamount River and where the Abenooki Indians, back before the whites came north from Massachusetts and drove the Indians away to Canada, had built their fishing weirs. It was a sleek, sixty-eight-foot-long Marlette with a mansard roof, very fancy, a replacement for the one that had burned to the ground a few years ago. A young newly married couple, Ginnie and Claudel Bing, had moved in, and only three months later, returning home from a weekend down on the Maine coast, had found it leveled and still smouldering in the ground, the result of Ginnie's having left the kitchen stove on. They had bought the trailer, financed through the Granite State Realty Development Corporation, and were renting only the lot and services, and their insurance on the place hadn't covered half of what they owed (as newlyweds, they were counting on a long and increasingly rewarding future, so they had purchased a new car and five rooms of new furniture all on time). Afterward, they broke up, Claudel lost his job, became something of a drunk and ended up living alone in a room at the Hawthorne House and working down at the tannery. It was a sad story, and most people in the park knew it, and remembered it whenever they passed the shining new trailer that the Corporation had moved in to replace the one that the Bings had burned down. Because the new trailer had been so expensive, the rent was high, which made it difficult for Marcelle to find a tenant for it, but the Corporation didn't mind, since it was being paid for anyhow by Claudel Bing's monthly checks. Corporations have a way of making things come out even in the end.

There was in the park one trailer, an old Skyline, that was situated more favorably than any other in the park, number 8, and it was out at the end of the shoreside line, where the road became a cul-de-sac and the shore curved back around toward the swamp and state forest. It was a plain, dark gray trailer, with the grass untended, uncut, growing naturally all around as if no one lived there. A rowboat lay tilted on one side where someone had drawn it up from the lake behind the trailer, and there was an ice-fishing shanty on a sledge waiting by the shore for winter, but there were no other signs of life around the yard, no automobile, none of the usual junk and tools lying around, no piles of gravel, crushed stone or loam to indicate projects underway and forsaken for lack of funds, no old and broken toys or tricycles or wagons, nothing out back but a single clothesline stretching from one corner of the trailer back to a pole that looked like a small chokecherry tree cut from the swamp. This was where the man Merle Ring lived.

Merle Ring was a retired carpenter, retired by virtue of his arthritis, though he could still do a bit of finish work in warm weather, cabinetmaking and such, to supplement his monthly social security check. He lived alone and modestly and in that way managed to get by all right. He had outlived and divorced numerous wives, the number varied from three to seven, depending on who Merle happened to be talking to, and he had fathered on these three to seven women at least a dozen children, most of whom lived within twenty miles of him, but none of them wanted him to live with him or her because Merle would only live with him or her if, as he put it, he could be the boss of the house. No grown child would accept a condition like that, naturally, and so Merle lived alone, where he was in fact and indisputably the boss of the house.

Merle, in certain respects, was controversial in the park, though he did have the respect of Marcelle Chagnon, which helped keep the controversy from coming to a head. He was mouthy, much given to offering his opinions on subjects that involved him not at all, which would not have been so bad, however irritating it might have been, had he not been so perverse and contradictory with his opinions. He never seemed to mean what he said, but he said it so cleverly that you felt compelled to take him seriously anyhow. Then, later, when you brought his opinion back to him and tried to make him own up to it and take responsibility for its consequences, he would laugh at you for ever having taken him seriously in the first place. He caused no little friction in the lives of many of the people in the park. When one night Doreen Tiede's ex-husband arrived at the park drunk and threatening violence, Merle, who happened to be nearby, just coming in from a long night of hornpouting on the lake, stopped and watched with obvious amusement, as if he were watching a movie and not a real man cockeyed drunk and shouting through a locked door at a terrorized woman and child that he was going to kill them both. Buck Tiede caught sight of old Merle standing there at the edge of the road, where the light just reached him, his string of hornpout dangling nearly to the ground (he was on his way to offer his catch to Marcelle, who had a deep-freeze and would hand the ugly fish out next winter when, rolled in batter and fried in deep fat, they would be a treat that reminded people of summer and got them to talking about it again). "You old fart!" Buck, a large and disheveled man, had roared at Merle. "What the hell you lookin' at! G'wan, get the hell outa here an' mind your own business!" He made a swiping gesture at Merle, as if he were chasing off a dog.

Then, according to Marcelle, who had come up behind him in the darkness with her shotgun, Merle said to the man, "Once you kill her, it's done. Dead is dead. If I was you, Buck, and wanted that woman dead as you seem to, I'd just get me some dynamite and blow the place all to hell. Or better yet, just catch her some day coming out of work down to the tannery, snipe her with a high-powered rifle from a window on the third floor of the Hawthorne House. Then she'd be dead, and you could stop all this hollering and banging on doors and stuff."

Buck stared at him in amazement. "What the hell are you saying?"

"I'm saying you ought to get yourself a window up in the Hawthorne House that looks down the hill to the tannery, and when she comes out the door after work, plug her. Get her in the head, to be sure. Just bang, and that'd be that. You could do your daughter the same way. Dead is dead, and you wouldn't have to go around like this all the time. If you was cute about it, you'd get away with it all right. I could help you arrange it. Give you an alibi, even." He held up the string of whiskery fish. "I'd tell 'em you was out hornpouting with me."

"What are you telling me to do?" Buck took a step away from the door toward Merle. "You're crazy."

"Step aside, Merle, I'll take care of this," Marcelle ordered, shouldering the tiny man out of the way and bringing her shotgun to bear on Buck Tiede. "Doreen!" she called out. "You hear me?"

Buck made a move toward Marcelle.

"Stay right where you are, mister, or I'll splash you all over the wall. You know what a mess a twelve-gauge can make?"

Buck stood still.

A thin, frightened voice came from inside. "Marcelle, I'm all right! Oh God, I'm sorry for all this! I'm so sorry!" Then there was weeping, both a woman's and a child's.

"Forget sorry. Just call the cops. I'll hold Mister Bigshot here until they come."

And she did hold him, frozen and silent at the top of the steps, while Doreen called the police, who came in less than five minutes and hauled Buck off to spend the night in jail. Merle, once Marcelle and her shotgun had taken charge of the situation, had strolled on with his fish, gutting them and skinning them quickly in Marcelle's kitchen, then neatly wrapping and depositing them in her deep-freeze. The cops came and went, blue lights flashing, and later Marcelle returned home, her shotgun slung over her thick arm, and when she entered her kitchen, she found Merle sitting over a can of Budweiser reading her copy of *People* magazine.

"You're crazy, dealing with Buck Tiede that way," she said angrily.

"What way?"

"Telling him to shoot Doreen from a room in the Hawthorne House! He's just liable to do that, he's a madman when he's drinking!" She cracked open a can of beer and sat down across from the old man.

He closed the magazine. "I never told him to kill her. I just said how he might do it, if he wanted to kill her. The way he was going about it seemed all wrong to me." He smiled and showed his brown teeth through his beard.

"What if he actually went and did it, shot her from the Hawthorne House some afternoon as she came out of work? How would you feel then?"

"Good."

"Good! Why, in the name of Jesus, Mary and Joseph, would you feel good?"

"Because we'd know who did it."

"But you said you'd give him an alibi!"

"That was just a trick. I wouldn't, and that way he'd be trapped. He'd say he was with me all afternoon fishing, and then I'd come out and say no, he wasn't. I'd fix it so there'd be no way he could prove he was with me, because I'd make sure someone else saw me fishing alone, and that way he'd be trapped and they'd take him over to Concord and hang him by the neck until dead."

"Why do you fool around like that with people?" she asked, genuinely curious. "I don't understand you, old man."

He got up, smiled and flipped the copy of *People* magazine across the table. "It's more interesting than reading this kind of stuff," he said and started for the door. "I put an even dozen hornpouts in your freezer."

"Thanks. Thanks a lot," she said absently, and he went out.

*   *   *

MERLE HEARD ABOUT FLORA'S GUINEA PIGS FROM NANCY Hubner, the widow in number 7, who heard about them from her daughter, Noni, who was having a love affair with the college boy, Bruce Severance. He told her one night in his trailer after they had made love and were lying in darkness on the huge waterbed he'd built, smoking a joint while the stereo played the songs of the humpback whale quietly around them. Noni had been a college girl in northern California before her nervous breakdown, so she understood and appreciated Bruce more than anyone else in the park could. Most everyone tolerated Bruce good-humoredly—he believed in knowledge and seemed to be earnest in his quest for it, and what little knowledge he had already acquired, or believed he had acquired, he dispensed liberally to anyone who would listen. He was somberly trying to explain to Noni how yogic birth control worked, how "basically feminist" it was, because the responsibility was the man's, not the woman's.

"I wondered how come you never asked me if I was protected," she said.

"Yeah, well, no need to, man. It's all in the breathing and certain motions with the belly, so the sperm gets separated from the ejaculatory fluid prior to emission. It's really quite simple."

"Amazing."

"Yeah."

"Overpopulation is an incredible problem."

"Yeah. It is."

"I believe that if we could just solve the overpopulation problem, all the rest of the world's problems would be solved, too. Like wars."

"Ecological balance, man. The destruction of the earth."

"The energy crisis. Everything."

"Yeah, man. It's like those guinea pigs of Flora Pease's. Flora, she's got these guinea pigs, hundreds of them by now. And they just keep on making new guinea pigs, doubling their numbers every couple of months. It's incredible, man."

Noni rolled over on her belly and stretched out her legs and wiggled her toes. "Do you have that record of Dylan's, the one where he sings all those country and western songs, way before anyone even *heard* of country and western? What's it called?"

"*Nashville Skyline?*"

"Yeah, that's it. Isn't it incredible, how he was singing country and western way before anyone even heard of it?"

"Yeah, he's really incredible, Dylan. Anyhow . . ."

"Do you have it, the record?" she interrupted.

"No, man. Listen, I was telling you something."

"Sorry."

"That's okay, man. Anyhow, Flora's guinea pigs, it's like they're a *metaphor*. You know? I mean, it's like Flora is some kind of god and the first two guinea pigs, the ones she bought from the five-and-dime in town, were Adam and Eve, and that trailer of hers is the world. Be fruitful and multiply, Flora told them, and fine, they go out and do what they're programmed to do, and pretty soon they're taking over the world, the trailer, so that Flora can't take care of them anymore. No matter how hard she works, they eat too much, they shit too much, they take up too much room. So what happens?"

Silence.

"What happens?" Bruce repeated.

"Oh. I don't know. A flood, maybe?"

"No, man, it's not that literal, it's a metaphor. What happens is Flora moves out, leaves the trailer to the guinea pigs. Twilight of the gods, man. God is dead. You know.''

''Yeah. That's really incredible.''

''Yeah,'' Bruce said, drifting into still deeper pools of thought.

After a few moments, Noni got up from the bed and drew on her clothes. ''I better get home, my mother'll kill me. She thinks I'm at the movies with you.''

''Naw, man, she knows where you are. All she's got to do is walk three doors down and see my van's still here. C'mon, she *knows*. She knows we're making it together. She's not that out of it.''

Noni shrugged. ''I don't know. She believes what she wants to believe. Sometimes I think she still doesn't believe Daddy's dead, and it's been over four years now. There's no point in forcing things on people. You know what I mean?''

Bruce understood, but he didn't agree. People needed to face reality, it was good for them and good for humanity as a whole, he felt. He was about to tell her why it was good for them, but Noni was already dressed and heading for the door, so he said good night instead and waved from the bed as she slipped out the door.

WHEN LATER THAT SAME EVENING SHE TOLD HER MOTHER that Flora Pease was raising hundreds of guinea pigs in her trailer, it was not so much because Noni herself was interested in Flora or the guinea pigs as it was because her mother Nancy was quizzing her about the movie she was supposed to have seen with Bruce.

''That's not true,'' the woman said.

''What's not?'' Noni switched on the TV set and sat down cross-legged on the floor.

''About the guinea pigs. Where'd you hear such a thing?''

"Bruce. Do you think I could study yoga somewhere around here?"

"Of course not. Don't be silly." Nancy lit a cigarette and sat down on the sofa, where she'd been reading this month's Book-of-the-Month Club selection, a novel that gently satirized the morals and mores of Westchester County's smart set. "Bruce. I don't know about that boy. How can he be a college student when the nearest college is the state university in Durham, which is over forty miles from here?"

"I don't know." Noni was sliding into the plot intricacies of a situation comedy about two young women who worked on an assembly line in Milwaukee and made the kind of comically stupid errors of judgment and perception that Chester A. Riley used to make in *The Life of Riley* twenty-five years before. "It's a correspondence school or something, in Vermont. He has to go there and see his teachers for a couple of weeks twice a year or something. It's the new thing in education."

Well, Nancy didn't know how it could be much of an education, and it certainly didn't explain why Bruce lived where he did and not at his college or even at his parents' home, as Noni did.

"I don't know," Noni said.

"Don't you ever ask, for heaven's sake?"

"No."

That was all their conversation for the night. At eleven, Nancy yawned and went to bed in her room at the far end of the trailer, the rooms of which were carpeted and furnished lavishly and resembled the rooms of a fine apartment. Around midnight, Noni rolled a joint and went to her room, next to her mother's, and smoked it, and went to sleep. She bought her marijuana from Bruce. So did Terry buy his from Bruce. Also Leon LaRoche, who had never tried smoking grass before but certainly did not reveal that to Bruce, who knew it anyhow and charged him twice the going rate. Doreen Tiede bought grass from Bruce, too. Not often, however; about once every two or three months. She liked to smoke it in her trailer with men she went out with and came home with, so she called herself a "social smoker," but Bruce knew what that meant. Over the years, Bruce had bought his grass from several people, most recently from a Jamaican named Keppie who lived in the West Roxbury area of Boston but who did business from a motel room in Revere. Next year, Bruce had decided, he would harvest the hemp crop Flora Pease had discovered, and he would sell the grass back, running it the other direction, to Keppie and his Boston friends. He figured there must be five hundred pounds of the stuff growing wild out there, just waiting for a smart guy like him to cut, dry, chop and pack. He might have to cut Terry Constant in, but that would be fine, because in this business you often needed a partner who happened to be black.

THE NEXT MORNING, ON HER WAY TO TOWN TO HAVE HER hair cut and curled by Ginnie Bing (now Ginnie Leeke, after having married the plumber Howie Leeke), Nancy Hubner picked up Merle Ring. Merle was walking out from the trailerpark and had almost reached Old Road, when he heard the high-pitched whirr of Nancy's powerful Japanese fastback coupe and without turning around stepped off the road into the light, leafless brush. There had been an early snow in late October that winter, and then no snow throughout November and well into December, which had made it an excellent year for ice-fishing. After the first October snow, there was a brief melt and then a cold snap that had lasted for five weeks now, so that the ice had thickened daily, swiftly becoming iron-hard and black and smooth. Then all over the lake shanties had appeared, and all day and long into the night men and sometimes women sat inside the shanties, keeping warm from tiny kerosene or coal-burning heaters, sipping from bottles of whiskey, watching their lines and yakking slowly to friends or meditating alone and outside of time and space, until the flag went up and the line got yanked and the fisherman would come crashing back into that reality from the other. The ice had hardened sufficiently to bear even the weight of motor vehicles, and now and then you could look out from the shore and see a car or pickup truck creeping across the slick ice and stopping at one of the shanties, bringing society and a fresh six-pack or pint of rye. No one ever visited Merle's shanty, though he certainly had plenty of friends of various ages and both sexes. He had made it known that, when he went ice-fishing, it was as if he were going into religious withdrawal and meditation, a journey into the wilderness, as it were, and if you were foolish or ignorant enough to visit him out there on the ice in his tiny, windowless shack with the stovepipe chimney sticking up and puffing smoke, you would be greeted by a man who seemed determined to be left alone. He would be cold, detached, abstracted, unable or unwilling to connect to the person standing self-consciously before him, and after a few moments you would leave, your good-bye hanging unanswered in the air, and Merle would take a sip from his fifth of Canadian Club and drift back into his trance.

Nancy braked her car to a quick stop next to Merle, and reaching over, cranked down the window and asked if he wanted a lift into town. She liked the old man, or perhaps it would be more accurate to say that the old man intrigued her, as if she believed he knew something about the world they all lived in together that she did not know and that would profit her greatly if she did know. So she courted him, fussed over him, seemed to be looking after his comfort and welfare, behaving the way, as she once said to Noni, his daughters ought to behave.

Merle apparently knew all this, and more, though you could never be sure with him. He got inside the low, sleek car, slammed the door shut and surrounded himself with the smell of leather and the pressure of fan-driven heat. "Morning, Mrs. Hubner. A fine, crispy morning, isn't it?" he said.

She agreed and asked him where she could drop him. A fast, urgent driver, she was already flying past the intersection of Old Road and Main Street and was approaching the center of town. She drove so as to endanger, but she didn't seem to know it. It was as if her relation to the physical act of driving a motor vehicle was the same as her relation to poverty—abstract, wholly theoretical, and sentimental—which made her as dangerous a driver as she was a citizen. She was the type of person that believes poor people lead more wholesome lives than rich people and what poor people lack, and rich people have, is education. It was almost impossible for her to understand that what poor people lack, and rich people have, is money. And as for the wholesomeness of the lives of the poor, her notions were not all that different from Bruce Severance's, since the basis for both sets of ideas was a fear and loathing of the middle class that they themselves so perfectly embodied.

Merle and Nancy exchanged brief remarks, mostly solicitous on her part as to the present condition of Merle's arthritis and mostly whining on his part as to the same thing. Merle probably knew that by whining he could put Nancy at her ease, and in encounters as brief as this one he, like most people, surely enjoyed being able to put people at their ease. It made things more interesting for him later on. Stopping in front of Hayward's Hardware and Sporting Goods Store, where Merle was headed for traps, she suddenly asked him a direct question (since she was now sufficiently at her ease to trust that he would answer directly and honestly and in that way might be brought to reveal more than he wished to): "Tell me, Mr. Ring, is it true that that woman Flora in number eleven, you know the one, is raising hundreds of guinea pigs in her trailer?"

"Yes," he said, lying, for he had heard nothing of it. "Though I'm not sure of the numbers. It's hard to count 'em over a certain point, sixty, say."

"Don't you think that's a little . . . disgusting? I mean, the *filth*. I think the woman ought to be put away, don't you?" she asked, still trying to get information.

"What would you do with all those guinea pigs then?"

"Why, let the S.P.C.A. take them, I suppose. They know how to handle these things, when things like this get out of hand. Imagine, all those tiny animals crowded into a trailer, and remember, number eleven is not one of the larger trailers in the park, as you know."

"I guess you're right, the S.P.C.A. could kill 'em for us, once we'd got Flora locked up someplace. The whole thing would probably drive her right over the edge anyhow, taking away her animals and killing 'em like that, tossing 'em into that incinerator they got. That'd push ol' Flora right over the edge. She'd be booby-hatch material for sure then, whether she is now or not."

"You're making fun of me, Mr. Ring. Aren't you?"

"No, no, no, I'm not making fun of you, Mrs. Hubner," he said, opening the door and stepping out, not without difficulty, however, because of the shape of the car and his stiff back. "I'll check into it for you, ma'am. Get the facts of the situation, so to speak. Because you're probably right. I mean, something will have to be done, eventually, by someone. Because those kind of animals, rodents and such, they breed fast and before you know it a hundred is two hundred, two hundred is four, four is eight, and so on. So I'll check into it for you."

"Thank you so much, Mr. Ring," she said with clear relief. He was such a nice man. She wondered if there was some way she could make his life a little easier. At his age, to be alone like that, it was simply awful.

Merle closed the door, waved and walked into Hayward's, and Nancy drove on to Ginnie's Beauty Nook, on Green Street across from Knight's Paint Store, where Ginnie and her ex-husband Claudel had lived in the upstairs apartment back when their trailer had burned down. That was over three years ago, maybe four. Nancy couldn't remember, until it came back to her that it had happened in the summer, when Ginnie and Claudel had returned from a weekend on the Maine coast to discover that their fancy trailer had burned to the ground in their absence, and then she remembered that was the summer Noni turned fifteen and started having migraines and saying she hated her, and then she remembered that was the summer her husband had died. So it must be over four years now since Ginnie and Claudel moved into town and rented that apartment over Knight's Paint Store. Isn't it amazing, how time flies when you're not paying attention, she reflected.

A WEEK LATER, MERLE WOKE LATE AFTER HAVING SPENT most of the night out on the lake in his ice-house, and because the sun was shining, casting a raw light that somehow pleased him, he decided to visit Flora Pease and determine if all this fuss over her guinea pigs was justified. Since talking with Nancy Hubner, he had spoken only to Marcelle Chagnon about the guinea pigs, and her response had been to look heavenward, as if for help or possibly mere solace, and to say, "Just don't talk to me about that crazy woman, Merle, don't start in about her. As long as she don't cause any troubles for me, I won't cause any troubles for her. But if *you* start in on this, there'll be troubles. For me. And that means for her, too, remember that.''

"Makes sense," Merle said, and for several days after he had succeeded in going about his business—ice-fishing, eating, cleaning, reading the *Manchester Union-Leader*, puttering with his tools and equipment—slow, solitary activities that he seemed to savor. He was the kind of person who, by the slowness of his pace and the hard quality of his attention, appeared to take a sensual pleasure from the most ordinary activity. He was a small, lightly framed man and wore a short white beard which he kept neatly trimmed. His clothing was simple and functional, flannel shirts, khaki pants, steel-toed work-shoes—doubtless the same style of clothing he had worn since his youth, when he first became a carpenter's apprentice and determined what clothing was appropriate for that kind of life. His teeth were brown, stained from a lifetime of smoking a cob pipe, and his weathered skin was still taut, indicating that he had always been a small, trim man. There was something effeminate about him that, at least in old age, made him physically attractive, especially to women but to men as well. Generally, his manner with people was odd and somewhat disconcerting, for he was both involved with their lives and not involved, both serious and not serious, both present and absent. For example, a compliment from Merle somehow had the effect of reminding the recipient of his or her vanity, while an uninvited criticism came out sounding like praise for having possessed qualities that got you singled out in the first place.

Though seasonably cold (fifteen degrees below freezing), the day was pleasant and dry, the light falling on the bone-hard ground directly, so that the edges of objects took on an unusual sharpness and clarity. Merle knocked briskly on Flora's door, and after a moment, she swung it open. She was wrapped in a wool bathrobe that must have been several decades old and belonged originally to a very large man, for it flowed around her blocky body like a carpet. Her short hair stuck out in a corolla of dark red spikes, and her eyes were red-rimmed and watery-looking, as, grumpily, she asked Merle what he wanted from her.

"A look," he chirped, smiling.

"A look. At what?"

"At your animals. The guinea pigs I heard about."

"You heard about them? What did you hear?" She stood before the door, obstructing his view into the darkened room beyond. An odor of fur and straw, however, seeped past and merged warmly with the cold, almost sterile air outdoors.

Merle sniffed with interest at the odor, apparently relishing it. "Heard you got a passel of 'em. I never seen one of these guinea pigs before and was wondering what in hell they look like. Pigs?"

"No. More like fat, furry chipmunks," Flora said, easing away from the door. She still had not smiled, however, and clearly was not ready to invite Merle inside. "Mrs. Chagnon send you over here?" she suddenly demanded. "That woman is putting me on a spot. I can't have any friends anymore to visit or to talk to me here, or else I'll get into trouble with that woman."

"No, Marcelle didn't send me, she didn't even want to talk about your guinea pigs with me. She just said as long as they don't cause her any trouble, she won't cause you any trouble."

"That's what I mean," Flora said, defiantly crossing her short, thick arms over her chest. "People come around here and see my guinea pigs, and then I get into trouble. If they don't come around here and don't see nothing, then it's like the guinea pigs, for them, don't exist. That kid, Terry, the black one, he started it all, when all I was doing was trying to be friendly, and then he went and dragged the other kid, the white one, in here, and they got to smoking my hemp, and then pretty soon here comes Mrs. Chagnon, and I get in trouble. All I want is to be left alone,'' she said with great clarity, as if she said it to herself many times a day.

Merle nodded sympathetically. ''I sure understand how you feel. It's like when I won the lottery, that was back a ways, before you come here, and everybody thought I had a whole heap more money than I had, so everyone was after me for some.''

That interested Flora. She had never met anyone who had won the lottery. In fact, she was starting to believe that it was all faked, that no one ever won, that those people jumping up and down hysterically in the TV ads were just actors. Now, because of Merle's having won, her faith in the basic goodness of the world was magically restored. ''This means they probably went to the moon, too,'' she said with clear relief.

''Who?''

''The astronauts.''

''You didn't believe that, the rocket to the moon? I thought you used to be in the Air Force.''

''That's why I had so much trouble believing it,'' she said and stood aside and waved him in.

Inside, when his eyes had grown accustomed to the dim light of the room, this is what Merle saw: large, wood-framed, chicken-wire pens that were waist-high and divided into cubicles about two feet square. The pens were placed in no apparent order or pattern throughout the room, which gave the room, despite the absence of furniture, the effect of being incredibly cluttered, as if someone were either just moving in or all packed to move out. As far as Merle could see, the rooms adjacent to this one were similarly jammed with pens, and he surmised that the rooms he couldn't see, the bedroom at the back and the bathroom, were also filled with pens like these. In each cubicle there was a pair of grown or nearly grown guinea pigs or else one grown (presumably female) pig and a litter of two or three piglets. Merle could see and hear the animals in the cubicles a short distance away from him scurrying nervously about their cages, but the animals nearer him were crouched and still, their large round eyes rolling frantically and their noses twitching as, somehow, Merle's own odor penetrated the heavy odor of the room.

Flora reached down and plucked a black and white spotted pig from the cage it shared with a tan, long-haired mate. Cradling it in her arm and stroking its nose with her free hand, she walked cooing and clucking over to Merle and showed him the animal. "This here's Ferdinand," she said. "After the bull."

"Ah. May I?" he said, reaching out to take Ferdinand.

Merle held the animal as Flora had and studied its trembling, limp body. It seemed to offer no defense and showed no response to the change in environment except that of stark terror. When Merle placed it back into its cubicle, it remained exactly where he had placed it, as if waiting for a sudden, wholly deserved execution.

"How come you like these animals, Flora?"

"Don't *you* like them?" she bristled.

"I don't feel one way or the other about them. I was wondering about you."

She was silent for a moment and moved nervously around the cages, checking into the cubicles as she moved. "Well, somebody's got to take care of them. Especially in this climate. They're really not built for the ice and snow."

"So you don't do it because you like them?"

"No. I mean, I like looking at them and all, the colors are pretty, and their little faces are cute and all. But I'm just taking care of them so they won't die, that's all."

There was a silence, then Merle said, "I hate to ask it,

but how come you let them breed together? You know where that'll lead?"

"Do you know where it'll lead if I *don't* let them breed together?" she asked, facing him with her hands fisted on her hips.

"Yup."

"Where?"

"They'll die out."

"Right. That answer your question?"

"Yup."

Merle stayed with her for the next half-hour, as she showed him her elaborate watering system—a series of interconnected hoses that ran from the cold water spigot in the kitchen sink around and through all the cages, ending back in the bathroom sink—and her cleverly designed system of trays beneath the cages for removing from the cages the feces and spilled food, and her gravity-fed system of grain troughs, so that all she had to do was dump a quart a day into each cage and the small trough in each individual cubicle would be automatically filled. Because she had constructed the cages herself, she explained, and because she was no carpenter, they weren't very fancy or pretty to look at. But the basic idea was a good one, she insisted, so that, despite her lack of skill, the system worked and consequently every one of her animals was clean, well-fed and watered at all times. "You can't ask for much more in this life, can you?" she said proudly as she led Merle to the door.

He guessed no, you couldn't. "But I still think you're headed for troubles," he told her, and he opened the door to leave.

"What do you mean? What's going on?" Suddenly she was suspicious of him and frightened of Marcelle Chagnon again, with her suspicion of the one and fear of the other swiftly merging to become anger at everyone.

"No, no, no. Not troubles with Marcelle or any of the

rest of the folks in the park. Just with the breeding and all. I mean, Flora, in time there will be too many of them. They breed new ones faster than the old ones die off. It's simple. There will come a day when you won't have any more room left in there. What will you do then?"

"Move out."

"What about the animals?"

"I'll take care of them. They can have the whole trailer, they'll have lots of room if I move out."

"But you don't understand," Merle said calmly. "It goes on forever. It's numbers, and it doesn't change or level off or get better. It gets worse and worse, faster and faster."

"*You* don't understand," she said to him. "Everything depends on how you look at it. And what looks worse and worse to you might look better and better to me."

Merle smiled, and his blue eyes gleamed. He stepped down to the ground and waved pleasantly at the grim woman. "You are right, Flora. Absolutely right. And I thank you for straightening me out this fine morning!" he exclaimed, and whistling softly, he walked off for Marcelle's trailer, where he would sit down at her table and drink a cup of coffee with her and recommend to her that the best policy was no policy, in the matter of Flora and her guinea pigs, because Flora would be more than capable of handling any problem that the proliferation of the guinea pigs might create.

Marcelle was not happy with Merle's advice. She was a woman of action and it pained her to sit still and let things happen, especially things that seemed to her to have no other possible consequence, if let go, than disaster. But, as she told Merle, she had no choice in this matter of the guinea pigs. If she tried to evict Flora and the animals, there would be a ruckus and possibly a scandal; if she brought in the health department, there was bound to be a scandal; if she evicted Flora and not the guinea pigs, then she'd have the problem of disposing of the damn things herself. "It's just gone too far," she said, scowling.

"But everything's fine right now, at this very moment, isn't it?" Merle asked, stirring his coffee.

"I suppose you could say that."

"Then it hasn't gone too far. It's gone just far enough."

AT THIS STAGE, JUST BEFORE CHRISTMAS THE FIRST YEAR of Flora Pease's residence at the trailerpark, everyone had an opinion as to what ought to be done with regard to the question of the guinea pigs.

Flora Pease: Keep the animals warm, well-fed, clean and breeding. Naturally, as their numbers increase, their universe will expand. (Of course, Flora didn't express herself that way, for she would have been speaking to people who would have been confused by language like that coming from her. She said it this way: "When you take care of things, they thrive. Animals, vegetables, minerals, same with all of them. And that makes you a better person, since it's the taking care that makes *people* thrive. Feeling good is good, and feeling better is better. No two ways about it. All people ever argue about anyhow is how to go about feeling good and then better.")

Doreen Tiede: Evict Flora (she could always rent a room at the Hawthorne House, Claudel Bing had and, God knows, he was barely able to tie his own shoes for a while, he was so drunk, though of course he's much better now and may actually move out of the Hawthorne House one of these days, and in fact the man was starting to look like his old self again, which was not half-bad), and then call in the S.P.C.A. to find homes for the animals (the ones that couldn't be placed in foster homes would have to be destroyed—but really, all they are is animals, rodents, rats, almost).

Terry Constant: Sneak into her trailer one day when she's in town buying grain, and one by one, set the animals free. Maybe you ought to wait till spring and then just set them free to live in the swamp and the piney woods and fields between Old Road and the trailerpark. By the time winter came rolling around again, they'd have figured out how to tunnel into the ground and hibernate like the rest of the warm-blooded animals. The ones that didn't learn how to survive, well, too bad for them. Survival of the fittest.

Bruce Severance: The profit motive. That's what needs to be invoked here. Explain to Flora that laboratories pay well for clean, well-fed guinea pigs, especially those bred and housed under such controlled conditions as Flora has established. Explain this, pointing out that this will enable her to continue to breed guinea pigs for both fun and profit for an indefinite period of time, for as long as she wants, when you get right down to it. Show her that this is not only socially useful but it will provide her as well with enough money for her to take even better care of her animals than she does now.

Noni Hubner: Bruce's idea is a good one, and so is Leon LaRoche's, and Captain Knox has a good idea too. Maybe we ought to try one first, Captain Knox's, say, since he's the oldest and has the most experience of the world, and if that doesn't work we could try Leon LaRoche's, and then if that fails, we can try Bruce's. That would be the democratic way.

Leon LaRoche: Captain Knox's idea, of course, is the logical one, but it runs certain risks and depends on his being able to keep Flora, by the sheer force of his will, from reacting hysterically or somehow "causing a scene" that would embarrass the trailerpark and we who live in it. If the *Suncook Valley Sun* learned that we had this kind of thing going on here, that we had this type of village eccentric living here among us at the trailerpark, we would all suffer deep embarrassment. I agree, therefore, with Doreen Tiede's plan. But my admiration, of course, is for Captain Knox's plan.

Carol Constant: I don't care what you do with the damned things, just do something. The world's got enough problems, real problems, without people going out and inventing new ones. The main thing is to keep the woman happy, and if having a lot of little rodents around is what makes her happy and they aren't bothering anyone else yet, then for God's sake, leave her alone. She'll end up taking care of them herself, getting rid of them or whatever, if and when they start to bother her—and they'll bother her a lot sooner than they bother us, once we stop thinking about them all the time. Her ideas will change as soon as the guinea pigs get to the point where they're causing more trouble than they're giving pleasure. Everybody's that way, and Flora Pease is no different. You have to trust the fact that we're all human beings.

Nancy Hubner: Obviously, the guinea pigs are Flora's substitutes for a family and friends. She's trying to tell us something, and we're not listening. If we, and I mean all of us, associated more with Flora on a social level, if we befriended her, in other words, then her need for these filthy animals would diminish and probably disappear. It would be something that in the future we could all laugh about, Flora laughing right along with us. We should drop by for coffee, invite her over for drinks, offer to help redecorate her trailer, and so on. We should be more charitable. It's as simple as that. Christian charity. I know it won't be easy—Flora's not exactly socially "flexible," if you know what I mean, but we are, at least most of us are, and therefore it's *our* responsibility to initiate contact, not hers, poor thing.

Captain Dewey Knox: It's her choice, no one else's. Either she goes, or the animals go. She decides which it's to be, not us. If she decides to go, fine, she can take the animals with her or leave them behind, in which case I'm sure some more or less humane way can be found to dispose of them. If she stays, also fine, but she stays without the animals. Those are the rules—no pets. They're the same rules for all of us, no exceptions. All one has to do is apply the rules, and that forces onto the woman a decision that, however painful it may be for her, she must make. No one can make that decision for her.

Marcelle Chagnon: If she'd stop the damned things from breeding, the whole problem would be solved. At least it would not bother me anymore, which is important. The only way to get her to stop breeding them, without bringing the Corporation or the health board or the S.P.C.A. or any other outsiders into it, is to go in there and separate the males from the females ourselves, and when she comes back from town, say to her, okay, Flora, this is a compromise. Sometimes people don't understand what a compromise is until you force it on them. It's either that or we sit around waiting for this thing to explode, and then it'll be too late to compromise, because the outsiders will be in charge.

Merle Ring: Let Flora continue to keep the animals warm, well-fed, clean and breeding. Naturally, as their numbers increase, their universe will expand. And as a result, all the people in the trailerpark, insofar as they observe this phenomenon, will find their universe expanding also. (It's understood that Merle did not express himself this way, for he would have been expressing himself to people who would have been offended by language like that. Here's how he put it: "It should be interesting to see what the woman does with her problem— if it ever actually becomes a problem. And if it never becomes a problem, that should be interesting too.")

*   *   *

FLORA'S LIFE UP TO NOW OUGHT TO HAVE PREPARED HER FOR what eventually happened with the guinea pigs. It had been a hard life, beginning when Flora was barely a year old with the death of her mother. Her father was what often in these parts is called a rough carpenter, meaning that he could use a hammer and saw well enough to work as a helper for a bona fide carpenter during the summer months. Usually he was the one who nailed together the plywood forms for making cellar walls and then, when the cement had set, tore the forms apart again. During the fall and winter months, when it was too cold for cement to pour, the bona fide carpenters moved to interior work, which required a certain skill and a basic fluency with numbers, and Flora's father was always among the first to be laid off, so that he would have to collect unemployment until spring.

There were three older children, older by one, two and three years, and after the mother died, the children more or less took care of themselves. They lived out beyond Shackford Corners in a dilapidated house that appeared to be falling into its own cellar hole, an unpainted, leaky, abandoned house heated in winter by a kerosene stove, with no running water and only rudimentary wiring. The father's way of raising his children was to stay drunk when he was not working, to beat them if they cried or intruded on his particular misery, and when he was working, to leave them to their own devices, which were not especially healthful devices. When Flora's older brother was six and she was three, while playing with blasting caps he had found near the lumber camp a half-mile behind the house in the woods, he blew one of his arms off and almost died. When Flora's only sister was eleven, she was raped by an uncle visiting from Saskatchewan and after that could only gaze blankly around you when you tried to talk to her or get her to talk to you. Flora's other brother, when he was fourteen and she thirteen, sickened and died of what was determined by the local health authorities to have been malnutrition, at which point the remaining three children were taken away from the father and placed into the care of the state, which meant, at that time, the New Hamphire State Hospital over in Concord, where they had a wing for juveniles who could not be placed in foster homes or who were drug addicts or had committed crimes of violence but were too young to be tried as adults. Four years later, Flora was allowed to leave the mental hospital (for that is what it was) on the condition that she join the United States Air Force, where she spent the next twenty years working in the main as a maid, or steward, in officers' clubs and quarters at various bases around the country. She was not badly treated by the Air Force itself, but numerous individual servicemen, enlisted men as well as officers, treated her unspeakably.

Despite her life, Flora remained good-naturedly ambitious for her spirit. She believed in self-improvement, believed that it was possible, and that not to seek it, not to strive for it, was reprehensible, was in fact a sin. And sinners she viewed the way most people view the stupid or the poor—as if their stupidity or poverty were their own fault, the direct result of sheer laziness and a calculated desire to exploit the rest of humankind, who, of course, are intelligent or well-off as a direct result of their willingness to work and not ask for help from others. This might not seem a particularly enlightened way to view sinners, and it certainly was not a Christian way to view sinners, but it did preserve a kind of chastity for Flora. It also, of course, made it difficult for her to learn much, in moral terms, from the behavior of others. There was probably a wisdom in that, however, a trade-off that made it possible for her to survive into something like middle age without having fallen into madness and despair.

Within a week of having moved into the trailerpark, Flora had purchased her first pair of guinea pigs. She bought them for fifteen dollars at the pet counter of the five-and-dime in town. She had gone into the store looking for goldfish, but when she saw the pair of scrawny, matted animals in their tiny, filthy cages at the back of the store, she had forgotten the goldfish, which looked relatively healthy anyhow, despite the cloudiness of the water in their tank. She built her cages herself, mostly from castoff boards and chicken wire she found at the town dump and carried home. The skills required were not great, were, in fact, about the same as had been required of her father in the construction of cement forms. At the dump she also found the pieces of garden hose she needed to make her watering system and the old gutters she hooked up as grain troughs.

Day and night she worked for her guinea pigs, walking to town and hauling back fifty-pound bags of grain, dragging back from the dump more old boards, sheets of tin, gutters, and so on. As the guinea pigs multiplied and more cages became necessary, Flora soon found herself working long hours into the night alone in her trailer, feeding, watering and cleaning the animals, while out behind the trailer the pyramid of mixed straw, feces, urine and grain gradually rose to waist height, then to shoulder height, finally reaching to head height, when she had to start a second pyramid, and then, a few months later, a third. And as the space requirements of the guinea pigs increased, her own living space decreased, until finally she was sleeping on a cot in a corner of the back bedroom, eating standing up at the kitchen sink, stashing her clothing and personal belongings under her cot so that all the remaining space could be devoted to the care, housing and feeding of the guinea pigs.

By the start of her third summer at the trailerpark, she had begun to lose weight noticeably, and her usually pinkish skin had taken on a gray pallor. Never particularly fastidious anyhow, her personal hygiene now could be said not to exist at all, and the odor she bore with her was the same odor given off by the guinea pigs, so that, in time, to call Flora Pease the Guinea Pig Lady (as did the people in town, having learned at last of the secret— through several sources: it's a small town, Catamount, and one sentence by one person can be placed alongside another sentence by another person, and before long you will have the entire story) was not to misrepresent her. Her eyes grew dull, as if the light behind them was slowly going out, and her hair was tangled and stiff with dirt, and her clothing seemed increasingly to be hidden behind stains, smears, spills, drips and dust.

"Here comes the Guinea Pig Lady!" You'd hear the call from outside where the loafers leaned against the glass front of Briggs' News & Variety, and a tall, angular teen-ager with shoulder-length hair and acne, wearing torn jeans and a Mothers of Invention tee shirt, would stick his long head inside and call out your name, "C'mere, take a look at this, will ya!"

You'd be picking up your paper, maybe, or because Briggs' was the only place that sold it, the racing form with yesterday's Rockingham results and today's odds. The kid might irritate you slightly—his gawky, dim-witted pleasure at staring at someone undeniably less sociable-looking than he, his slightly pornographic acne, the affectation of his tee shirt and long hair—but still, your curiosity up, you'd pay for your paper and stroll to the door to see what had got the kid so excited.

In a low, conspiratorial voice borne on bad breath, the

kid would say, "Take a look at that, will ya? The Guinea Pig Lady."

She would be on the other side of the street, shuffling rapidly along the sidewalk in the direction of Merrimack Farmers' Exchange, wearing her blue, U.S. Air Force, wool, ankle-length coat, even though this would be in May and an unusually warm day even for May, and her boot lacings would be undone and trailing behind her, her arms chopping away at the air as if she were a boxer working out with the heavy bag, and she would be singing in a voice moderately loud, loud enough to be heard easily across the street, "My Boy Bill" from *Carousel*.

"Hey, honey!" the kid would wail, and the Guinea Pig Lady, though she ignored his call, would stop singing. "Hey, honey, how about a little nookie, sweets!" The Guinea Pig Lady would speed up a bit, her arms churning faster against the air. "Got something for ya, honey! Got me a licking-stick, sweet lips!" Then, in a wet whisper, to you: "A broad like that, man, you hafta fuck 'em in the mouth. You can get a disease, ya know."

If you already knew who the woman was, Flora Pease of the Granite State Trailerpark out at Skitter Lake, and knew about the guinea pigs and, thereby, could reason why she was headed for the grain store, you would ease past the kid and away. But if you didn't know who she was, you might ask the kid, and he would say, "The Guinea Pig Lady, man. She lives with these hundreds of guinea pigs in the trailerpark out at Skitter Lake. Just her and all these animals. Everybody in town knows about it, but she won't let anyone inside her trailer to see 'em, man. She's got these huge piles of shit out behind her trailer, and she comes into town all the time to buy feed for 'em. She's a fuckin' freak, man! A freak! And nobody in town can do anything about 'em, the guinea pigs, I mean, because so far nobody out at the

trailerpark will make a formal complaint about 'em.
Though you can bet your ass if I lived out there I'd sure
as shit make a complaint. I'd burn the fucking trailer to
the ground, man. I mean, that's disgusting, all them
animals. Somebody ought to go out there some night
and pull her outa there and burn the place down, complaint or no complaint. It's a health hazard, man! You
can get a disease from them things!"

IN SEPTEMBER THAT YEAR, AFTER ABOUT A WEEK OF NOT
having seen Flora leave her trailer once, even to empty
the trays of feces out back, Marcelle Chagnon decided
to make sure the woman was all right, so one morning
she stepped across the roadway and knocked on Flora's
door. The lake, below a cloudless sky, was deep blue,
and the leaves of the birches along the shore were yel-
lowing. There had already been a hard frost, and the
grass and weeds and low scrub shone dully gold in the
sunlight.

There was no answer, so Marcelle knocked again,
firmly this time, and called Flora's name. Under her
breath, she muttered, "Jesus, Mary and Joseph. Just
what I need."

Finally she heard a low, muffled voice from inside.
"Go away." Then silence, except for the breeze off the
lake.

"Are you all right? It's me, Marcelle!"

Silence.

Marcelle reached out and tried the door. It was locked.
She called again, "Flora, let me in!" and stood with her
hands in fists jammed against her hips. She breathed in
and out rapidly, her large brow pulled down in alarm. A
few seconds passed, and then she called out, "Flora,
I'm coming inside!"

Moving quickly to the top step, she pitched her shoulder against the door just above the latch, which immediately gave way and let the door blow open, causing Marcelle to stagger inside, off balance, blinking in the darkness and floundering in the odor of the animals as if in a huge wave of warm water. She reacted like a fireman entering a house filled with smoke. "Flora!" she yelled. "Flora, where are you!" Bumping against the cages, she made her way around them and into the kitchen area, shouting her name and peering in vain into the darkness. In several minutes, she had made her way to the bedroom in back, and there in a corner she found Flora on her cot, wrapped in a blanket, looking almost unconscious, limp, bulky, gray. Her hands were near her throat clutching the top of the blanket, like the hands of a frightened, beaten child, and she had her head turned toward the wall, with her eyes closed. She looked like a sick child to Marcelle, like her own child, Joel, who had died when he was twelve—the fever had risen and the hallucinations had come until he was out of his head with them, and then suddenly, while she was mopping his body with damp washcloths, the wildness had gone out of him and he had turned on his side, drawn his skinny legs up to his belly, and died.

Flora was feverish, though not with as high a fever as the boy Joel had endured, and she had drawn her legs up to her, bulking her body into a lumpy heap beneath the filthy blanket. "You're sick," Marcelle announced to the woman, who seemed not to hear her. Marcelle straightened the blanket, brushed the woman's matted hair away from her face, and looked around the room to see if there wasn't some way she could make her more comfortable. The room was jammed with the large, odd-shaped cages, and Marcelle could hear the animals rustling back and forth on the wire flooring, now and then chittering in what she supposed was protest against hunger and thirst.

Taking a backward step, Marcelle yanked the cord and opened the venetian blind, and sunlight tumbled into the room. Suddenly Flora was shouting, "Shut it! Shut it! Don't let them see! No one can see me!"

Obediently, Marcelle closed the blind, and the room once again filled with the gloom and shadow that Flora believed hid the shape of the life being lived here. "I got to get you to a doctor," Marcelle said quietly. "Doctor Wickshaw's got office hours today, you know Carol Constant, his nurse, that nice colored lady who lives next door? You got to see a doctor, missy."

"No. I'll be all right soon," she said in a weak voice. "Just the flu, that's all." She pulled the blanket up higher, covering most of her face but exposing her dirty bare feet.

Marcelle persisted, and soon Flora began to curse the woman, her voice rising in fear and anger, the force of it pushing Marcelle away from the cot, as she shouted, "You leave me alone, you bitch! I know your tricks, I know what you're trying to do! You just want to get me out of here so you can take my babies away from me! Get out of here! I'm fine, I can take care of my babies fine, just fine! Now you get out of my house! Go on, get!"

Marcelle backed slowly away, then turned and walked to the open door and outside to the sunshine and the clean fall air.

DOCTOR WICKSHAW, CAROL TOLD HER, DOESN'T MAKE housecalls. Marcelle sat at her kitchen table, looked out the window and talked on the telephone. She was watching Flora's trailer, number 11, as if watching a bomb that was about to explode.

"Yeah, I know that," Marcelle said, holding the receiver between her shoulder and cheek so both hands could be free to light a cigarette. "Listen, Carol, this is Flora Pease we're talking about, and there's no way I'm going to be able to get her into that office. But she's real sick, and it could be just the flu, but it could be meningitis, for all I know. My boy died of that, you know, and you have to do tests and everything before you can tell if it's meningitis." There was a silence for a few seconds. "Anyhow, I don't want some infectious disease breaking out here, and Doctor Wickshaw could save us a lot of trouble if he'd just drive out here for ten minutes and take a look at this crazy woman so we could know how to handle her. I mean, I maybe should call the ambulance and get her over to the Concord Hospital, for all I know right now! I need somebody who knows something to come here and look at her," she said, her voice rising.

"Maybe on my lunch hour I'll be able to come by and take a look," Carol said. "At least I should be capable of saying if she should be got to a hospital or not."

Marcelle thanked her—not without first laying down a curse against doctors who set themselves up like bankers—and hung up the phone. Nervously tapping her fingers against the table, she thought to call in Merle Ring or maybe Captain Knox, to get their opinions of Flora's condition, and then decided against it. That damned Dewey Knox, he'd just take over, one way or the other, and after reducing the situation to a choice between two courses, probably between leaving her alone in the trailer and calling the ambulance, he'd insist that someone other than he do the choosing, probably Flora herself, who, of course, would choose to be left alone. Then he'd walk off believing he'd done the right thing, the *only* right thing, without it ever occurring to him that he'd missed the point of the whole dilemma. Merle would be just as bad, she figured, with all his smart-ass comments about illness and death and leaving things alone until they have something to say to you that's completely clear. Some illnesses lead to death, he'd say, and some lead to health, and we'll know before long which this is, and when we do, we'll know how to act. Men. Either they take responsibility for everything, or else they take responsibility for nothing.

Around one, Carol Constant arrived in her little blue Japanese sedan, dressed in a white nurse's uniform and looking, to Marcelle, very much like a medical authority. Marcelle led her into Flora's trailer, after warning her about the clutter and the smell—"It's like some kinda burrow in there," she said as they stepped through the door—and Carol, placing a plastic tape against Flora's forehead, determined that Flora was indeed quite ill, for her temperature was 105 degrees. She turned to Marcelle and told her to call the ambulance.

Immediately Flora went wild, bellowing and moaning about her babies and how she couldn't leave them, they needed her. She thrashed against Carol's strong grip for a moment and then gave up and fell weakly back into the cot.

"Go ahead and call," Carol told Marcelle, "and I'll hold on to things here until they come." When Marcelle had gone, Carol commenced talking to the ill woman in a low, soothing voice, stroking her forehead with one hand and holding her by the shoulder with the other, until, after a few moments, Flora began to whimper and then to weep, and finally, as if her heart were broken, to sob. By now Marcelle had returned from calling the ambulance and was standing in the background almost out of sight, while Carol soothed the woman and crooned, "Poor thing, you poor thing."

"My babies, who'll take care of my babies?" she wailed.

"I'll get my brother Terry to take care of them,"

Carol promised, and for a second that seemed to placate the woman.

But then she began to wail again, because she knew it was a lie and when she came back her babies would be gone.

No, no, no, no, both Carol and Marcelle insisted. When she got back, the guinea pigs would be here, all of them, every last one. Terry would water and feed them, and he'd clean out the cages every day, just as she did.

"I'll make sure he does," Marcelle promised, "or he'll have his ass in a sling."

That calmed the woman, but just then two young men dressed in white, the ambulance attendants, stepped into the room, and when Flora saw them, their large, grim faces and, from her vantage point, their enormous, uniformed bodies, her eyes rolled back and she began to wail, "No, no, no! I'm not going! I'm not going!"

The force of her thrashing movements tossed Carol off the cot onto the floor, and moving swiftly, the two young men reached down and pinned Flora against her cot. One of them, the larger one, told the other to bring his bag, and the smaller man rushed out of the trailer to the ambulance parked outside.

"I'm just going to give you something to calm yourself, ma'am," the big man said in a mechanical way. The other man was back now, and Carol and Marcelle, looking at each other with slight regret and apprehension, stepped out of his way as he pushed through with the black satchel.

In seconds, Flora had been injected with a tranquilizer, and while the two hard-faced, large men in white strapped her body into a four-wheeled, chromium and canvas stretcher, she descended swiftly into slumber. They wheeled her efficiently out of the trailer, as if she were a piece of furniture, and slid her into the back of the ambulance, and then, with Marcelle following in her car, they were gone.

Alone by the roadway outside Flora's trailer, Carol watched the ambulance and Marcelle's battered old Ford head out toward Old Road and away. After a moment or two, drifting from their trailers one by one, came Nancy Hubner, her face stricken with concern, and Captain Dewey Knox, his face firmed to hear grim news, and Merle Ring, his face smiling benignly.

"Where's my brother Terry?" Carol asked the three as they drew near.

IT WAS NEAR MIDNIGHT THAT SAME NIGHT. MOST OF THE trailers were dark, except for Bruce Severance's, where Terry, after having fed, watered and cleaned the ravenous, thirsty and dirty guinea pigs, was considering a business proposition from Bruce that would not demand humiliating labor for mere monkey-money, and Doreen Tiede's trailer, where Claudel Bing's naked, muscular arm was reaching over Doreen's head to snap off the lamp next to the bed—when out by Old Road the woman Flora Pease, the Guinea Pig Lady, came shuffling along the lane between the pine woods. She moved quickly and purposefully, just as she always moved, but silently now. She wore the clothes she was wearing in the morning, when the men had taken her from her cot and strapped her onto the stretcher—old bib overalls and a faded, stained, plaid flannel shirt. Her face was ablaze with fever. Her red hair ringed her head in a stiff, wet halo that made her look like an especially blessed peasant figure in a medieval fresco, a shepherd or carpenter rushing to see the Divine Child.

When she neared the trailerpark sufficiently to glimpse the few remaining lights and the dully shining, geometric shapes of the trailers through the trees and, here and there, a dark strip of the lake beyond, she cut to her left and departed from the roadway toward the swamp. Without hesitation, she darted into the swamp, locating even in darkness the pathways and patches of dry ground, moving slowly through the mushy, brush-covered muskeg, emerging from the deep shadows of the swamp after a while at the edge of the clearing directly behind her own trailer. Soundlessly, she crossed her back yard, passed the head-high pyramids standing like dolmens in the dim light, and stepped through the broken door into the trailer.

The trailer was in pitch darkness, and the only sound was that of the animals as they chirped, bred and scuffled in their cages through the nighttime. With the same familiarity she had shown cutting across the swamp, Flora moved in darkness to the kitchen area, where she opened a cupboard and drew from a clutter of cans and bottles a red one-gallon can of kerosene. Then, starting at the farthest corner of the trailer, she dribbled the kerosene through every room, looping through and around every one of the cages, until she arrived at the door. She placed the can on the floor next to the broken door, then stepped nimbly outside, where she took a single step toward the ground, lit a wooden match against her thumbnail, tossed it into the trailer, and ran.

Instantly the trailer was a box of flame, roaring and snapping in rage, sending a dark cloud and poisonous fumes into the night sky as the paneling and walls ignited and burst into flame. Next door, wakened by the first explosion and terrified by the sight of the flames and the roar of the fire, Carol Constant rushed from her bed to the road, where everyone else in the park was gathering, wide-eyed, confused, struck with wonder and fear.

Marcelle hollered at Terry and Bruce, ordering them to hook up garden hoses and wash down the trailers

next to Flora's. Then she yelled to Doreen. Dressed in a
filmy nightgown, with the naked Claudel Bing standing
in darkness behind her, the woman peered through her
half-open door at the long, flame-filled coffin across the
lane. "Call the fire department, for Christ's sake! And
tell Bing to get his clothes on and get out here and help
us!" Captain Knox gave orders to people who were
already doing what he ordered them to do, and Nancy
Hubner, in nightgown, dressing gown and slippers, hauled
her garden hose from under the trailer and dragged it
toward the front, screeching as she passed each window
along the way for Noni to wake up and get out here and
help, while inside, Noni slid along a stoned slope of
sleep, dreamless and genuinely happy. Leon LaRoche
appeared fully dressed in clean and pressed khaki
workclothes with gloves and silver-colored hardhat, looking like a cigarette ad's version of a construction worker.
He asked the Captain what he should do, and the Captain pointed him toward Bruce and Terry, who were
already hosing down the steaming sides of the trailers
next to the fire. At the far end of the row of trailers, in
darkness at the edge of the glow cast by the flames,
stood Merle Ring, uniquely somber, his arms limply at
his sides, in one hand a fishing rod, in the other a string
of hornpout.

In a few moments, the fire engines arrived, but it was
already too late to save Flora's trailer or anything that
had been inside it. All they could accomplish, they realized immediately, was to attempt to save the rest of the
trailers, which they instantly set about doing, washing
down the metal sides and sending huge, billowing col-
umns of steam into the air. Gradually, as the flames
subsided, the firemen turned their hoses and doused the
dying fire completely. An hour before daylight, they had
left, and behind them, where Flora's trailer had been,

was a cold, charred, shapeless mass of indistinguishable materials—melted plastic, crumbled wood and ash, blackened, bent sheet metal, and flesh and fur.

BY THE PINK LIGHT OF DAWN, FLORA EMERGED FROM THE swamp and came to stand before the remains of the pyre. She was alone, for the others, as soon as the fire engines had left, had trudged heavily and exhausted to bed. Around nine, Marcelle Chagnon was stirred from her sleep by her telephone—it was the Concord Hospital, informing her that the woman she had signed in the day before, Flora Pease, had left sometime during the night without permission and they did not know her whereabouts.

Marcelle wearily peered out the window next to her bed and saw Flora standing before the long, black heap across the lane, and she told the woman from the hospital that Flora was here. She must have heard last night that her trailer burned down, over the radio, maybe, and hitchhiked back to Catamount. She assured the woman that she would look after her, but the woman said not to bother, she only had the flu and probably would be fine in a few days, unless, of course, she had caught pneumonia hitchhiking last night without a hat or coat on.

Marcelle hung up the phone and continued to watch Flora, who stood as if before a grave. The others in the park also, as they rose from their beds, looked out at the wreckage, and seeing her there, stayed inside and left her alone. Eventually, around midday, she slowly turned and started back toward the swamp.

Marcelle saw her leaving and ran out to stop her. "Flora!" she cried, and the woman turned back and waited in the middle of the clearing. Marcelle trotted heavily across the open space, and when she came up to her, said to Flora, "I'm sorry."

Flora stared at her blankly, as if she didn't understand. "Flora, I'm sorry . . . about your babies." Marcelle put one arm around the woman's shoulders, and they stood side by side, facing away from the trailerpark.

Flora said nothing for a few moments. "They wasn't my babies. Babies make me nervous," she said, shrugging the arm away. Then, when she looked up into Marcelle's big face, she must have seen that she had hurt her, for her tone softened. "I'm sorry, Mrs. Chagnon. But they wasn't my babies. I know the difference, and babies make me nervous."

That was in September. The fire was determined to have been "of suspicious origin," and everyone concluded that some drunken kids from town had set it. The several young men suspected of the crime, however, came up with alibis, and no further investigation seemed reasonable.

By the middle of October, Flora Pease had built a tiny, awkwardly pitched shanty on the land where the swamp behind the trailerpark rose slightly and met the pine woods, land that might have belonged to the Corporation and might just as well have belonged to the state of New Hampshire, but it was going to take a couple of lawyers and a pair of surveyors before anyone could say for sure, so as long as neither the Corporation nor the state of New Hampshire fussed about it, neither the Corporation nor the state of New Hampshire was willing to make Flora tear down her shanty and move.

She built the shack herself, from stuff she dragged down the road and into the woods from the town dump—old boards, galvanized sheet metal, strips of tarpaper, cast-off shingles—and furnished it the same way, with a discolored, torn mattress, a three-legged card table, an easy chair with the stuffing blossoming at the seams, and a moldly rug that had been in a children's play-house. It was a single room, with a tin woodstove for cooking and heat, a privy out back, and for light a single kerosene lantern.

For a while there were a few people from the trailerpark who went out there to the edge of the swamp and visited her. You could see her shack easily from the park, as she had situated it right where she had the clearest view of the charred wreckage of old number 11. Bruce Severance, the college kid, went fairly often to visit her, especially in early summer, when he was busily locating the feral hemp plants in the area and needed her expert help, and Terry Constant went out there, "just for laughs," he said, but even so, he used to sit peacefully with her in the sun and get stoned on hemp and rap with her about his childhood and dead mother. Whether or not Flora talked about her childhood and her dead mother Terry never said, but then, no one asked him, either. It quickly got hard to talk about Flora. She was just there, exactly the way she was, the Guinea Pig Lady, even though she didn't have any guinea pigs, and there wasn't much anyone could say about it anymore, since everyone more or less knew how she had got to be who she was and everyone more or less knew who she was going to be from here on out. Merle used to walk out there in warm weather, and he continued to visit Flora long after everyone else had left off and had gone about his and her business quite as if Flora no longer even existed. The reason he went out, he said, was because you got a different perspective on the trailerpark from out there, practically the same perspective he said he got in winter from the lake when he was in his ice-house out on the lake. And though Marcelle never went out to Flora's shack, every time she passed it with her gaze, she stopped her gaze and for a long time looked at the place and Flora sitting outside on an old metal folding chair, smoking her cob pipe and staring back at the trailerpark. She gazed at Flora mournfully and with an anger longing for a shape, for Marcelle believed that she alone knew the woman's secret.

Cleaving, and Other Needs

WHEN DOREEN TIEDE MARRIED BUCK TIEDE SHE DID not have to change her name. Her grandfather Sam Tiede, a well driller from Northwood, and Buck's father Norman Tiede, a house painter from Catamount, were brothers. They had been born and raised in Catamount, along with a half-dozen more Tiedes of the same generation, and when Sam had moved to Northwood ten miles away and had become a well driller and after a few years had managed to borrow enough money from the bank in Concord to set him and his son up with their own drilling rig, he was regarded from then till now as the successful son of old Warren Tiede, for none of the remaining children had moved that far from Catamount and made money. Doreen, then, was descended directly from the Tiedes who had risen in the world, whereas her second cousin Buck was from the Tiedes who, generation after generation, had plowed the same old row. This is important to know, because it helps explain why Doreen didn't have to change her last name when, a seventeen-year-old virgin, she married, and it also helps explain why they acted the way they did after they were married and divorced. It doesn't much help explain Buck's alcoholism, of course, and it doesn't tell you why Doreen had such a craving for sexual love that Buck, who wasn't much interested in sex in the beginning, got to be obsessed with it, but it does tell you why Doreen thought Buck was a better man than he perhaps thought he was, and it tells you a little something about his anger.

In the first year of their marriage, Doreen made love with three men other than her husband, who knew about only one of the men, Howie Leeke, and when it came right down to it, didn't know about Howie for sure and was made to think that he was imagining the worst parts, the parts, that is, where Howie rides wildly atop Doreen on the waterbed he's supposed to have out there in his trailer on Cush Meadow Road, rides her bouncing, arching, tautly sprung, eighteen-year-old body as if it were a horse he were breaking, rubbing and drifting through her while she works against him the other way in perfectly thrilling countertime, until she can't control her movements any longer and . . . Well, you know the rest.

Buck knew the rest, too, but only from what he had read about sex in *Playboy* and other such magazines, not from what he had experienced with women himself, for he had very little experience when he married Doreen—teen-age sex in the back seat of his Chevy Nomad with girls he had gone to high school with, which meant mainly kissing and biting and then plucking and pulling and poking at each other's private parts and sometimes sucking on each other's private parts, which, even though such activities usually brought him and sometimes his girlfriend a deep shudder and a wet spot, nevertheless left him feeling dazed with guilt and overall feelings of inferiority; and then, later, in the service, sex with prostitutes in towns near the bases where he was stationed, in Texas and South Carolina, sex that left him feeling like a man who has just walked out to the neon-lit street from a pornographic movie; and after he had come back to New Hampshire and had gone to work for Doreen's father and grandfather, his cousin and uncle, drilling wells in Northwood and living at his parents' home in Catamount, sex with Doreen, who was then a senior in high school, five years younger than he. Because Buck was afraid he would get Doreen pregnant before she graduated from high school, and probably also because he wanted Doreen's father and grandfather to think well of him, Buck Tiede of the Catamount Tiedes who never amount to a tinker's dam anyway, sex with Doreen remained more or less of the back-seat kind, enlivened of course with a lot of talk, for they were, after all, in love.

Both Doreen and Buck were good-looking, and people thought of them as sexy because they looked the way sexy people are supposed to look, clean and healthy and symmetrical. Doreen was tall and broad-shouldered with full breasts and a firm, round bottom. She had silky-smooth, dark brown hair that hung loosely over her shoulders, and in the summer she tanned easily and evenly to a shade that made people think she might have a little Mediterranean blood in her. Her face was large, with a full, broad mouth that was good-humored, and because of the crispness of her full lips, sensual, and her brown eyes, shaded by a prominent but serious-looking brow, were set wide on her face. Her nose wasn't quite right—a little short and narrow for such a large face, but it certainly was not unattractive. Buck's most unattractive feature in those days was the wide gap between his front teeth. The gap was wide enough for him to spit through, which he did habitually, wide enough even for him to clamp a cigarette with, which, as a joke, he sometimes did, so that he could go on talking while his cigarette remained attached to his upper jaw by the gapped front teeth. Then he would pluck the cigarette away, and you would see that the gap was actually kind of sexy, kind of inviting, like an open door or gate, and if you were a man, you'd think, "Hmmm, I bet old Buck gets a lot of women," and if you were a woman, you'd think, "Hmmm, I wonder what it would be like to run my tongue into that gap between his teeth." He was also tall, a little over six feet, and in those days in good shape from his work on the drilling rig, and with his ash-brown hair cut in the military style and his clear blue eyes and straight, narrow nose, he was clean-looking, too.

Their wedding night and honeymoon—a week in a motel near Franconia Notch in the White Mountains— weren't much fun for Doreen. They weren't much fun for Buck, either. He was awkward and too quick and then impotent for a while and then impatiently passionate and grabby, his head so full of blood from shame and lust that he couldn't think, so finally, because she could think, Doreen just gave herself over to him and, without feeling, let him have his ways with her. There were several ways, because of all the false starts and false stops and his difficulties with the condom, and it was with barely hidden relief for both of them when, finally, lodged up inside her, Buck grunted and his pelvis whimpered of its own accord, and he was freed to withdraw from her. Her hymen he had broken easily, without even realizing it, earlier, and though she had felt a stab of pain, it was a hot, quick and almost pleasurable pain, so she had said nothing to him. Then next morning when he got out of bed to pee, he saw the specks of blood on the sheet beneath where he had slept, and he quickly covered them with the top sheet and went straight into the shower, while she lay curled on her side sleeping peacefully.

Throughout the honeymoon week, Doreen watched and understood Buck, and she loved him. She hated to see him suffer so, and in a way she wished he would just forget all about making love to her and just let her look at him, as if he were a movie actor or maybe a stranger she had met here in the White Mountains while on vacation alone, a tall, athletic-looking man with bright blue eyes and a sexy gap between his front teeth. She could watch him at breakfast in the International Pancake House across the road from the motel. Or she could watch him in the chair in front of her as they both rode the aerial tramway to the top of Wildcat Mountain. Or, at the viewing platform at Echo Lake below the Old Man of the Mountain, he could be peering through the telescope next to hers. His quarter's worth of viewing and hers would run out at the same time, and both their telescopes would droop at the same instant. He would turn to her and their eyes would meet above their telescopes, and he would say, "I've been watching you all week. I think you're beautiful, and I want to make love to you." The music would rise, she would let go of her telescope and take a single, delicate step forward, he would reach out his hand and take hers, and . . . Well, you know the rest.

Doreen knew the rest, too, but she wasn't all that interested in the rest. And everything she was going through in bed with Buck only served to formalize her lack of interest. When they returned to Catamount and moved into the trailerpark at Skitter Lake, it only got worse. Buck tried to make love to her about once a week at first, and then once every two weeks, and then only once a month, always with the same frustrating results for her, the same depressing results for him. It wasn't that either one of them was technically incompetent in the act. What was wrong was inside their heads. Her fantasies and his fears had no way of meshing together or of helping one another go away or even of becoming known to one another. The one thing that kept their attempts at lovemaking even remotely tender was her understanding of his fears, for when he grew angry at himself for his awkwardness or the unpredictability of his body, its sudden flights from itself, he would turn on her, suddenly snarling through the darkness that lay between them, "Goddamn it, Doreen, if you didn't just lay there like a log I might be able to get myself more excited about the idea of making love to you," and if, as a result of that scolding, she started licking him over his chest, fondling his inner thighs, grasping his muscular buttocks in her hands, digging into his white, tight flesh with her sharp fingernails, he'd slump and say in a low voice, "I don't know, Doreen, it frightens me when you're like this. All I can think of is your doing it with another man." Doreen understood these remarks and during the days while Buck was at work in Northwood drilling artesian wells with her father and grandfather, she plotted strategies that she hoped would allay Buck's fears at last and thereby would make him into the kind of man who could lift her up and out of her real life into the world where she knew she truly belonged, the world in which she was the recipient of a handsome stranger's utter devotion.

Within six months, however, the only time Buck would make love to her was when he was drunk, but not every time he was drunk, for by that time he was getting drunk often. All Doreen's strategies had failed by then—filmy negligees, soft music, flattery, faked orgasms, even marijuana. But nothing she did allowed Buck to come to her directly, good-humoredly, with simple hunger and tenderness and admiration neatly intertwined. If anything, her strategies only made it worse, because Buck always noticed them immediately and grew either desperate to respond to them or else grew angry and accused her of accusing him of being unable to function sexually without atmosphere and stimulants. That was when she committed adultery for the first time—after Buck had grabbed the two marijuana cigarettes from her hand and had flushed them down the toilet and stomped out of the trailer, leaving her alone in bed. She had got out of bed and had walked to the trailer next door in her nightgown, barefoot, to the kid she had bought the marijuana cigarettes from, Bruce Severance, thinking that what she wanted was to buy another cigarette, this one to smoke alone, defiantly in front of the TV, so that when Buck came back smelling of booze and still angry at her, she wouldn't much care. But she and Bruce had got to talking, he loved to talk, especially about marijuana, and she had not realized that marijuana was such an interesting subject, that there was so much to know about it, and for about five minutes, standing against the wall of his trailer, the kid had made love to her. He had simply come up against her when she had started to leave, had pulled her nightgown to her hips, and then, with one quick hand, had unzipped his fly, releasing his erect penis, which he had inserted. It was over before she had realized it had begun.

"What . . . what if I get pregnant?" she whispered into his ear.

"Don't worry, man. You won't."

"I won't?"

"Tantric birth control, man. It takes years to learn, but it works. You won't get pregnant," he promised.

She felt his semen dribbling down the inside of her thigh, and she drew her nightgown back down and stepped away.

''Just don't forget to wash, man,'' the kid said, and he asked if she wanted to use his bathroom.

She stammered no, no, she'd better get back, because her husband could be coming in any minute and he would be drunk and mean.

The kid agreed and opened the door for her. He kissed her on the nape of her neck as she passed by him and went out, but she barely felt his kiss, for she was terrified that she had been impregnated by him.

For a month after that night she felt dirty and almost evil, but when she discovered that she was not pregnant, she no longer felt dirty or almost evil. In fact, she felt downright eager to do it again. Not with Bruce Severance, however, for, even though he was a few years older than she, he was a kid to her, a long-haired pretentious kid, and what she wanted was a man, a grown man who was sure of himself and had a broad smile and could explain things to her and would be kind and tolerant and patient with her when she could not understand what he explained. That was why she made love to Leon LaRoche, who lived in number 2, two trailers down from where she lived with Buck.

Leon was in his late twenties then, and he dressed nicely, because of his job as a teller at the Catamount Savings and Loan, and he was a bachelor who smiled easily and who liked to explain things slowly, methodically, calmly, with tolerance and even affection for Doreen when she seemed not to know what he was talking about. He talked politics with her, for there was an election that fall, and though her family had always voted Republican, Doreen was thinking of registering as a Democrat for this, her first election, and Leon explained to her what she should tell her family when they found out she had registered as a Democrat, which they surely would do, since the lists of registered voters and their party affiliations were required by law to be posted in public places. He told her about Roosevelt and Jack Kennedy and civil rights, which she thought fascinating, for, even though she had heard of all three, no one had ever explained them to her slowly, carefully, and with a sure, precisely accurate knowledge of what she did not know, which meant that no one had ever told her about these things without confusing her or else condescending to her.

She touched his knees with hers—she was wearing a plaid cotton shirtwaist dress, and he wore his shirt and tie and dark brown suit pants (his jacket he had carefully hung in the closet on arriving home from the bank for lunch, which he preferred to fix for himself at home rather than spend the extra $475 a year he had calculated it would cost to eat lunch in town at the Copper Skillet). Then she reached forward between their chairs and touched his knees with the palms of her hands, running her fingertips up the insides of his legs, until she was touching his crotch. He reached out and took her by the shoulders and drew her forward and down, so that her face was laid against his tightening thigh. Then he unzipped his fly, and she dove both her hands in, working and massaging him until the red head of his penis was shoving its way past the folds of cloth toward her mouth.

Afterward, Leon hurriedly drew his crotch away from Doreen's mouth and said something about having to fix his lunch and get back to work on time, and Doreen had left his trailer in tears and had gone back to her own place and had vomited. As with Bruce, she felt dirty for about a month, although of course this time her guilt was not compounded by a fear of being pregnant, and then one morning she woke up, Buck was gone to work, and as she looked down her long, muscular legs to her feet and wiggled them deliciously, she felt fine again. It was a cold February morning, two weeks before the presidential primary, and when she went into the bathroom to shower, she discovered that during the night the cold water line to the shower had frozen solid. Water ran smoothly through all the other pipes, so she reasoned that, as the day warmed, the shower line would thaw on its own and probably was not frozen solidly enough to burst the pipe. She knew that by noon at the latest everything would be working properly again. But she also thought of Howie Leeke, the recently divorced plumber who was awfully good-looking and had a funny, raspy way of talking and quick gray eyes, so she called the plumber.

Howie liked to please women. "I always like to leave 'em crying for more," he said with a grin (when asked how he did it, how he managed to have so many women calling him in the morning to come and fix pipes or blocked drains or broken appliances that, when he arrived, seemed to need little or no repair at all). In Doreen's case, however, Howie was unable to leave her crying for more. She very quickly discovered that she had too much of him, that his persistent, tireless weight was smothering her, and the longer they bounced and thrashed across her bed, onto the floor, on the coffee table in the living room, on and on and on, for what seemed to her like whole days and nights, the more she wished she had never called him, had never come to the door in her blue nightgown, had never leaned over behind him when he squatted down by the tub to try the faucets. When he finally left, which he would do only after she had moaned and cried out like an animal with its leg caught in a trap, she had shut the door on him with enormous relief and gratitude for his absence. He had said, as he stepped out the door, "I'll be back, don't worry," and she had answered, "No, you can't. I love my husband," and he had winked and strolled across the frozen ground to his pickup truck.

But Howie was a braggart, and it wasn't a week before Buck had got told by one of the kids who worked on his crew that Howie Leeke was making cracks about Doreen Tiede down at the Hawthorne House the other night. At first Buck couldn't believe it, that his wife, the teen-aged angel Doreen, had let that big-mouthed, nervous, skinny, twice-divorced plumber near her perfect body, that she had listened to his line, that she had seen his sex organ! That he had seen hers! That their sex organs had actually made contact with one another! Then, of course, he couldn't believe anything else, and he knew it was because Howie was a giant in bed, a titan, while he was a shrimp, a child, and, driving home from work, as the snow started falling, Buck began to cry, to sob, to groan, to call out her name, Doreen! Doreen! while his car slipped on the snow and skidded from side to side, drifting dangerously into long, slow slides coming down the long hill from Northwood to Catamount.

Most people can either only give love or receive it, rarely both, and there's nothing wrong with that, so long as you attach yourself to your opposite number, that is, so long as, if you are the one who can only give love, you attach yourself to someone who can only receive it. You will be able then to make each other happy. If, by the same token, you are like Doreen Tiede and can only receive love, if you have no vision of a person's needing you more than you need that person, then you had better not hook up with someone like Buck Tiede, or you will quickly end up as they ended up—with Buck on his knees in front of his wife, snow-covered, for he had crashed his car at the turnoff from Old Road and had walked in from the road to the trailerpark, sobbing hysterically, blindly, all the way in.

Doreen was unmoved, but she stroked his head mechanically and listened to his cries, until after a while, his cries turned to wet, begging queries as to what, exactly, she had done with Howie. In her own words, he said, he wanted to hear it from her own lips. He didn't care how bad it was, he just wanted to hear it from her own lips. He knew, no matter how bad it was, no matter where it led, even if it led to her running off with Howie, he deserved it, for he had not been a good lover for her, he had been a weak and boyish man in bed, and she was a young woman who needed steady loving, just like all the sad songs said, so go ahead, give it to him straight, at least give him that much, so he could know the truth and wouldn't go around the rest of his life being laughed at because everyone knew what he didn't know.

"The rice is burning," she said, and she pushed his head off her lap and got up. In a few seconds she came back from the stove and sat down again, and he put his head back on her lap, and she told him that she hadn't slept with Howie, she had only let him kiss her, once, and then she had felt awful and she had sent him away.

"Kissed you? That's all?"

"Yes."

He didn't believe her, of course, and his despair turned suddenly to anger, for she was lying to him, lying so she could go out tomorrow as soon as he had gone to work and do all kinds of disgusting things with her and Howie Leeke's bodies. He saw them sweating against each other, naked and twined around each other, heads where genitals are supposed to be, genitals where heads are supposed to be, arms and hands where legs and feet should be, stomachs against backs, backs against stomachs, everything backward and upside-down, and the two of them laughing deliriously as they swallowed each other whole. "You whore, I'm going to shoot you dead," he declared, and he got to his feet and stomped down the narrow hallway to their bedroom, returning a minute later, just as she lit a cigarette, with his .20 gauge shotgun. "You lying bitch, you deserve to die! You first, and then I'm going to shoot that sonofabitch Howie Leeke, and then I'm going to shoot myself!" He drew the gun up and aimed at her chest, which had begun to heave.

"Good," she said. "I want you to shoot me. But don't shoot Howie, and please, Buck, don't shoot yourself. You're a good man, and it's not Howie's fault that he kissed me, it's mine. I'm everything you say I am, I deserve to be shot by a jealous husband, even if all I did was let another man kiss me, but you don't deserve to die. You're a good man, Buck, and someday you'll make something of yourself, someday you'll be running your own well-drilling business and you'll be just like Daddy and Grandpa, happy and with children and a good wife and all that a good man can wish for. But I'm a rotten wife, I haven't been good to you, I've let another man kiss me . . ." She got up from the chair and crossed the room slowly, evenly, until she drew near the barrel of the shotgun. "I let another man's lips touch mine." She placed her chest lightly against the mouth of the gun barrel. "A strange man's lips were placed and pressed against mine, and I permitted it. I invited it." Buck pulled the trigger.

They say that time stops, or goes away, and your body and the world's body cross into one another. You have no thoughts, for once, no memories and no plans for the future, they say it's like being born, though of course you have no memory of that and cannot know if the comparison is apt, and they say that it's like dying, but you have not quite done that either and so cannot know if they are right, and people who have died cannot come back and tell you what it was like to die, so you will just have to imagine what Doreen felt for that instant when Buck pulled the trigger and the hammer fell, and the only noise was a gasp from Doreen as she clamped her hands onto the barrel of the gun and pressed it as tightly as she could against the exact center of her chest and then collapsed into a pile on the floor, the shotgun clattering to the floor beside her, as Buck came forward toward her, his trousers already to his knees, his hands yanking at her clothing, drawing it away from her body, until he had her naked from the waist down, her legs spread wide on either side of him, and he was moving swiftly, sweetly, smoothly into her, the two of them crooning sly obscenities and gross compliments into each other's ears.

Doreen got pregnant that night, and both she and Buck knew it the instant it happened, or at least they claimed to know it afterward. But they did not live happily ever after. Their second year of marriage was worse than the first, and when the baby was born, a girl they named Maureen, Doreen stopped sleeping with Buck altogether, and he took to staying out late almost every night, usually at the Hawthorne House, where he would drink himself into a sullen stupor that often led him to beat his wife when he arrived home and found her sleeping peacefully alone. Doreen had three or four lengthy affairs over the next few years, none of them satisfactory to her, all of them resulting in an increased distance from her husband Buck. They were divorced in the fifth year of their marriage, when their little girl was four and right after Buck had been fired by Doreen's father and grandfather because she had been forced to call the police one night to stop him from beating her. Doreen and Buck never forgot that snowy night and the shotgun, however, and in later years, alone, they would wish they could speak of it to each other, but they never did speak of it to each other, not even the night that it happened.

Black Man
and White Woman
in Dark Green Rowboat

IT WAS THE THIRD DAY OF AN AUGUST HEAT WAVE. WITHIN
an hour of the sun's rising above the spruce and pine
trees that grew along the eastern hills, a blue-gray haze
had settled over the lake and trailerpark, so that, from
the short, sandy spit that served as a swimming place for
the residents of the trailerpark, you couldn't see the far
shore of the lake. Around seven, a man in plaid bathing
trunks and white bathing cap, in his sixties but still
straight and apparently in good physical condition, left
one of the trailers and walked along the paved lane to
the beach. He draped his white towel over the bow of a
flaking, bottle-green rowboat that had been dragged onto
the sand and walked directly into the water, and when
the water was up to his waist, he began to swim,
smoothly, slowly, straight out in the still water for two
hundred yards or so, where he turned, treaded water for

a few moments, and then started swimming back toward shore. When he reached the shore, he dried himself and walked back to his trailer and went inside. By the time he closed his door, the water was smooth again, a dark green plain beneath the thick, gray-blue sky. No birds moved or sang; even the insects were silent.

In the next few hours, people left their trailers to go to their jobs in town, those who had jobs—the nurse, the bank teller, the carpenter, the woman who worked in the office at the tannery and her little girl who would spend the day with a babysitter in town. They moved slowly, heavily, as if with regret, even the child.

Time passed, and the trailerpark was silent again, while the sun baked the metal roofs and sides of the trailers, heating them up inside, so that by midmorning it would be cooler outside than in, and the people would come out and try to find a shady place to sit. First to appear was a middle-aged woman in large sunglasses, white shorts and halter, her head hidden by a floppy, wide-brimmed, cloth hat. She carried a book and sat on the shaded side of her trailer in an aluminum and plastic-webbing lawn chair and began to read her book. Then from his trailer came the man in the plaid bathing trunks, bare-headed now and shirtless and tanned to a chestnut color, his skin the texture of old leather. He wore rubber sandals and proceeded to hook up a garden hose and water the small, meticulously weeded vegetable garden on the slope behind his trailer. Every now and then he aimed the hose down and sprayed his boney feet. From the first trailer in from the road, where a sign that said MANAGER had been attached over the door, a tall, thick-bodied woman in her forties with cropped, graying hair, wearing faded jeans cut off at midthigh and a floppy tee shirt that had turned pink in the wash, walked slowly out to the main road, a half-mile, to get her mail. When she returned, she sat on her steps and read the letters

and advertisements and the newspaper. About that time
a blond boy in his late teens with shoulder-length hair,
skinny, tanned, shirtless and barefoot in jeans, emerged
from his trailer, sighed and sat down on the stoop and
smoked a joint. At the last trailer in the park, the one
next to the beach, an old man smoking a cob pipe and
wearing a sleeveless undershirt and beltless khaki trousers slowly scraped paint from the bottom of an over-
turned rowboat. He ceased working and watched carefully as, walking slowly past him toward the dark green
rowboat on the sand, there came a young black man
with a fishing rod in one hand and a tackle box in the
other. The man was tall and, though slender, muscular.
He wore jeans and a pale blue, unbuttoned, shortsleeved
shirt.

The old man said that it was too hot for fishing, they
wouldn't feed in this weather, but the young man said he
didn't care, it had to be cooler out on the lake than here
on shore. The old man agreed with that, but why bother
carrying your fishing rod and tackle box with you when
you don't expect to catch any fish? Right, the young
man said, smiling. Good question. Placing his box and
the rod into the rowboat, he turned to wait for the young
woman who was stepping away from the trailer where,
earlier, the middle-aged woman in shorts, halter and
floppy hat had come out and sat in the lawn chair to
read. The young woman was a girl, actually, twenty or
maybe twenty-one. She wore a lime-green terry cloth
bikini and carried a large yellow towel in one hand and a
fashion magazine and small brown bottle of tanning lotion in the other. Her long, honey-blond hair swung
from side to side across her tanned shoulders and back
as she walked down the lane to the beach, and both the
young man and the old man watched her as she approached them. She made a brief remark about the heat
to the old man, said good morning to the young man,

placed her towel, magazine and tanning lotion into the dark green rowboat and helped the young man shove the boat off the hot sand into the water. Then she jumped into the boat and sat herself in the stern, and the man, barefoot, with the bottoms of his jeans rolled to his knees, waded out, got into the boat and began to row.

For a while, as the man rowed and the girl rubbed tanning lotion slowly over her arms and legs and across her shoulders and belly, they said nothing. While he pulled smoothly on the oars, the man watched the girl, and she examined her light brown skin and stroked it and rubbed the oily, sweet-smelling fluid onto it. Then, holding to the gunwales with her hands so that her entire body got exposed to the powerful sun, she leaned back, closed her eyes and stretched her legs toward the man, placing her small, white feet over his large, dark feet. The man studied the wedge of her crotch, then her navel, where a puddle of sweat was collecting, then the rise of her small breasts and her long throat glistening in the sunlight. The man was sweating from the effort of rowing now and he said he should have brought a hat. He stopped rowing, let the blades of the oars float in the water, and removed his shirt and wrapped it around his head like a turban. The girl, realizing that he had ceased rowing, looked up and smiled at him. "You look like an Arab. A sheik."

"A galley slave, more likely."

"No, really. Honestly." She lay her head back again and closed her eyes, and the man took up the oars and resumed rowing. They were a long way out now, perhaps a half-mile from the trailerpark. The trailers looked like pastel-colored shoeboxes from here, six of them lined up on one side of the lane, six on the other, with a cleared bit of low ground and marsh off to one side and the outlet of the lake, the Catamount River it was called, on the other. The water was deep there, and below the surface and buried in the mud were blocks of stone and wooden lattices, the remains of fishing weirs the Indians had constructed here and used for centuries until the arrival of the Europeans. In the fall when the lake was low you could see the tops of the huge boulders the Indians had placed into the stream to make channels for their nets and traps. There were weirs like this all over northern New England, most of them considerably more elaborate than this, so no one here paid much attention to them, except perhaps to mention the fact of their existence to a visitor from Massachusetts or New York. It gave the place a history and a certain significance, when outsiders were present, that it did not otherwise seem to have.

The girl had lifted her feet away from the man's feet, drawing them back so that her knees pointed straight at his. She had turned slightly to one side and was stroking one cheekbone and her lower jaw with the fingertips and thumb of one hand, leaning her weight on the other forearm and hand. "I'm already putting on weight," she said.

"It doesn't work that way. You're just eating too much."

"I told Mother."

The man stopped rowing and looked at her.

"I told Mother," she repeated. Her eyes were closed and her face was directed toward the sun and she continued to stroke her cheekbone and lower jaw.

"When?"

"Last night."

"And?"

"And nothing. I told her that I love you very much."

"That's all?"

"No. I told her everything."

"Okay. How'd she take it? As if I didn't already know." He started rowing again, faster this time and not as smoothly as before. They were nearing a small, tree-covered island. Large, rounded rocks lay around the island, half-submerged in the shallow water, like the backs of huge, coal-colored pigs. The man peered over his shoulder and observed the distance to the island, then drew in the oars and lifted a broken chunk of cinderblock tied to a length of clothesline rope and slid it into the water. The rope went out swiftly and cleanly as the anchor sank, then suddenly stopped. The man opened his tackle box and started poking through it, searching for a deep-water spinner.

The girl was sitting up now, studying the island with her head canted to one side, as if planning a photograph. "Actually, Mother was a lot better than I'd expected her to be. If Daddy were alive, it would be different," she said. "Daddy . . ."

"Hated niggers."

"Jesus Christ!"

"And Mother loves 'em." He located the spinner and attached it to the line.

"My mother likes you. She's a decent woman, and she's tired and lonely. And she's not your enemy, any more than I am."

"You're sure of that." He made a long cast and dropped the spinner between two large rocks and started winding it back in. "No, I know your mamma's okay. I'm sorry. No kidding, I'm sorry. Tell me what she said about you and me."

"She thought it was great. She likes you. I'm happy, and that's what is really important to her, and she likes you. She worries about me a lot, you know. She's afraid for me, she thinks I'm *fragile*. Especially now, because I've had some close calls. At least that's how she sees them."

"Sees what?"

"Oh, you know. Depression."

"Yeah." He cast again, slightly to the left of where he'd put the spinner the first time.

"Listen, I don't know how to tell you this, but I might as well come right out and say it. I'm going in to do it this afternoon. Mother's coming with me. She called and set it up this morning."

He kept reeling in the spinner, slowly, steadily, as if he hadn't heard her, until the spinner clunked against the side of the boat and he lifted it dripping from the water, and he said, "I hate this whole thing. Hate. Just know that much, will you?"

She reached out and placed a hand on his arm. "I know you do. So do I. But it'll be all right again afterward. I promise."

"You can't promise that. No one can. It won't be all right again afterward. It'll be lousy."

"I suppose you'd rather I just did nothing."

"That's right."

"Well. We've been through all this before. A hundred times." She sat up straight and peered back at the trailerpark in the distance. "How long do you plan to fish?"

"An hour or so. Why? If you want to swim, I'll row you around to the other side of the island and drop you and come back and get you later."

"No. No, that's all right, there are too many rocks anyhow. I'll go in when we get back to the beach. I have to be ready to go by three-thirty."

"Yeah. I'll make sure you get there on time," he said, and he made a long cast off to his right in deeper water.

"I love to sweat," she said, lying back and showing herself once again to the full sun. "I love to just lie back and sweat."

The man fished, and the girl sunbathed. The water was as slick as oil, the air thick and still. After a while, the man reeled in his line and removed the silvery spinner and went back to poking through his tackle box. "Where the hell is the damn plug?" he mumbled.

The girl sat up and watched him, his long, dark back twisted toward her, the vanilla bottoms of his feet, the fluttering muscles of his shoulders and arms, when suddenly he yelped and yanked his hand free of the box and put the meat of his hand directly into his mouth. He looked at the girl in rage.

"What? Are you all right?" She slid back in her seat and drew her legs up close to her and wrapped her arms around her knees.

In silence, still sucking on his hand, he reached with the other hand into the tackle box and came back with a pale green and scarlet plug with six double hooks attached to its sides and tail. He held it as if by the head delicately with thumb and forefinger and showed it to her.

The girl grimaced. "Ow! You poor thing."

He took his hand from his mouth and clipped the plug to his line and cast it toward the island, dropping it about twenty feet from the rocky shore, a ways to the right of a pair of dog-sized boulders. The girl picked up her magazine and began to leaf through the pages, stopping every now and then to examine an advertisement or photograph. Again and again, the man cast the flashing plug into the water and drew it back to the boat, twitching its path from side to side to imitate the motions of an injured, fleeing, pale-colored animal.

Finally, lifting the plug from the water next to the boat, the man said, "Let's go. Old Merle was right, no sense fishing when the fish ain't feeding. The whole point is catching fish, right?" he said, and he removed the plug from the line and tossed it into his open tackle box.

"I suppose so. I don't like fishing anyhow." Then after a few seconds, as if she were pondering the subject, "But I guess it's relaxing, even if you don't catch anything."

The man was drawing up the anchor, pulling in the wet rope hand over hand, and finally with a splash he pulled the cinderblock free of the water and set it dripping behind him in the bow of the boat. They had drifted closer to the island now and were in the cooling shade of the thicket of oaks and birches that crowded together over the island. The water was suddenly shallow here, only a few feet deep, and they could see the rocky bottom clearly.

"Be careful," the girl said. "We'll run aground in a minute." She watched the bottom nervously.

The man looked over her head and beyond, all the way to the shore and the trailerpark. The shapes of the trailers were blurred together in the distance so that you could not tell where one trailer left off and another began. "I wish I could just leave you here," the man said, still not looking at her.

"What?"

The boat drifted silently in the smooth water between a pair of large rocks, barely disturbing the surface. The man's dark face was somber and ancient beneath the turban that covered his head and the back of his neck. He had leaned forward on his seat, his forearms resting wearily on his thighs, his large hands hanging limply between his knees. "I wish I could just leave you here," he said in a soft voice, and he looked down at his hands.

She looked nervously around her, as if for an ally or a witness.

Finally, the man slipped the oars into the oarlocks and started rowing, turning the boat and shoving it quickly away from the island. Facing the trailerpark, he rowed along the side of the island, then around behind it, out of sight of the trailerpark and the people who lived there, emerging again in a few moments on the far side of the island, rowing steadily, smoothly, powerfully. Now his back was to the trailerpark, and the girl was facing it, looking grimly past the man toward the shore.

He rowed, and they said nothing more, and in a while they had returned to shore and life among the people who lived there. A few of them were in the water and on the beach when the dark green rowboat touched land and the black man stepped out and drew the boat onto the sand. The old man in the white bathing cap was standing in waist-deep water, and the woman who was the manager of the trailerpark stood near the edge of the water, cooling her feet and ankles. The old man with the cob pipe was still chipping at the bottom of his rowboat, and next to him, watching and idly chatting, stood the kid with the long blond hair. They all watched silently as the black man turned away from the dark green rowboat and carried his fishing rod and tackle box away, and then they watched the girl, carrying her yellow towel, magazine and bottle of tanning lotion, step carefully out of the boat and walk to where she lived with her mother. It was very hot, and no one said anything.

Dis Bwoy,
Him Gwan

IT WAS MID-OCTOBER. THE LEAVES WERE ALREADY OFF THE trees and were leathery brown on the frozen ground, and in the gray skies and early darkness you could feel winter coming on, when one afternoon around four-thirty a blue, late model Oldsmobile sedan with Massachusetts plates slowly entered the trailerpark. It was dark enough so that you couldn't see who was inside the car, but strange cars, especially out-of-state cars, were sufficiently unusual an event at the trailerpark that you wanted to see who was inside. Terry Constant had just left the manager's trailer with his week's pay for helping winterize the trailers, as he did every year at this time, when the car pulled alongside him on the lane, halfway to the trailer he shared with his sister, and Terry, who was tall, wearing an orange parka and Navy watch cap, leaned over and down to see who was inside and saw the face of a black man, which naturally surprised him, since Terry and his sister were the only black people for miles around.

The car stopped, and the man inside rolled down the window, and Terry saw that there was a second man inside, a white man. Both looked to be in their late thirties and wore expensive wool sweaters and smoked cigarettes. The black man was very dark, darker than Terry, and not so much fat as thick, as if his flesh were packed in wads around him. The white man was gray-faced and unshaven and wore a sour expression, as if he had just picked a foul-tasting substance from behind a tooth.

"Hey, brudder," the black man said, and Terry knew the man was West Indian.

"What's happening," Terry said. He kept his hands in his jacket pockets and looked down from his full height.

"Me wan fine a particular youth-mon, him cyall himself Seberonce, mon. You know dis a-mon, me brudder?" The man smiled and showed Terry his gold.

"Bruce Severance?"

"Dat de mon."

"He ain't here."

The man smiled steadily up at Terry for a few seconds and finally said, "But him lib here."

"Yeah."

"Where him lib, tell me dat."

"That trailer there," Terry said, pointing at a pale yellow Kenwood with a mansard roof. The trailer sat on cinderblocks next to a dirt driveway, and the yard was unkempt and bare, without shrubbery or lawn.

"Okay, mon, many tanks," the black man said, still smiling broadly, and he rolled the window up, stopped smiling, backed the car into the driveway of the trailer opposite, and headed slowly back out to the main road.

Terry stood and watched the car leave, then walked

on, turning in at his sister's trailer, which was dark, for she wasn't home from work yet, and made to unlock the door, when he heard his name coming at him from the darkness.

"Terry!" A blond, long-haired kid in a faded Levi jacket stepped around from the back end of the trailer and came up to him.

"Hey, man, some dudes was just looking for you."

"I know, get inside," the kid said urgently, and he pushed at Terry's shoulder.

"Take it easy, man." He unlocked the door and stepped inside, and the skinny kid followed him like a shadow.

"Don't turn on the lights. No, go back to your room and turn on one light, then come here. If they know you were coming here and then no lights go on, they'll figure something's up."

"What the hell you talking about? You high?"

"Do it. I'll explain."

Terry did as he was told and came back to the darkened kitchen, where the kid, Bruce Severance, was standing at the window peeking out at the entrance to the trailerpark. Terry opened the refrigerator, throwing a wedge of yellow light into the room.

"Shut that fucking thing!" the kid cried.

"Take it easy. Want a beer?"

"No. Yeah, okay, just shut the door, will you?"

"Sure." He took out two cans of Miller's and shut the refrigerator door, dropping the room into darkness again. Handing the kid one of the cans, he slid onto a tall stool at the kitchen counter and snapped open his beer and took a long swallow. Across the room by the window the kid opened his beer and started slurping it down.

"I thought you was down in Boston," Terry said.

"I was, but I came back up this morning."

"Where's your van?"

"I put it someplace."

"You put it someplace."

"Yeah. Listen, man, there's some heavy shit going down. When's your sister come home?"

"Around five-thirty," Terry said.

They sat in silence for a few seconds, and then Terry said in a low voice, "Your deal came apart, huh? That's your Jamaican out there, and his friend, right?"

"Right."

"They didn't want to buy your New Hampshire home-grown? Good old Granite State hemp grown wild in the bushes ain't smoke enough for the big boys. Funny." He paused and sipped his beer. "I'm not surprised."

"You're not."

"No. When those kinda guys set something up and it's running smoothly along like it's been doing, with you doing the dealing and them doing the supplying for as long as this setup's been working, they get mad if you try to change the rules. But you, I guess you know that now."

The kid said nothing. A minute passed, and then he said almost in a whisper, "If you're not surprised, how come you never said anything?"

"You wouldn't have heard me."

"They just said they didn't want to buy, they wanted to sell."

"You let 'em try some smoke?"

"Yeah, sure. We met, just like usual. In the motel in Revere. And I gave them both a joint without telling them what it was, you know?"

"And first whack, they knew you had something they didn't sell you, right?"

"Yeah. But they didn't believe it was hemp. They thought I was dealing for somebody else. They knew it wasn't red or gold or ganja or anything they'd smoked before, but they wouldn't believe this shit is growing wild all over the place up here. I told them all about the

war, and the stuff about the Philippines and the government paying the farmers to grow hemp for rope back
then and how the stuff went wild after the war, all of it!
But they thought I was shitting them, man.''

''I wouldn't have believed you, either.''

''But you know it's true! You've seen it, you even
helped me dry the damned stuff and brick and bale it!
You even smoke it yourself!''

''No more, man. The shit makes me irritable.''

''It makes you high, too,'' the kid said quickly.

''So how come those dudes are up here now?''

''I told them I have five one-hundred pound bales of
the stuff,'' the kid said in a low voice.

Terry sat in silence, took a sip of his beer and said,
''You're stupid. Stupid. You oughta be selling insurance, not dope.''

''I thought it would let them know I was in business
for myself and not dealing for some other supplier, if
they knew I had five bales of my own. The Jamaican,
Keppie, he just looked at me like I wasn't there anymore and said I should go to California, and I knew the
whole thing had come apart. So I left them at the motel
and drove back up. My van's parked on one of the
lumber roads in the state park west of the lake. I walked
in through the woods, and then I saw them. I was
coming to get you,'' the kid added.

''Me! What do you want me for? I wouldn't touch this
with a stick, man!''

''I need to get rid of the stuff.''

''No shit. What are you going to do with it, throw it in
the lake?''

''We can lug it into the woods, man. Just leave it.
Nobody'll find it for months, and by then it'll be rotted
out and nobody'll know what the hell it is anyhow.''
After a pause, the kid said, ''I need you to help me.''

''You're strong enough to carry one of those bales

five times. You don't need me." Terry's voice was cold and angry. "You're an asshole. You know that?"

"Please. You can take your sister's car and we can do it in one trip. It'll take me all night alone on foot, maybe longer, and someone may see me." He was talking rapidly, like a beggar explaining his poverty. He whined, and his voice almost broke with the fear and the shame. He was a nice enough kid, and most people liked him right away, because he enjoyed talking and usually talked about things that at first were interesting, organic gardening, solar energy, transcendental meditation, but he tended to lecture people on these subjects, which made him and the subjects soon boring. Terry hung out with him anyhow, smoked grass and drank in town with him at the Hawthorne House, mainly because the kid, Bruce, admired Terry for being black. Terry knew what that meant, but he was lonely and everyone else in town either feared or disliked him for being black. The kid usually had plenty of money, and he spent it generously on Terry, who usually had none, since, except for the occasional chores and repair work tossed his way by Marcelle Chagnon, the manager of the trailerpark, it was impossible for him to find a job here. Outside of his sister, who was his entire family and who, through happenstance, had located herself here in this small mill town in New Hampshire working as a nurse for the only doctor in town, Terry had no one he could talk to, no one he could gossip or grumble with, no one he could think of as his friend. When you are a long way from where you think you belong, you will attach yourself to people you would otherwise ignore or even dislike. In that way Terry had attached himself to Bruce Severance, the kid who sold grass to the local high school students and the dozen or so adults in town who smoked marijuana, the kid who drove around in the posh, black and purple van with a painting of a Rocky Mountain sunset on the sides and the bumper stickers attacking nuclear energy and urging people to heat their homes with wood, the kid who had furnished his trailer with a huge waterbed and Day-Glo posters of Jimi Hendrix and Bob Dylan, the kid who, to the amusement of his neighbors, practiced the one hundred twenty-eight postures of T'ai Chi outside his trailer every morning of the year, the kid who was now sitting across the darkened kitchen of the trailer owned by Terry's sister, his voice trembling as he begged Terry, four years older than he, a grown man despite his being penniless and dependent and alone, to please, please, please, help him.

Terry sighed. "All right," he said. "But not now."

"When?" The kid peered out the window again. "They probably went back to town, to drink or for something to eat. We should do it now. As soon as your sister gets home with the car."

"No. That's what I mean, I don't want my sister to know anything about this. This ain't her kind of scene. We can go over to your place and wait awhile, and then I'll come home and ask her for the car for a few hours, and then we'll load that shit into the car and get it the hell out of here, and you can tell those dudes you were only kidding or some damned thing. I don't care what you tell them. Just don't tell them I helped you. Don't even tell them I know you." Terry got off the stool and headed for the door. "C'mon. I don't want to be here when my sister gets home."

"Terry," the kid said in a quick, light voice.

"What?"

"What *should* I tell them? I can't say I was only kidding. They know what that means."

"Tell them you were stoned. Tripping. Tell them you took some acid. Beg."

"Yeah. Maybe that'll cool it with them," he said somberly, and he followed Terry out the door.

Keeping to the shadows behind the trailers, they walked to the far end of the park, crossed the short beach there and came up along the lake, behind the other row of trailers, until they were behind the trailer where Bruce lived. "Go on in," Terry instructed him. "They couldn't see you now even if they were parked right at the gate."

The kid made a dash for the door, unlocked it and slipped in, with Terry right behind. When the kid had locked the door again, Terry suggested he prop a chair against the knob.

"Why? You think they'll try to break in?"

"A precaution. Who knows?"

"Jesus, maybe we should've waited out in the woods till your sister got home!"

"No, man, forget it, will you?" Terry walked through the room, stumbling against a beanbag chair and giving it a kick. "You got any beer here? I shoulda grabbed a couple of beers from my sister."

"No. Nothing. Don't open the refrigerator. The light."

"Yeah," Terry said, his voice suddenly weary. He sat down heavily in the beanbag chair, and it hissed under his weight. "Jesus, it's cold in here. Can't you get some heat into this place?"

"I can't make a fire. They'll see the smoke."

"Forget the fucking stove, you goddamn freak. Turn up the damn thermostat. You got an oil heater, don't you?"

"Yeah, but no oil. I only use wood," the kid said with a touch of his old pride.

"Jesus." Terry wrapped his arms around himself and tried to settle deeper into the chair. He was wearing his orange parka and knit cap, but sitting still like this had chilled him. Bruce had gone down the hall to a window from which he could see the entrance to the trailerpark.

"Hey, man!" Terry called to him. "Your fucking pipes are gonna freeze! You can't put a woodstove in a trailer and not have any oil heat and keep your pipes from freezing! It's a known fact!''

There was a knock at the door, softly, almost politely.

Terry stood up and faced the door. He whispered Bruce's name.

When the second knock came, louder, the kid was standing next to Terry.

"Oh, my God," the kid said.

"Shut up!"

A clear voice spoke on the other side of the door. "Seberonce! Come, now."

Then there was the sound of a metal object working against the latch, and the lock was sprung, and the door swung open. The Jamaican stepped quickly inside, and the white man followed, showing the way with a flashlight.

"Too dark in here, mon," the Jamaican said.

The man with the flashlight closed the door, then found the wall switch and flicked it on, and the four men faced each other.

"Ah! Seberonce, we gots to hab some more chat, mon," the Jamaican said. Then to Terry, "So, my brudder soul-bwoy. You gwan home now, me doan got no bidniss wid you, mon." He flashed his gold teeth at Terry. Inside the small space of the trailer both the Jamaican and his companion seemed much larger than they had in the car. They were, indeed, both taller and thicker than Terry, and in their presence Bruce looked like an adolescent boy.

"I was just telling him you were asking for him," Terry said slowly. Bruce was moving away, toward the kitchen area.

"Wait, mon! Stan still!" the Jamaican ordered.

The other man switched off his flashlight and leaned his sweatered bulk against the door. "You," he said to Terry. "You live here?"

"No, man. Across the way, with my sister. She's a nurse in town."

"Whad a black mon lib up here wid rednecks for, mon?"

"My sister. She . . . she takes care of me."

"Gwan home now, mon," the Jamaican said, suddenly no longer smiling. The sour-faced man opened the door for Terry, and he took a step toward it.

"Wait, Terry!" the kid cried. "Don't leave me alone!"

"Shut you face, Seberonce. We gots to hab some more chat, me and you. Dis bwoy, him gwan."

Terry stepped out the door, and the sour-faced man closed it behind him. It was cold outside. He stepped to the hard, cold ground and walked quickly across the lane to his sister's trailer and went inside, locking the door carefully behind him. He crossed the room and stood by the window where Bruce had stood earlier and in the darkness watched the trailer he had just fled. After a few moments, he saw the two men leave and walk down the lane, past the manager's trailer and through the gate. For a second they were silhouetted by the headlights of a car coming from the other direction, and after the car had passed the men, Terry realized it was his sister's.

Swiftly, he left the window and then ran from the trailer and across the lane. The lights were still on in the living room of Bruce's trailer, and the door was wide open, and as he came up the steps he looked into the room and saw the kid slumped over in the beanbag chair, the back of his head scarlet where the bullets had entered.

Terry turned around and walked away. His sister was pulling a heavy bag of groceries from the front seat of her car. He came up behind her and said, "You want help?"

"Yeah," she said. "Was that you just now running over to Bruce's?" she asked over her shoulder as she backed away from the bag of groceries.

"No," he said. "No. I was just getting my pay from Marcelle. I . . . I haven't seen Bruce, not for a couple of days. Not since he went down to Boston."

"Good," she said. "I wish you'd stay away from that kid. He's trouble," she said sighing.

What Noni Hubner Did Not Tell the Police About Jesus

SHE DID NOT REVEAL THAT TWO DAYS PRIOR TO HIS ARRIVAL at the trailerpark she spoke with Him on the telephone. She was alone in her mother's trailer at the time, which was approximately 10:30 PM, and because she expected her mother, Nancy Hubner, to return from a meeting of the Catamount Historical Society around 11:00, Noni had just rolled and smoked a single marijuana cigarette, which she was accustomed to doing when left alone at this time of night, for while she had come to require for sleep the kind of sedation provided by a single marijuana cigarette, her mother had forbidden her to use the weed, particularly since Noni's psychiatrist had happily provided her with enough Valium to put her to sleep for the rest of her natural life. Noni was in the bathroom flushing down the roach, when the phone rang, and it was Jesus. More precisely, He claimed to be Jesus. He had a surprisingly high voice, kind of thin, almost Oriental, and He spoke in a New Hampshire accent that was sufficiently local for her to think at first that He was originally from around here, but then of course she quickly remembered that He was Jewish and from Bethlehem and that, therefore, His use of a local New Hampshire accent in speaking English with her was merely a typically Christian courtesy designed to make her feel more at ease than she would have with someone speaking in a foreign accent or, as surely would have been understandable, in a foreign language altogether, ancient Hebrew, for God's sake. She would have thought He was some kind of nut and hung up.

"This Noni Hubner?" were His first words to her.

"Yes."

"This is Jesus. Been thinking of giving a visit."

"Jesus?"

"Yup."

"I must be dreaming," she said. "You sound like my father."

"I am."

"No, I mean my real father."

"I see. Your mother's dead husband."

"Oh my God! How could you know about that?"

"Check your Bible," He said.

"Oh, listen, I . . . I've really had problems, my mother says I'm fragile, and she's right. You shouldn't call up and fool around like this. I've been very depressed lately," she reminded Him.

"I know that. That's why I been thinking of giving a little visit. Might turn things around for you, Noni."

"Okay, fine. Really," she said, her voice trembling. "You do that. I . . . I've got to go now, I hope it's okay to go now."

"Fine. Good-bye."

"Bye."

And that was all. She hung up, her mother came home around 11:00, and Noni kissed her good night and went into her room at the back of the trailer and fell immediately to sleep, dreaming, as might be expected, of her dead father. It was one of those dreams that are so easy to interpret you feel sure your interpretation is wrong, that is, assuming you respect the intelligence of dreams. Noni and her father were standing in the lobby of a large hotel, the Hyatt Regency in Nashville, Tennessee, and Noni's father kissed her good-bye, and when the elevator door opened, he led her forward into it, stepping back himself just as the door closed. The elevator was suspended in a round glass tube, and it shot up for forty or fifty floors, then came to an abrupt stop. The door opened, and standing in front of her, with His hand extended toward her in the same position as her father's when he had led her into the elevator way below, was Jesus. He was wearing a white robe, as He's usually portrayed, and was smiling. He wasn't very tall, about her height, five foot six, and He was smiling with infinite understanding and sweetness. She stepped out of the elevator and placed her hand in His. Then she woke up, and it was morning, a late February morning, gray and cold and lightly snowing.

SHE DID TELL THE POLICE WHAT DAY IT WAS THAT SHE FIRST saw Jesus, February 22, 1979, but she did not reveal to them when exactly on that day or where exactly at the trailerpark. They probably were a little embarrassed by the line of questioning they were caught in and, as a consequence, accepted approximate answers when exact answers would have been more revealing and possibly more convincing. It was the second afternoon following her phone conversation with Him that she actually saw Jesus. The light snow of the previous day had built to a snowstorm that had abated the next morning, leaving six inches of new powdery snow on top of two feet or more of the old, crusted stuff, and Noni in boots and parka had shoveled a path out to the driveway, which had been cleared early that morning by the kid from town who plowed out most everybody in the park that winter, and afterward she had walked down the freshly cleared lane under a darkly overcast sky, one of those weighted, low skies that make you think winter will never end, that it will surely press on and down, bearing you beneath it, until finally you lie down in the snow and go to sleep. At the end of the lane she came to the lake, and with the trailers behind her and the wind off the lake in her face, she stood and gazed across the silver-gray ice to the island and, beyond the island, to the humped, pale blue hills. The wind had scraped most of the snow off the lake, drifting it against the shore and the trees and here at the trailerpark against the sides of the trailers. Her pale, pinched face grew paler and drew in upon itself as the steady wind drove against the shore, and as she later said, it seemed to her at that moment more than any other that her life was not worth anything, for she was a stupid, unimaginative young woman who had no gifts for the world and who did not believe in herself enough to believe that her love was worth giving. She had discovered in college that she was stupid and flunked out after two semesters, and she had learned on the commune that she was unimaginative and after taking a lot of acid tried to stab one of the people who truly was imaginative, and in the hospital she had found out that she had no gifts for the world because her dependencies were so great, so she stopped eating and almost died of starvation, and then last summer with Terry she had learned that her love was worth nothing so she refused to have his baby and sent him away. She opened her eyes, wishing the lake were not covered with ice so that she could walk straight into the water and drown, when she saw a man approaching her at a distance, walking slowly over the ice directly toward her. Even from this distance she knew the man was Jesus, and trembling, suddenly warm, all her dark thoughts gone, she raised her hand and waved. But when He waved back, she grew frightened. He was more or less the same as He had been in the dream, except that He wore a heavy maroon poncho over His shoulders, and His feet were wrapped in some kind of bulky mucklucks. He was hatless, and His long, dark brown hair swirled around His bearded face. Turning away from Him, she ran in terror back up the lane to her mother's trailer, dashed breathlessly inside, locking the door behind her, and when she had pulled off her boots and parka, she switched on the television set and sat down in front of it and tried to watch. Her mother was in the kitchen, preparing dinner. "Have a nice walk, dear?" she called. Noni said no, she had seen Jesus walking across the lake toward her, so she had run home. "Oh, dear," her mother said.

TIME PASSED, AND WINTER DID INDEED TURN EVENTUALLY into spring, soggy and swollen and ravaged, which is almost always the case with New Hampshire springs. Renewal seems almost impossible, except as survival alone indicates a potential for it. Noni saw no more of Jesus during these months, but she thought of Him frequently, and she read her Bible, and along about the end of March she started attending services at a small white building located on one of the side streets in town. It was a single-story building that once had been a paint store, just a half-block off Main Street, and the two large windows facing the street had been painted over dark green and a sign in white, wobbly letters had been made

in each of them. The one on the right said: CHURCH OF
THE NEW HAMPSHIRE MINISTRY OF JESUS CHRIST; on the
other side were the words, FOR WHERE TWO OR THREE ARE
GATHERED TOGETHER IN MY NAME, THERE AM I IN THE MIDST
OF THEM. The people who attended prayer meetings and
listened to sermons here were all local people, about
twenty in all, and except for Noni, working people.
Noni didn't work because she was supported by her
mother who, in turn, was supported by her dead husband who, in his turn, had been supported by the selling
of life insurance. Nevertheless, she felt comfortable with
these people, mostly because they had been unhappy
once, too, and now they were not, and when they talked
about their time of unhappiness she knew they had felt
then just as she felt now, stupid and unimaginative, with
no gifts for the world and no belief that her love was
worth giving. It was Jesus, they said, who had changed
their lives, for He had found their love to be of infinite
worth and their gifts, no matter how slight, to be of great
value, and their intelligence and imaginative powers to
be apocalyptically superior to the intelligence and imagination of the rest of the people in town. They said to
her, when she wept, "Did you never read in the Scrip-
tures, 'The stone which the builders refused is become
the head stone of the corner. This is the Lord's doing; it
is marvelous in our eyes'?" And then in mid-April,
shortly after Easter, Noni saw Jesus a second time, this
time in the form of a body of light. He appeared to her
one night late while she lay in her bed and tried to sleep.
Since joining the Church of the New Hampshire Ministry of Jesus Christ she had given up smoking marijuana,
along with alcoholic beverages, sex, cigarette smoking,
cursing and cosmetics. All her anxieties and grief fell
immediately away, and she came to be filled with the
light of Jesus, and when He had passed through her and
had gone from her room, she remained filled—but filled

now with love, her love of Jesus Himself, and the inescapable logic of that love. From then until now Noni Hubner was a different person. That much was obvious to anyone who knew her, and that much, of course, she told the police when they interrogated her.

SHE DID NOT QUOTE HIM DIRECTLY, AND NOT JUST BECAUSE they didn't happen to ask her what, exactly, Jesus had asked her to do for Him. It was at the Wednesday evening prayer services, while Brother Joel was preaching, that she had received her instructions, or what she regarded as instructions. Brother Joel was in the front of the room, holding the open Bible in one hand, pointing at the ceiling with the other, shouting and beseeching, berating and explicating, imploring and excoriating to the assembled group of about seventeen or eighteen persons, mostly women of middle age and a few men of various ages, and several of the women were shaking their bodies up and down and rolling their heads back and around, as Brother Joel, a young man from Maine who had settled here last year to commence his ministry, moved to the text of Matthew, chapter eighteen, and read the words of Jesus that begin, "Verily I say unto you, Except ye be converted, and become as little children, ye shall not enter the kingdom of heaven," and when he reached the place where Jesus says, "For the Son of man is come to save that which was lost," Noni felt herself leave her body behind, watched it fall like an emptied husk to the floor next to her chair, as she ascended into a rosy cloud, where she saw the outstretched hand of Jesus, and into His hand she placed her own, while He pointed with His other hand beyond the cloud and down. She thought for a second to check for the wounds in His hands, as Thomas had done, and a cold wind blew against her and took the doubting thoughts with it. She let her gaze flow to where Jesus indicated, beyond the cloud and down, and in the far distance she saw her father's grave. It was a summer afternoon, just as it had been when they had buried him, and she knew it was her father's grave, all right, even though it was covered with grass now and the stone, a common gray granite stone, was too far away for her to read the inscription, for she knew the location, even though she had not been out to his grave in the cemetery on the hill above the river since the afternoon of his burial. Nor had her mother. His grave was at the top of the hill, near a grove of young maple trees, and when the service had been completed by Reverend Baum, her mother's Congregational minister, Noni and her mother had turned and had got quickly into her mother's Japanese fastback coupe, and they had driven away and had not come back. From that day till now, almost five years later, Noni's mother had spoken of her head husband as if he were merely absent, as if he had driven downtown to get the paper, and Noni had screamed at her several times that first year, "He's *dead!* Face it, Mother, Daddy's *dead! Dead! Dead!*" And then, after the first year, Noni had ceased screaming, had ceased correcting her mother, had ceased even to reflect on it, and in the end had ceased to observe that, to her mother, the man was neither dead nor alive, for to Noni that's how it was also—her father was neither dead nor alive. But when she came back to her body lying there on the wood floor of the Church of the New Hampshire Ministry of Jesus Christ, she knew her father was waiting for her, his hand reaching out to her, so she rose to her feet, and she left the building.

AT THE CEMETERY, STANDING WITH THE SHOVEL IN THE CIR-cle of light cast by her mother's coupe, she waited and listened and heard Jesus moving in the darkness behind her, heard His bare feet press against the wet grass, while He watched over her, and when the policemen came forward and crossed into the circle of light, walking over her father's grave to her, one of them taking the shovel from her hands, the other holding her arms tightly, as if she might run away, she had no fear. The one holding her arm asked what she thought she was doing, and she told him that she had come to show her mother that her father was dead, so that her mother could be free, as she was free. When they asked where her mother was, Noni was silent for a second and heard Jesus shift His weight in the shadows, and then she told them. While the second policeman went to the coupe and released Noni's mother from her bonds, Noni silently thanked Jesus for His guidance.

THE CONCEIT THAT CERTAIN PEOPLE, ESPECIALLY FEMALE people, resemble certain flowers is not very original, but then, it's not without its uses either. Especially if you can obtain enough significant information about the flower to gain at the same time significant information about the person. For instance, Noni Hubner was like a kind of orchid that grows in northern New England—the pink lady's-slipper, *Cypripedium acaule*. It may surprise you that orchids actually appear in these latitudes, but they do. And the pink lady's-slipper, as it happens, is one of the more common members of the orchid family to appear in New Hampshire, Vermont and Maine, so that you often discover it in open pine woods, or on the east-facing slopes of riverbanks. It blooms in June when the plant's delicate throat swells and turns pink. Sometimes the orchid is white, but then you'll go back the following June and discover that it has bloomed a deep shade of pink, as if it had suffered a wound in your absence. People who love the sight of these orchids know that regardless of how plentiful they seem, you must not pick them. Nor should you transplant them, as they seldom survive a change of habitat for longer than a few years. In fact, most people who know where you can find such a lovely, fragile flower will not tell you the location, because they are afraid you will go there, and in your affection and delight, will pick the beautiful pink lady's-slipper or will try to transplant it nearer your home.

Comfort

LEON LAROCHE, THE BANK TELLER, TRIED TO TELL THIS
story once to his friend and neighbor, Captain Dewey
Knox (U.S. Army, ret.). Leon was in his late twenties
when he made the attempt, and he had been drinking
beer with the Captain in the Captain's trailer for several
hours, so he was slightly drunk, or he probably would
not have tried to tell it at all. It's not so much that you
will say things when drunk that you'd never say when
sober, as much as you will try to say things you'd
ordinarily know simply could not be said. It's your judgment about the sayable that goes, not your inhibitions.

The two men had been talking about a kid who used
to live at the trailerpark, Buddy Smith, who had been a
thief and a liar and whose father, Tom Smith, had finally
thrown him out of the trailer he'd shared with his son for
most of the kid's life. Six months after the son had

departed, the father shot himself, and nobody understood any of it. The son never showed up in Catamount again, not even for the funeral, and that had been the end of the matter, except when folks now and then wondered about what might have happened to Buddy Smith and wondered why his father, a sociable though utterly private man, had killed himself. Most people believed that by now the kid was locked up in jail somewhere out West, where his mother was supposed to live, and that Tom Smith had shot himself in the mouth with his shotgun because, since he had been living alone, his drinking had got out of hand, and you know how too much drinking alone can make you depressed. Nobody thought the two events, the son's departure and the father's suicide, were connected. At least not in such a way as to think the suicide could have been avoided, which is to say, at least not in such a way as you could blame the son for the death of the father.

"I liked Buddy," Leon said, gazing into his glass. The two men were seated at the Captain's kitchen table, the television set still rumbling behind them in the living room, for when Leon had knocked on the door and had offered to share a six-pack of beer with him, the Captain had been watching the evening news and in his pleasure had neglected to shut the machine off. The older man had been grateful for the interruption—it was a frosty November night, and people generally didn't go calling on people on nights like this—and when the first six-pack had been drunk, the Captain had started offering beer from his refrigerator, until they had found themselves working their way through a third six-pack. The Captain said he didn't mind, it was a Friday night anyhow, and he was restless and felt like having company, so what the hell, crack open another, Leon, and relax, for chrissakes, you're too uptight, boy. You remind me of myself when I was your age, he told Leon. Some people have to learn to relax, have to force themselves to do it, and then after a while it comes naturally, he said laughing, as if to prove how finally it had come naturally to him.

"No, I really liked Buddy, although I can't say I knew him very well. He was a chess player. I never knew that until one night after work I went into the Hawthorne House for a drink, because I was angry, pissed off, from having been yelled at once too often by Bob Fosse at the bank. You wouldn't believe that man, *I* don't believe that man. After what, seven years, and he still treats me like shit. Anyhow, I went into the Hawthorne House, which is unusual for me, because that place can be kind of rough, you know, and I hate the smell of it, like urine and old beer, but like I said, I was angry at Bob Fosse and needed a drink to calm down.

"Buddy was in a corner playing one of the pinball machines, alone, as usual. He never seemed to have any friends in town, even though there are plenty of kids his age in town, too many of them, who don't seem to do anything except hang around drinking beer and flexing their muscles and getting themselves tattooed. Buddy was like that, or at least he seemed like that, but even so, he kept pretty much to himself. But then, too, Buddy didn't exactly look like those guys, either. I mean, he was always clean-looking, and he wore his hair short, and he took good care of his clothes. He looked like a recruit in the army home on leave. Even so, he never seemed to do much except hang around the trailerpark or up at the Hawthorne House, as if waiting for someone supposed to pick him up there and take him to someplace far away and very different from this place. Those other guys his age were made in Catamount, New Hampshire, to stay in Catamount, New Hampshire, and eventually to die in Catamount, New Hampshire. It was stamped all over their faces, all over their bulky muscles, all over the way they talked and laughed and punched each other around."

The Captain knew the type. He shoved his paw across his white crewcut and sighed. Bring back the draft, he intoned, and in a year the streets of America will be cleared of that type and safe to walk in again.

"Buddy had spent a year in the service, the Marines, I think he told me, and just as he was about to be shipped overseas to Germany or someplace, he was in an automobile accident that put a metal plate into his head and got him discharged. He told me that while we were sitting at the bar, but I don't think I believed him, because while he was telling me all this, he kept smiling at me and watching my eyes, as if he was putting me on, just to see if I'd believe some lie.

"He was a chess player. He said he wasn't very good, but he liked to play, which is true as well for me, so I said we should get together to play chess sometime, and he thought that was a great idea. He knew no one who played chess around here, and neither did I. He had a way of watching the point of his cigarette while he smoked that was unusual. I bought him a second beer, and we talked about how hard it was living in a small town in New Hampshire, how boring it was and how mean-minded the people were. He said he was leaving for the West Coast as soon as he got some money that was owed him by a guy in the Marines, and then he asked me why I stayed here, living in Catamount, going back and forth every day from the trailerpark to the bank. My mother lives in Concord, where I grew up, and this was the best job I could find when I got out of New Hampshire Commercial College, and I go to Boston sometimes on weekends, I told him. He was curious about that, about what I do in Boston on weekends, and I told him the truth, that I go around to the bars and maybe take a meal at a fancy restaurant and go to a movie. That's all. He didn't believe me, but he was very nice, very cheerful and friendly. He said I probably stayed home every weekend and watched TV.

"By then the place was filling up and had got pretty noisy. The juke box was playing and two or three couples were dancing, and you had to holler to be heard, so I asked Buddy if he wanted to come back to my place for some supper and a few games of chess. He asked me if I had anything to drink, apologizing as he asked, explaining that he was broke or else he'd have offered to buy the beer. I had plenty of beer in the refrigerator, plus a bottle of scotch I keep around, and I had planned to go on home and cook up a couple of hamburgers for myself anyhow. I hadn't played any chess in over a year, not since my brother was back East visiting my mother two Thanksgivings ago. Buddy said fine, so I paid, and we left in my car.

"When we got to the trailer, he opened a beer and set up the chessboard in the living room while I cooked hamburgers. He had the television on and was watching it and drinking beer and seemed very relaxed to me. But he seemed sad, too. It's hard to explain. He probably reminded me of myself somehow, sitting there alone, with the television set on and a chessboard set up in front of him. I walked into the living room to say something to him, I don't know what, just something that wouldn't make him seem so sad and alone to me, maybe, and when I passed behind his chair, I lay my hand on his shoulder in a friendly way. You know? Just lay my hand on his shoulder as I passed behind his chair.

"What happened then was . . . embarrassing. I don't know why I'm telling this to you, I've never told anyone else, but it's bothered me ever since. He grabbed at my hand as if it were an insect, a spider or something, and threw it off his shoulder. When he stood up and turned to face me, he was red-faced and enraged, sputtering at me, calling me a fairy, all kinds of names. He knocked over the chessboard, made a few wild moves around the room as if he was trying to find a way out without passing me, and finally went by me as if I had some kind of disease he could catch, and slammed the door."

The Captain was at the refrigerator and had drawn out a pair of beers. He let the door shut on its own and stood facing it. "Well . . . so he decided you had . . . unnatural desires, eh?"

"Apparently. Yes, he did. But I didn't."

Of course. The Captain was still facing the closed refrigerator door.

"It was just that he had looked so sad and alone there, so pitiful. I can't describe it. Sometimes you can have a feeling toward a person that makes you want to do that, to place a hand on him and that's all, just to comfort him, even though he doesn't know he needs comfort—no, especially because he doesn't know he needs comfort. But I don't know why I'm telling you this. I must need comfort and not know it or something," Leon said, and he laughed lightly, nervously.

The Captain laughed with him and turned and sat back down at the table. Leon, his face pinched in thought, opened the bottle and filled his glass, then studied the glass carefully, watching the bubbles rise inside and the moisture drip down the outside. The Captain filled his pipe from a brown leather pouch and lit it, drawing in the smoke rapidly until he had it going on its own. Then he asked Leon if it was true, was he a fairy?

Leon slowly looked up at the older man, the way you would look at a falling tree if you had got unexpectedly caught beneath it. It was too late to step out of its path. "Yes," he said. "I suppose I am."

The Captain smiled and revealed that he had always thought so, but Leon was not to worry, because his secret was safe. He understood that sort of thing, it happened all the time in the service. Well, not all the time, but often enough that you had to learn to be tolerant, so long as people kept these things to themselves. He continued talking a few seconds longer, but Leon was already standing and pulling on his jacket, then moving for the door.

At the door, he apologized for having drunk so much of the Captain's beer, and then stepped outside to the cold night air. It was a clear sky, with falling stars and a crescent moon that looked like a narrow streak against the dark blue sky.

God's Country

THE REAL ESTATE MAN HAROLD DAME WAS DYING. DOCTOR Wickshaw gave him one month to six, and when he explained what few remaining services there were available for the real estate man, whether they kept him in the hospital or put him in a nursing home, and the costs of those services, the real estate man's son and daughter-in-law, who had been running the business alone for nearly a year anyhow, decided to bring him home, to install him in his bedroom on the second floor and to hire a nurse to take care of him for the one month to six he had left. She could administer the drugs he required, she could clean and feed him and take care of his bedding, she could watch after his dying, and when he was dead, she could leave.

Decisions like this are hard, the son of the real estate man explained to his wife, who had reservations about

having the old man in the house for one to six months, a
living corpse, practically (though out of respect for her
husband's feelings she did not exactly put it that way), a
total invalid drugged against pain, helpless and dependent as a newborn infant and daily becoming more so,
shrinking into himself, unable to speak coherently or
even to recognize who was in the room—it probably
meant they wouldn't be able to go to Florida for the
month of January the way they'd planned.

Nonsense, the husband assured her, unless of course
the old man happened to die during that particular month,
in which case there would be the funeral to take care of,
but they could fly back for that, if necessary. All they
had to do was be sure that the nurse they hired was
honest, competent and pleasant to be around, for after
all, they themselves would have to be around her for
one to six months, not counting the month of January,
when they would be in Florida. The wife wondered if
the nurse would have to eat with them. Of course not.
She could take the room next to the old man's, and she
could eat there. The son and daughter-in-law would continue living downstairs in their wing of the house, where
they had lived ever since the son had been brought into
the business, and they would practically never see the
woman.

There are several ways to go about hiring a private
nurse to provide this kind of care, but when you live in a
small town in a rural state like New Hampshire, probably the easiest way is to let your physician take care of
it. Harold Dame's son and daughter-in-law were busy
people, especially with the old man so sick and for the
last year unable to run the business the way he used to,
so they had explained at great length to Doctor Wickshaw,
an intelligent and tactful man, precisely what kind of
woman they were looking for, and he had proceeded to
find them just such a woman.

Doctor Wickshaw was what you might call an artistic man, in that he was the president of the Catamount Drama Club, the coordinator for the annual Suncook Valley Arts Festival, and owned a large collection of works by contemporary New Hampshire painters and sculptors. His wife was a potter and wore smocks and sandals and large gold hoops in her pierced ears. He had a white Vandyke beard, a rosy complexion, and the kind of round belly on a slender body that a man who enjoys exotic food and interesting wine often wears. He was good-natured, affluent (for he had been the only physician in town for over twenty-five years and had invested heavily and wisely in real estate), and somewhat eccentric. In the summer months he frequently wore Bermuda shorts and shortsleeved shirts to the office.

For over a year, he had been looking for a nurse who could double as a receptionist, and he had interviewed and rejected every local person even remotely qualified for the job and then had advertised in Concord, twenty-five miles away, and after interviewing and rejecting the few applicants who had come out from Concord, he had nearly given up the search. Very few people who have qualifications for such specialized work as nursing are willing to live in a small mill town like Catamount, a town that has been dying for a half-century, a town where the poor are not only always with you but where annually they seem to increase in geometric proportion to the rich. The old buildings, designed and constructed when labor was cheap and materials plentiful, grow older and shabbier and eventually fall, to be replaced by asphalt lots or else by corrugated iron, sheet metal and plastic structures whose function, regardless of the name of the building or the owner, seems to be strictly that of temporary storage. It occurred to Doctor Wickshaw, however, that if somehow a nurse could be lured to this town and could be made to stay for several seasons, she would discover, as he himself had discovered years ago, that it offered numerous advantages and pleasures not obtainable in the cities and attractive suburbs to the south. There was the beauty of the landscape, the lakes and forests, the rivers and mountains, the flowers and wildlife; there was the comfort of living among people whose names and family histories you knew, people who would come to your aid when you needed it and who would leave you alone when you desired it; there was the security of living in a community that still honored the old-fashioned virtues of thrift, honesty, independence and respect for the independence of one's neighbors, love of God, love of country, and love of family.

"There has got to be someone left in the world who has a decent education and still cares for this kind of life," the doctor told his wife.

She agreed, but all she'd seen lately of people with educations and options who happened to opt for living "up here among the savages," as she put it, were hippies and real estate developers. Everyone else, she reminded him, if it's possible, leaves.

"We haven't left," Doctor Wickshaw proudly announced.

"No," she said. "We haven't."

Along about the time the doctor no longer felt able to hold this type of conversation with his wife—due to his failure to find a nurse willing to come out here to Catamount and work for little more than half of what she could make in Concord or down in Manchester, New Hampshire—the son and daughter-in-law of Harold Dame, the real estate man, had come to him and asked him to locate and hire for them a private nurse for the old man's final one to six months. They were willing to pay whatever it cost—for they already knew how much it would cost to keep the old man in the hospital or in a nursing home, and there wasn't a private nurse in the world who would charge them that much.

The doctor pondered a moment and informed them that he probably could get someone to come out of Boston, thanks to certain collegial connections he maintained there, and if they wished, he would do all the interviewing and hiring himself, for after all, who knew the medical and personal needs of Harold Dame better than he, Sam Wickshaw, his personal physician and his old friend and hunting companion of days gone by?

The son and daughter-in-law were relieved and went quickly on to their scheduled meeting with a surveyor out at Suncook Pond. The doctor picked up his phone and dialed Doctor Furman Bisher in Brookline, Massachusetts, a heart specialist with a summer home on Lake Winnepesaukee, and that is how Harold Dame, the real estate man, came to be cared for in his dying months by Carol Constant, a twenty-eight-year-old, recently divorced black woman from West Roxbury, Massachusetts, an unemployed nurse trying to return to the profession she had left three years ago to marry a man and care for his sick and aged mother. The mother had died, the man had gone to New York with a girl who wrote for TV, and Carol, after filing for divorce, had started looking for work. One of the physicians who had interviewed her, since many of his patients were black professional people and he was therefore in the market for a black nurse, was Doctor Furman Bisher. He had declined to hire her because Carol was not, to his eyes, an especially pretty woman. She was extremely dark, with a broad flat nose and liquid brown eyes. Her hair she kept cropped close to her head, almost like a skullcap. Also, she was a large woman, well muscled and tall, almost masculine, a little frightening to a man like Doctor Furman Bisher. But he had admired her obvious intelligence, and her credentials were impeccable, and she seemed to be an extremely pleasant woman, good-natured and kind, so he had not hesitated to recommend her to his New Hampshire colleague. "She's a black woman," he warned Doctor Wickshaw, "but she's sensible. She needs a long-term private job like this to build up her file, which frankly was a little thin for me to take her on here. But she ought to be perfect for your needs up there in the boondocks," he joked.

When Carol was first led into Harold Dame's room on the fourth floor of the Concord Hospital, she knew immediately that he could not see her, and she was relieved. Doctor Wickshaw had met her at the bus station downtown, and he had stared at her whenever he thought she wasn't looking, and at the hospital the receptionists, nurses and orderlies, even the elevator operator, had noticeably marked her presence as a foreign presence, and she had started to worry about her clothing, her shoes, her handbag—they were wrong, loud, shabby, large. Of course, she knew what the real problem was, and she knew too that it was not a problem as such, the way loud or shabby clothing was a problem, that is, as something that could be solved. No, this was a fact, a condition. She had not seen a human face that was not gray or pink or peach-colored since the moment she had boarded the bus in Park Square in Boston. All right, then. It was a condition, a working condition, and she would endure it. She had known it would be this way. She was no fool, and she knew her geography; she also knew herself and knew that to live and work wholly among white people would continually embarrass her, which in turn would anger her. Beyond that, she knew her anger would end up defeating her true purposes here, and, therefore, to avoid being angry, she would have to accept being embarrassed.

The nearly dead man in the hospital bed relieved her of her embarrassment, however, and for a moment she forgot the portly, red-faced doctor with the ostentatiously pointed beard, and the blond, square-faced head nurse who had imperiously demanded to know her business with the patient, requiring the doctor to explain elaborately that she was being considered for a position as Mr. Dame's private nurse. The shrunken, ash-gray man lay inertly beneath the sheet, a short, narrow mound encircled by tubes and chrome-plated armatures. His wrinkled lids closed over bulbous eyes like onion skins, and his small, open, toothless mouth was sharp-edged and dark, like a hole punched in dry ground.

"He's sleeping," Doctor Wickshaw mumbled, as he flipped open Harold Dame's file, perused it momentarily, and then passed it on to Carol. "His heart and lungs are strong," he said smiling. "So unless he catches pneumonia, he could last six or seven months. Of course, he may go tomorrow, too. The surgeon's report is right there," he said, pointing over her shoulder to a faded, photocopied sheet with scribbling across it.

Carol read the file slowly, page by page—notes by the attending physician, Doctor Samuel F. Wickshaw, notes from the half-dozen laboratories consulted, notes from the surgeon who had done the exploratory, notes from the anesthesiologist, remarks and observations from the nutritionist, instructions from Doctor Wickshaw to the square-faced head nurse, and on down the line—so that, by the time she had finished reading, she had imagined a body for this man lying in front of her, an old, diseased, misused but still somehow stubbornly sturdy body. Yes, she decided, she could administer to that body the few services it would require until it expired. They weren't technically difficult to administer, and the man would not interfere much, she knew, for he would be conscious only intermittently, and less so with each passing week.

And the pay—they had discussed it on the telephone, she and the Doctor, and had agreed on a figure that was almost the same as she would have received in Boston—was satisfactory. She asked a few questions about the son and daughter-in-law, learned that they were working people who would be living in the house but in a separate wing of the house, that in fact they would be away much of the time and would most definitely not interfere with her whatsoever, and agreed to take the job.

"Excellent!" Doctor Wickshaw exclaimed. He moved closer, his cheeks reddening with pleasure. "I'm sure you're going to enjoy it up here."

"I am?" She took a backward step toward the man in the bed.

"Yes, the fall! It's beautiful in the fall! The leaves! Look!" he said, pointing out the window.

Carol turned and looked out the large window to the hospital grounds below, and then beyond the grounds to the rippling, tree-covered hills spreading away to the west, a thick carpet of orange, yellow and red all the way to the horizon. It was late afternoon, and the sunlight touched the treetops and brought the colors forward as if on an outstretched hand.

"People drive hundreds of miles just to see these colors," he said in a reverent voice. "And all we have to do is look out our windows. Isn't it *something*?"

"Yes. Yes, it is something."

He took a step back. "Well, now, let's get ol' Harold out of here and back in Catamount where he belongs, eh? The Dame place is lovely," he assured her. "Up high, a lovely view of the lake, that's Skitter Lake, and even a view of the White Mountains on clear days. You're going to love it!" he promised.

*   *   *

FOR THE FIRST TWO DAYS AND NIGHTS AT THE HOUSE IT rained, a cold, raw, wind-blown rain, and when it cleared, most of the leaves had been driven from the trees and lay wetly on the ground, heavy and faded to dull shades of brown and yellow. The trees were now skeletal, black and boney and nervous-looking. That first afternoon, Carol had met Harold Dame's son and daughter-in-law, and they had approved of her, but she hadn't seen them since, though several times during those first days she heard them come and go, returning from the office in downtown Catamount for food and sleep. They did not check in on the old man, she knew, for her room connected to his through a bathroom and she slept with both doors open.

Doctor Wickshaw telephoned several times a day and once again every evening. "To see how the patient's doing," he said cheerfully. When she reported no change, he said, "Fine, fine," and then went on to ask her how she liked it up here in God's country.

"It's very pretty," she said.

"Yes, well, you've only seen a corner of it so far. I'll have to give you the guided tour some afternoon soon. No reason why you can't take off a few hours and have a look at some of our natural wonders, the lake, the Catamount River, the old Indian fishing weirs. The town is quite pretty, too," he told her. "The mill pond and the falls, several interesting old historical buildings, the park. A big difference from the city life," he told her.

"Yes."

"Safe! People leave their doors unlocked up here. 'Course, you better stay out of the woods in hunting season," he joked.

"Really? When's that?" From where she stood in her bedroom, she could see through the bathroom to Harold Dame's room. He was awake, blinking slowly, like a turtle. Near his chin his emaciated hands clutched the top sheet, as if he were trying to protect himself with it or were ashamed of what lay beneath and were trying to hide it from the rest of the world. Slowly he turned his face toward her, seeking the source of her voice.

"I'm sorry, Doctor," she interrupted, "but Mr. Dame's awake."

"Fine, fine, of course. Good girl," he said cheerfully. "And say, call me Sam, will you? Everyone in town does. Save that 'Doctor' business for the stuffed shirts down south. Okay?"

"Okay." She said good-bye and hung up, then walked quickly to her patient. Drawing up her chair, she sat next to the old man and gave him some water.

Taking care with his trembling mouth to use the plastic straw correctly, he studied the woman's large face for a few seconds, then seemed confused and withdrew his gaze, leaving her alone again.

Gently, she stroked his narrow forehead and pushed his lank, white hair back. His eyes, watery and pale blue, closed, and then he was asleep.

The next afternoon, a Sunday, Doctor Wickshaw arrived bearing a portable television set for Carol and immense good cheer. It was a bright, warm day, and the son and daughter-in-law were home, downstairs in the living room reading the Sunday papers and watching a football game on the large color TV. They had come upstairs that morning around nine, had taken a minute to study the old man in Carol's silent presence, and had asked her if she wanted to go to church. She said no, thanks, and with clear relief, they returned to their quarters.

Doctor Wickshaw, too, made a brief show of examining the patient, albeit with more precision than the old man's survivors had. He listened to his heart, took his blood pressure, studied Carol's notes on the man's temperature, medication, bodily functions, and so on. Then, clamping shut his black leather bag, he placed it at the foot of the bed, sighed and observed that it wouldn't hurt the old man if she took off for a few hours. "They'll be here all afternoon," he said, indicating with a nod toward the door the couple downstairs. "You must want a break." He was wearing a brown corduroy shooting jacket with tan leather patches at the elbows and over his right shoulder, green twill trousers and a tattersall shirt. His short, white hair and beard bristled like antennae, and he rubbed his hands together happily.

Carol thanked him for the use of the television set and said no, she'd be just as happy to stay here at the house. She might take a walk later. "You've already been plenty kind to me."

"No, no, you're coming with me," he said. "You need a break at least once a week or you'll get wacky out here with no one but ol' Harold for company." He grinned, showing her his excellent teeth. "C'mon, now, go in there and change into some civilian clothes," he said, pointing with his bearded chin toward her white uniform, "and I'll wait for you outside. It's a *gorgeous* day!" he exclaimed, darting a look out the window.

"All right."

"That's a good girl." He left, and she turned, glancing as she departed from the room at the body of the old man in the bed. He was awake, blinking his watery eyes and looking at the space in the room she had just filled. He had a puzzled expression on his gray face, as if he were wondering where she had gone.

She turned away from him, and when she went into her own bedroom, she closed the door.

Doctor Wickshaw, or "Sam," as he insisted on being called, talked steadily throughout the tour. He drove his huge, maroon Buick rapidly, nervously, waving his arms and pointing right and left at hills, trees and water as they passed Skitter Lake glistening in the sunlight and choppy in the breeze. They stopped for a minute at the Granite State Trailerpark so he could show her the remains of the old Indian fishing weirs, cruised through the center of town, with Sam enumerating, as they passed them, the several churches, the fire station, the police station, the town hall, the Hawthorne House, where, he told her, they often had first-class country and western bands playing, then stopped for a few moments at the park to watch a gang of teen-agers drink beer at a picnic table. On High Street, when they pased a large, white, Victorian house with a sign outside that said, SAMUEL F. WICKSHAW, M.D., the doctor slowed his car almost to a stop. Half the yard had been paved for cars, and the barn attached to the house in back had been converted into an office.

"I could run a clinic from that building," Sam said in a tone that was almost wistful.

"Why don't you?" Carol asked. It wasn't difficult to admire the meticulous, white buildings, the white picket fence that ran along the front, the carefully tended flower gardens covered with wood chips and awaiting the arrival of winter. Evergreen shrubs along the front of the house had been covered with burlap, and she could see on the side porch several neatly stacked cords of fireplace wood.

"Can't get the help."

"Really?"

"Would you believe that the woman who's been my nurse and receptionist for over a year now was trained as a *dietician*? Bless her, but she's fifty-nine and can't do much more than open a can of Band-Aids for me." He sighed and drove thoughtfully on.

Back at the house, he pulled into the circular drive and parked. Carol reached for the door, but Sam turned toward her, and slinging his right arm over the seat back, he grabbed on to her shoulder with his hand. "Wait," he said, suddenly serious.

His hand against her dark blue wool sweater was pink and blotched with liver spots, and his nails were white and carefully trimmed. She looked at the hand with curiosity, as if a leaf had unexpectedly fallen from a tree and landed there.

"I like you, Carol." He cleared his throat. "You're a fine nurse, and I like you as a person."

"Thank you, Doctor."

"Sam."

"Yes. Sam." With her right hand, she pulled the latch, and the heavy door of the Buick swung open.

"Well," he said, smiling broadly again and releasing her shoulder. "I just wanted you to know you're among friends up here in God's country."

"Yes. That's . . . that's nice of you." She stepped free of the car and closed the door solidly, walked around in front of the car and gave a little wave good-bye.

He rolled down his window and called to her. "Carol. We'll talk some more. Eh?"

"All right," she said, her voice rising. "And thank you."

He waved, closed his window, and drove swiftly off. For a moment she stood by the front door of the house watching him. A crow called harshly from the open field behind the house, and she could hear the afternoon breeze push through a stand of tall pines by the road. Then she opened the door and went quickly upstairs to her room.

Hurriedly, she shed her wool skirt, sweater and blouse and went to the closet and brought out her uniform, when, as if remembering something, she turned, padded barefoot across to the door that led to the bathroom and the room beyond, and opened it. She stood there in the doorway, holding her white uniform over one forearm, and looked at the man in the bed. His chest rose and fell slowly. His eyes were closed, and his mouth lay dry and open, his face slack as if being drawn by a great weight into the pillow. His gray hands twitched erratically above the sheet, his palms facing the ceiling, and he seemed to be pushing at a great, smothering blanket in his dreams.

NOVEMBER ARRIVED, AND WITH IT THE DEER-HUNTING SEAson, and all day long Carol heard gunfire coming from the woods behind the house. She could look out the window of her room and see miles of forest, leafless oak and maple trees, and along the ridges in the distance, blue spruce and balsam. Now and then she saw a red-suited figure with a rifle emerge from the woods and cross the brown field toward her and disappear at the side of the house. It had once been a farmhouse, with barns and outbuildings, but no longer. Modern plumbing and heating systems, picture windows, a pine-paneled recreation room and a large, renovated kitchen with a breakfast nook and gleaming new appliances had eliminated from the interior of the house all traces of the families that had owned the house before Harold Dame. It sat on a rise of land two miles west of town. Looking east, you could see the spires of the churches and here and there among the trees shining bits of the mill pond and, a ways farther, the lake. Spotted in the distance on the hills and ridges were houses and barns, old farms, most of them no longer farms but the renovated residences of people who made their livings in town from selling insurance, real estate, automobiles, snowmobiles and housetrailers to their neighbors and each other.

Though the weeks passed, Carol's relations with her employers remained the same—precisely distant, perfunctory, and utterly routine. They entered the kitchen in the morning immediately after she had left it and a

half-hour later departed for their office in town, returning in the evening to prepare their dinner, which they ate
in the recreation room in front of the television set. On
some nights they went out for several hours, but most
nights they remained at home retiring to their bedroom
downstairs early. She became deeply familiar with the
noises of their routines, as if the couple were performing
them in front of her. When she heard a toilet flush, she
knew which of the two had flushed it; when she heard
the shower, she knew who was bathing; when late at
night she heard the refrigerator door open and after a
few seconds close, she knew who had wanted a midnight snack. Once a day now, usually at dinnertime,
they entered the old man's room and asked about his
condition. She answered their simple questions briefly
and in general terms, which she knew was how they
wanted her to answer them, and then, satisfied, they
disappeared again. The son, Ed Dame, was in his
midthirties, thick-bodied and short, several inches shorter,
in fact, than Carol, with thinning, reddish hair that he
combed carefully sideways to cover his receding hair-
line. His nose was hooked and short, like his father's,
but his face was fleshy, freckled, and anxious. The
daughter-in-law, Sue, also short and anxious-looking,
was muscular and tight-bodied. Her dark hair she curled
nightly in blue plastic rollers, Carol knew, for one night
she had accidentally come upon her in the kitchen. Carol
had come downstairs hungry, around one in the morning
after the late movie, had walked into the darkened room
and discovered Sue already at the refrigerator, bent over
and poking through its bright, crowded interior. She was
wearing a pale blue dressing gown, large puffy slippers,
and several dozen blue plastic hair curlers.

Startled, Sue jumped back, and the refrigerator door
closed, leaving the room in darkness. For several seconds the two women stood silently in total darkness.

Then Sue opened the refrigerator door again, casting a wide beam of light over the floor, and said in an even voice, "I'll be out in a moment."

"I'm sorry," Carol said, and quickly went back upstairs.

The old man's condition had not changed for the first few weeks, but around midmonth, as the weather grew colder and day after day was overcast, windy, with scattered flecks of snow spitting from the low sky, he seemed to weaken somewhat. He woke from his sleep less frequently, and when he woke he simply gazed at the ceiling for a few moments and then drifted away again. There was an IV set up for him, now, with plastic tubes leading away from his body as well. Carol performed her duties carefully, mechanically, gracefully, as if the only sentient being in the room were she, but every now and then she would catch herself standing at the foot of the old man's bed staring at his withered, expressionless face. It was practically the face of a mummy now, a face long vacated, and yet she stared at it as if waiting for a response to her presence. But none came.

Sam Wickshaw telephoned daily, at first strictly on the pretext of checking on the condition of his patient, his old friend and hunting companion, Harold Dame, but then, after a few weeks, it seemed he called to report on his own day's activities. He described the patients he had seen that day, whether at his office in town or at the hospital in Concord, where he made early morning rounds; he referred to several real estate deals he was involved with, described his difficulties winterizing his summer cottage at Lake Winnepesaukee (mentioning his friend, and hers, Doctor Furman Bisher from Brookline, Massachusetts), and told her with great pleasure that he had bought a snowmobile, despite his wife's objections; and in late November, four days before Thanksgiving, he described to her in great detail how, that very morning, he had shot and killed an eight-point, one-hundred-fifty-pound deer. "It was up behind Shackford Corners, a few miles from where you are," he told her. "I was up on a ledge, a whole lot of larch trees around me, and all of a sudden, there he was, big as life, down below me tiptoeing through a grove of young ash trees. I gut-shot him, and he took off. Actually, even though I was above him a ways, I had a lousy shot," he explained. "Anyhow, luckily he cut around to my right, and when I came off the ledge, there he was again, so I got a second shot at him, and that time, he went down for good!"

They talked. She explained how she herself didn't like hunting or guns, but she didn't judge those who did, and he said he sure was glad of that. Sometimes he asked her questions about herself, her family, her ex-husband, her ambitions, and she answered his questions. Not in detail, however, but briefly and, as much as possible, in general terms, which she knew was how he wanted her to answer them.

Once a week, he drove out to the house and examined the patient. The examination usually took less than five minutes, but his visits took most of the afternoon, for the two of them talked, Sam doing most of the talking. Sometimes they walked down the road a ways or drove to a particularly scenic spot that Sam wanted to reveal to her. And inevitably, when they returned in his car to the house, Sam turned somber and tried for a moment to tell Carol how much and in what ways he liked her. Each time, Carol was able to ease out of the conversation without doing more than frustrating the man, so that, with a wave and a cheery remark, he could pretend to himself that he had never said anything that could be misconstrued as inappropriate.

There was a Sunday, however, when it did not go so smoothly. Carol had slipped out of the car, crossed in front of it and waved good-bye, and this time he had stepped out also.

"Wait a moment," he said seriously.

She stopped and stood before him, the same height as he but a larger person with a larger face, so that next to her he seemed suddenly fragile.

"Carol, I want to suggest something to you."

She smiled and reached out with one hand and patted his shoulder. "I know you like me as a person, Sam. I like you, too. Let's keep it that way," she said.

"No, no, no, that's not what I meant. What I mean is, I . . . ah . . . I'd like for you to work for me. I'd like you to stay up here, after Harold . . . after Harold is gone, and work for me. I like you . . . oh, hell, I know how that sounds. But I want you to work for me."

Carol said nothing. She studied the man's earnest, red face, as if searching for a lie.

"Well, you *think* about it," he blurted. "You *think* about it." He got back into the car and closed the door. Then he cranked down the window. "You *think* about it," he said. He started the motor, dropped the car into gear, and drove swiftly away, exhaust fumes trailing behind.

THE NIGHT BEFORE THANKSGIVING, HAROLD DAME THE REAL estate man died. At ten-thirty, Carol walked from her room to the old man's room, and as soon as she crossed the threshold, she knew he was dead. She had learned to hear his breathing without having to listen for it, so that when his breathing ceased, she knew. In the darkness, she reached forward and felt at his neck for his pulse, then turned and went back to her own room. She was in her nightgown, ready for sleep, with her bed already turned down. The portable television Sam had brought her was still on, and blue-gray figures flickered incoherently in front of her, as she sat down on the bed and picked up the telephone. She held the receiver in her lap for a moment and stared at the television screen. Finally, she dialed, and when Sam answered, she told him. "Harold died, Sam."

"Well. When, Carol?"

"In the last half-hour. I just went in to check him." Her voice was flat and without expression.

"Well. Are you all right?"

"I'm all right."

"What about Ed and Sue? Do they know?"

"No."

"Okay, then. I'll be right out there. I'll handle everything, Carol, don't worry."

"I'm not worried," she said.

"Listen, Carol, why don't you come in here tonight, stay here with us. I'll bring you back in with me. We have plenty of extra room," he said. "Maybe you'd like to have Thanksgiving dinner with us tomorrow," he said in a thin voice, as if talking to someone whose mind were already made up.

"All right. Thank you, Sam."

"You will? Wonderful! I'll be there in five minutes!"

She said good-bye and hung up. Then she rose from the bed and switched off the television, crossed the room and sat by the window, peering into the cold, familiar, New Hampshire darkness.

Principles

EVERY MAN OUGHT TO HAVE A PHILOSOPHY OF LIFE. THAT'S what Claudel Bing believed, and you might think that was his philosophy of life, but it wasn't. It was only a principle. It was like his father's principles, which people used to joke about and say were his philosophy of life, but they weren't. He used to tell his kids and Claudel's mother and anyone else who got him to talk seriously about life, "There are three things a man should never do. Swear in front of women, throw stones, and spit." But you won't find philosophy there. You won't find anything there that will get a man through a time of great suffering or moral confusion.

But when you're a kid you try to figure out your mother's and your father's philosophy, and you do it constantly, until either you've got it and can accept it for your own or cast it away, or else you never get it and

152

you end up sharing it with your mother and father anyway without even knowing it—which to Claudel seemed a shame. Because a man ought to be able to choose his own philosophy of life. That was another one of his principles.

Anyhow, for years he had struggled to figure out his father's philosophy of life, but all he could come up with were principles. Like the rule against spitting. What Claudel was looking for was something like Chisholm's Law, the one that says if things can get worse they will. Then, he figured, he could work out his own principles. A man can't have principles, he reasoned, unless he's got himself a philosophy of life.

It wasn't until he was nineteen and had finished basic training in the army and was shipping out for Vietnam—that was in 1965 or '66, when things were just starting to heat up over there—that he finally figured out his father's philosophy of life. It was his mother who gave him the information that tipped him off to it. He had taken a little kidding in basic training from the guys, especially the guys from the cities who had never heard of a man with the name of Claudel so they used to kid him about it, "Why not Claude?" and, "Claudelle, you sure that's a man's name?" He could never come back at them with a smart or truthful answer, so when he was home on furlough before shipping out, he asked his mother one day at breakfast how come she had named him Claudel.

His mother was fixing him some beans and eggs at the stove, and she turned around with a strange expression on her face, as if she was wondering herself why she had named him Claudel. After a few seconds she said, "It was your father named you. I wanted to call you Claude if you were a boy and Claudine if you turned out to be a girl. But he said no. Not that he didn't like both names. He said, 'Let's call it Claudel, regardless of whether it's a boy or a girl. No sense having two names ready when we're only expecting one baby.' "

"I can remember him saying that," Claudel's mother said, "just like it was yesterday. 'No sense having two names ready when we're only expecting one baby.' But that's your father, you know. All over. He likes to be efficient. When he was young and talked more about what he believed, maybe because he wasn't so sure of himself then and had to hear himself say things out loud before he could really believe they were true, he used to say, 'Too much is as bad as too little. Worse.' "

Right then and there at the breakfast table, Claudel finally got to understand his father's philosophy of life. If the old man believed that too much was as bad as, or worse than, too little, and if that belief had led him to give his son a name like Claudel, which he must have known would be an embarrassment to the boy for a long time, then the old man must have a pretty bleak view of life's offerings. It wasn't quite as bleak as Chisholm's Law, say, but it wasn't exactly optimistic either.

Your philosophy tells you what the world is like, gives you the long view, so to speak. And your principles tell you how to live in that world. And Claudel's father was telling him that the world was a tough and miserly place, and that the best way to live in that place was to be careful and relentlessly efficient. Don't waste a thing, don't take anything for granted. Don't put off for tomorrow what you can do today, because tomorrow might never come, and just in case it does, you better have something done today or else you're going to get beat tomorrow.

A hard view, Claudel knew. But when he was nineteen it seemed right to him. He loved his father and admired him, even though of course he thought his father was a little cracked on a few subjects, like spitting and throwing stones. But basically he thought his father knew the world a lot better than he himself did. The old man had pulled a hitch in the Navy in World War Two out there in the South Pacific, and after the war he'd worked for a few years down in Boston in the shipyards as a welder. At nineteen the son figured he'd do better listening to the father and taking on the father's philosophy of life than he would trying to work up one of his own. So he didn't mind being called Claudel anymore. Now that he knew there was a good reason for it.

2

THEN HE WENT OFF TO VIETNAM, AND OVER THERE HE learned a lot about the world that made him start to question his father's viewpoint, because what he saw over there made him start to believe in Luck. His father's philosophy had no place in it for Luck. But the war was teaching Claudel that there were lucky people, like him and the other guys who didn't get killed or blown half to bits, and there were unlucky people, like all those Vietnamese farmers, say, whose houses and land and children and whole families were getting wiped out for no reason they could name. Half the time they couldn't even see the bombers that dropped the bombs on them. It was like God was bombing them, instead of some foreigner looking into a bombardier's sight at 40,000 feet.

Claudel wasn't stupid, and he could see that the only difference between these farmers and the farmers back home was that one group was unlucky and the other group was lucky. And since he could see that, so far, he was a member of the lucky group, he started to expect more out of life than his father's philosophy had said he would get.

He could remember when it first came wholly clear to him that he was one of the lucky ones. His outfit used to sit around at night guarding the 105 howitzers with their M-14 automatic rifles, talking and smoking and looking out at the darkness for signs of life (signs of death for them, so they had to look very carefully). What they were looking for was flashlights. They never knew why, but those guys out there in the black pajamas were carrying flashlights. Every once in a while somebody would see a fleck of light way out there in the jungle, like a firefly, only half a mile away, and he'd start firing his M-14 full steam, and in a second everybody else would be blasting away at the jungle. They weren't supposed to fire those things except at an enemy they could see, but the guns were fun to shoot, because they were recoiling automatics and the barrel slid back onto a gas cartridge that took the recoil, so they would fire these things and just sit there watching the barrels slamming back and forth practically in their laps while the bullets soared through the night like stars. Then, after the shooting had stopped, all the men would be grinning. There'd be a sudden silence, and Claudel would look around and all his buddies would be grinning at nothing, and he'd realize that he was grinning at nothing too.

One night, though, after the shooting had stopped, he looked around him as usual and saw they were all grinning as usual, and all of a sudden they heard a baby crying. It was stone silent otherwise, so they could hear its bawling clearly even though it was coming from someplace way out there in the jungle. It went on and on, and there wasn't anything they could do about it. It started to make them edgy and nasty-tempered, and a few of the guys cursed the baby's mother for being out there in the night in the first place. A few other guys cursed the enemy for being out there with guns and booby traps, which were keeping them from going out and finding the baby and bringing it in to safety. And a few others cursed the enemy for setting the whole thing up. They said it was a trick to draw them away from the camp into an ambush in the jungle. That sounded plausible, but they weren't sure, so they just kept on being bothered by the baby's crying, which went on and on and seemed to grow louder and louder. Until finally one of the soldiers, a big square-faced guy from Chicago, jumped up and started firing his automatic into the bushes, as if he had seen a flash of light out there someplace. Then the others started firing with him, watching the barrels leap back and forth while the tracer bullets made icy arcs across the sky and dove into the darkness of the jungle a mile and a half away.

After a few minutes they stopped firing and sat down again. This time, when Claudel looked around, no one was grinning. Everyone wore a dark, somber expression on his face, and Claudel knew he looked the same as they did. That's when he started thinking he was lucky. He was young. It's how you explain things that are too complicated to explain. You call it Luck. Either you've got it or you haven't got it, but if you've got it, use it. That was the first principle of his new philosophy. If you've got it, use it.

3

So by the time he got home again, he was raring to go, hot to get started making big money, buy a fast and fancy car, get himself a pretty girl and maybe marry her and buy one of those sixty-five-foot mobile homes to live in. And he did precisely that. He got himself a job as a lineman for the Public Service Company and started pulling in a couple hundred bucks a week with overtime. Then he got himself a loan from the bank and bought one hell of an automobile, a white '68 GTO convertible that made everybody in town turn around and think a minute. He moved for a while with several different girls from town, one of them the daughter of a doctor, and after about a year he married Ginnie Branche, who ran Ginnie's Beauty Nook out on Route 28. They had a big wedding, lots of presents, electric blankets, electric corn popper, waffle iron, all the usual things you need, and moved right into a baby-blue sixty-eight-foot-long mobile home out on Skitter Lake. It was a fancy new Longwoods, one of the first mobile homes to come out with a cathedral ceiling and teakwood paneling in the living room. And after that, every morning when Claudel woke up in the master bedroom with that pretty young woman lying next to him, he'd slowly look across the room at his Danish modern bedroom suite, on to the framed pictures of mountains and streams, to the wall-to-wall green shag carpeting, the fancy fiber glass draperies shimmering in the morning breeze, and out the window to his GTO parked in the driveway, its top down, a huge white bird with its wings folded, and he'd say to himself, "Claudel Bing, you are one lucky son of a bitch!"

Now here's where you start to get to the point of his story. Because Claudel was wrong. He wasn't lucky. Not lucky at all. He only thought he was lucky. He thought the world was giving him a ride, and it was beginning to look like a good ride, so he figured all he had to do was just lie back and enjoy the passing scenery. And up to now, he'd been right. But then all of a sudden the scenery changed, and the road got bumpy, and then he knew he wasn't lucky.

But that didn't mean his father had been right, that the world was a chiseler and you had to be a miser to live in it. No, because Claudel wasn't *unlucky* either. He simply hadn't learned enough yet to have a view of the world that explained to him what happened to him, what he at first had called being lucky and what later he called being unlucky. Because for a while he did call it that, being unlucky, and if you had known him at that time or had just met him in a bar, you'd have heard him naming his life that way day and night, holding his glass up to let a bit of light from the Budweiser sign float through while he told his sad tale of bad luck to anyone who'd listen.

He'd tell you how the trailer had caught fire and burned to the ground because Ginnie had left the stove on, and how his insurance couldn't cover the loss so he was still paying off the damned mortgage to the bank. He and Ginnie had come home after a weekend down at York Beach, all sunburned and sandy from the beach and hungover from the good times they'd had the night before with some Canadians they'd run into at the motel bar, and when they pulled into the driveway, all there was next to it, where the trailer had been, was a sixty-eight-foot-long barbecue pit. The two of them just sat there in the car in their bathing suits and broke down and wept.

And after that Claudel would tell you how Ginnie had started running around with Howie Leeke, until everyone in town knew about it, except Claudel himself, of course, until one night he came into the Hawthorne House right after Howie had been there, and everybody started giving him a funny kind of grin, so he asked, "What the hell's wrong, my fly unzipped or something?"

Freddie Hubbard, a buddy of his from the Public Service Company, said, "No, nothing's wrong . . . It's just that Howie Leeke's been here and left . . . and he was telling stories again . . ."

"What kind of stories?" Claudel asked, thinking maybe one might be funny enough to repeat. He liked a good laugh as well as the next man, especially since his trailer burned down.

"Aw, you know," Freddie said. "Stories about him . . . and Ginnie."

Then all the people in the place sort of wiped their grins off and shifted in their seats and turned away, so Claudel knew what was happening, and what had been happening for a long time, probably ever since the trailer burned and he and Ginnie had moved into town and had taken the apartment over Knight's Paint Store, which happened to be across the street from Howie's pipefitting shop.

That's when Claudel started drinking every night after work at the Hawthorne House, hanging out there right up to closing time, stumbling home drunk and cursing his bad luck. Which of course only seemed to get worse. A man can't control his fate, but he does make his own luck. By calling it luck. But if he's a smart man, he won't call it luck at all. Of course Claudel didn't know that then. He called it luck, bad luck. So every night of the week he'd sit there on a stool at the bar of the

Hawthorne House, punching all the sad songs on the juke box, ordering beers and shots of Canadian Club over and over, until finally Gary the bartender would come over and say, "Hey, Claudel, it's midnight. I gotta lock up the joint."

Then he'd slide off the stool and head for the door, stumble down Main Street to Green Street, past the dark windows of the stores and restaurants and the few offices, till he came to Knight's Paint Store. Up the stairs he'd go, unlock the door, lurch in darkness to the bed, where Ginnie lay sleeping or pretending to sleep. Then, yanking off his clothes, smelling of beer and whiskey and cigarette smoke, he'd pull on her shoulder and paw at her body, even though he'd be too drunk to be much of a man, until finally she would jump out of bed, mad and afraid and disgusted.

In a month Ginnie had left him and had moved in with Howie Leeke, who had left his second wife the previous spring. In six weeks Claudel had got himself fired from the Public Service Company for coming in late so many times, late and hungover. And mad. All the time mad. He had got to be irritating to people. When he wasn't complaining about his bad luck, he was growling at people who looked, to him, to be having a run of good luck, like Freddie Hubbard, who had been his best friend since grade school. Freddie came into work one morning and told Claudel how he'd been promoted to foreman, and Claudel just sneered at him and said it was probably because they were afraid he'd fall off a pole if they didn't get him back down on the ground. "Keep lousing things up," he told his old friend as he walked off, "and they'll stick you in the front office."

People would say to him, "Hey, Claudel, how're you doing?" and he'd grump something like, "Depends on who I'm doing it to," or some other remark that was designed mainly to stop the conversation dead. It was like falling into a well that didn't seem to have a bottom. There is an end to a person's self, though, and you can reach it, but only if you're stupid enough or smart enough to try hard for a long, long time. And that's precisely what Claudel did, for over a year, and eventually he hit the bottom of that well.

4

IT HAPPENED ONE NIGHT AT THE HAWTHORNE HOUSE. He was living upstairs in a rented room by then, because after he'd got fired from the Public Service Company, he'd started collecting unemployment, and the bank had repossessed most of the furniture Ginnie had left him, the color TV and the bedroom suite and the couch. Besides, he wasn't able to pay the rent for the place over Knight's Paint Store anymore, so it seemed a reasonable thing to do. Maybe the only thing he could do. He'd go for days without shaving, letting his clothes get dirty and rumpled, eating Twinkies and potato chips for breakfast and cold canned beans for supper, getting himself drunk on boilermakers usually by three in the afternoon, and then sitting around in the Hawthorne House till closing time. He used to sit in one of the booths, and whenever someone would join him, because of having been a friend from the old days when, as Claudel still thought, his luck had been running good, he'd tell him over again how it all started with the fire and then his troubles with Ginnie and Howie Leeke, and how the Public Service Company had screwed him, probably because of Freddie Hubbard, who hated him, he was sure, and on and on into the night, until finally the friend would yawn and say he had to get home or someplace, and he'd leave, and Claudel wouldn't see him again for months, because the man would have been able to avoid him.

One night, a Friday, so there were a lot of drinkers in town that night, he was sitting in his usual booth, where he'd been sitting since three that afternoon, and he had nothing to think about, and no one to say it to, so he started listening to the conversation coming from behind him, where three young guys were sitting over beers and talking about state troopers and cars. A three-piece band had been playing for a while, country and western songs that had been popular about ten years ago. They had quit playing a few minutes earlier, had unplugged their instruments, two amplified guitars and a set of drums, and had headed for the bar. The Hawthorne House was laid out in a common way, a small bandstand in front that could accommodate no more than three musicians and their equipment, a dance floor the size of a kitchen, then along the walls a dozen plastic-covered booths and four long Formica-topped tables between them. At the back there was a bar with ten or twelve stools alongside it. On a Friday or Saturday night all the booths were usually taken and half the Formica tables were filled with drinkers, local men and women as well, and when the band played a danceable tune, eight or ten couples walked onto the dance floor and shoved each other around in approximate time to the music. But when the band took its break, there was a few minutes' silence, or relative silence, between the band's ceasing to play and someone's digging into his pocket for change for the juke box, and in that silence you could overhear conversations in the booths adjacent to yours. The rest of the time you couldn't hear anything said by anyone other than yourself unless it came from six inches away and was practically shouted into your face.

The music had stopped and the kid behind Claudel had gone on shouting into the faces of the two men sitting with him, men a few years older than he, all three of them wearing mechanic's uniforms from Steele's, the local Ford dealer, with their first names on the left breast pocket and Henry Ford's last on the other. The one talking, or rather shouting, was Deke, and the two he was shouting to were Art and Ron. "Nobody screws over me!" Deke told them. He had long, slack, blond hair that hung in greasy strands thick as twine over his collar, and his forearms wore tattoos, one a heart with a knife plunged into it and the words *Born to Love* emblazoned above the heart, the other a Confederate flag with the inscription *The South Will Rise Again!* "Nobody, but nobody, screws over me! I mean it, man, I don't give a shit how big he is, no goddamn state trooper puts me down!"

The kid's friends nodded, patiently waiting for the story of how nobody screwed over Deke once, because that's the way most stories get told when they're told in person. First the teller sets out his principles, and then he shows you how those principles get enacted in the world, usually by describing some incident or event in his recent past, so that what you end up with is the storyteller's philosophy of life. If you'd asked him straight out in the beginning to tell you what his philosophy of life was, he probably wouldn't have been able to tell you, any more than Deke could have. Sure he'd have one, at least he'd believe he had one, but unless he happened to be a professional philosopher, the chances are good he wouldn't be able to tell you what it was in so many words. And if he was a professional philosopher, the chances are just as good you wouldn't be able to understand what the hell he was talking about anyhow.

The same thing was happening with Deke. That's how Claudel looked at it. Deke started telling how the other night he was coming back to town from Concord in his LTD, hitting ninety-two as he left the traffic circle in Epsom, ninety-seven by the time he passed Webster's Mill Road where Frankie Marcoux was sitting in the dark, just waiting. Deke was a little bit drunk, but not much. He'd been drinking beer at the El Rancho in Concord since seven, and he was feeling ugly because he'd had a little run-in outside the El Rancho when he was leaving with a girl he'd picked up there. The girl turned out to be married and her husband turned out to be waiting for her in the parking lot, and the husband had given the girl hell and had taken her home with him. "Hey, I don't want some other guy's wife. Not like that, I mean. To me she was just some broad I picked up at the bar. To him she was his wife and the mother of his kids. So I just says to the guy, 'Sure,' I says, 'take her home where she belongs. Only next time,' I tell the guy, 'next time make sure she stays there,' I says, 'or maybe the next guy she walks out with won't be so agreeable.' You know what I mean?" he asked his friends.

They knew what he meant. Everybody took a pull on his beer, and Deke went on. "So, hey, here I am coming barrel-ass down Twenty-eight past Webster's Mill Road, and something tells me to check my mirror as I pass the intersection, and sure enough, I see Marcoux pulling out onto Twenty-eight with his blue light flashing and his siren wailing like an alley cat. Anyhow, *nobody* screws over me. So I jump on the LTD and I'm hitting a hundred and five when I pass Huckins Chevrolet, and just as I'm starting to put some real space between me and Marcoux, I see a goddamn semi, an eighteen-wheeler, for Christ's sake, slowing to turn off for town, and he's taking the whole damned road to make his cut, so I start hitting the brakes, right?"

"Right," Art said.

"Right," said Ron.

"Right. And pretty soon my ass end is letting go and I start to think maybe I'm going to roll, and I think, Jesus, I start to roll at a hundred and five and they'll be scraping me off Route Twenty-eight for a week. So I flip the wheel the same direction my ass is heading, bring her under control, at least I stop the slide, except that now I'm heading off the road into that big cornfield about a half-mile beyond Huckins, you know the one?"

Art, Ron, and Claudel, too, knew the one. It was a ten-acre, flat cornfield leased by a local dairy farmer, and at this time of year the corn was chest high. There was a shallow ditch between the field and the road, and then the ground was fairly flat and, except for the corn-stalks, smooth.

"So I barrel-ass into that goddamn field and I don't touch the brake or the gas, just let the goddamn car plow through the corn for a couple hundred yards, until it comes to a stop. I had enough sense to flick off my lights just as I left the road, so I was hoping Marcoux had been distracted by that semi jackknifing off the road, like I had been, and that he'd just keep on running down the road after me, while I cool it out in the middle of the cornfield. That's my plan, anyhow."

They all waited for him to tell them what had happened, Art, Ron, and Claudel. Show us how nobody screws over you, Deke.

"So I'm sitting there, waiting for Marcoux to flash by with his siren screaming and his blue light flashing, only all of a sudden I hear something that isn't a siren, it's a car engine, idling, and it's right behind me. And there isn't any blue light flashing, it's a set of headlights bouncing light off the corn that surrounds me, and I say, 'Shit, it's Marcoux.' And it is, it is that damned strutting sonofabitching horse's ass, and he's got me, because the only direction I can move is backward, and he's sitting there blocking me with his cruiser. He gets out, comes strolling up to my window, says, 'Hello, Deke,' real cool, you know, like he's seen it on TV. 'Out for your evening spin?' he asks me. Real funny. 'Ever think of trying the road, Deke? It's kinda hard to get much speed up, even in this LTD, when you're driving through a cornfield.' 'Ha ha ha,' I says to him. I mean, hey, *nobody* screws over me. You know what I mean?''

They knew.

"Did he run you in?" Art asked.

"Bet your ass!" Deke said defiantly. "Took me up to Laconia, made me take the breath test for drinking, but I passed the damned thing all right, so all he could do was hit me for speeding. I got my LTD out the next morning, but I was picking cornstalks out of the grill for days. Jesus, that car looked funny when I got it out, all those green stalks sticking out of the grill like that. I wanted to drive around town that way, you know, just to let people know."

"But you didn't," Ron said.

"Naw. No reason to. Besides, the only one I had to prove anything to was Marcoux, and I'd already done that, if you know what I mean."

They knew what he meant, all three of them. They were satisfied that nobody had screwed over him. They knew that even though he was barely twenty years old, Deke understood the world and knew how to live in it.

The band returned to the low stage in front, two middle-aged guitarists with their bellies hanging heavily over gaudy belt buckles and a skinny, balding drummer in his early sixties, all of them wearing matching purple cowboy shirts with pink fringes across their chests and along the backs of their arms.

They started the music again, and Claudel drifted back into his troubles, when all at once, as if entering a room he hadn't known existed, he realized that while he had been listening to Deke's story and thinking about it and while he had been watching the youth and attempting to understand him, he hadn't thought about himself once. Claudel had let young Deke become the center of his thoughts for a few minutes, and his mind and his heart now felt strangely refreshed for it. It was a feeling he couldn't remember having experienced before. Certainly not since Vietnam. A coherence had momentarily come over his life, and he understood it, knew where it had come from, which gave him a feeling of wholeness he hadn't even imagined possible before.

All those years of thinking he had held a philosophy of life, when in reality he had held nothing of the sort. And now, here in the bar at the Hawthorne House, after listening to a local kid tell a story of how he got arrested for speeding, Claudel suddenly felt he knew enough about the world to devise ways for getting along in the world. It's all in the way you pay attention to things! he said to himself. Oh, he knew nothing was going to change much. He wasn't going to get back his job at the Public Service Company, he knew that, and besides, the other day he'd agreed to go to work stacking hides down at the tannery. And he knew he'd never get Ginnie back, not now, because she was pregnant now and would probably marry Howie Leeke as soon as the divorce came through. And he knew he wasn't going to win the lottery or have some crazy kind of luck like that, which is what he'd need to pay off what he still owed the bank. No, he'd just go on—renting a room at the Hawthorne House, working days down at the tannery and spending his nights down here in the bar. Getting his life over with. But he also knew that it wouldn't bother him anymore. That made him very thankful. And that was the end of his story.

The Burden

BECAUSE OF THE SHABBY CHARACTER OF THE BOY'S MOTHER and also that of the man she had married the very day she found herself legally divorced and able to marry again, and because the two had determined to live far away from New Hampshire without even bothering to send him their address until several years later, Tom had raised Buddy practically by himself. And he had seen his son through hard times, especially as the boy got older, such as when he was in the service that one year and later when he got himself beat up by the guy with the baseball bat and spent six months flat on his back in Tom's trailer learning how to talk again. So of course when Tom walked into the Hawthorne House for a beer, even though, after the bright afternoon sunlight outside, he wasn't used to the darkness inside, he recognized the boy right away. You can do that with your children, you can tell who they are even in darkness, when all you can see of them is their height and the position they happen to be standing in. You just glance over, and you say, Oh yeah, there's my son.

Tom didn't know the girl with him, though. Not even when he drew close to her and could see her face clearly in the dim light of the bar. She was sitting alone in the booth next to the juke box where Buddy stood studying the songs. Tom could tell she was with Buddy and not alone because of the way she watched him while he studied the names of the songs on the juke box. It was the way girls always watched Buddy, as if they couldn't believe he wasn't going to disappear from in front of them any second—just poof! and he'd be gone, a curling thread of smoke hanging in the air where a second ago he had been smiling and chattering in that circular way of his. Nobody knew where Buddy got it from, his good looks and that way he had of talking so interestingly that people hated to see him come to a stop or ask a question, even, because his mother Maggie, Tom's ex-wife, had been pretty (back when she was Buddy's age, that is) but she had never been as outstandingly good-looking as Buddy was, and Tom, even though he had a square and regular-featured face, was not the kind of man you'd compliment for his looks, and of course neither Tom nor his ex-wife owned what you'd call a gift for gab, especially not Tom, who usually seemed more interested in listening than in talking anyway.

Tom walked past the girl, who looked to be around twenty-five, which made her four years older than Buddy and which was also usual for him. The girl was dark-haired and pretty, but actually more stylish than pretty when you got up close, with a round face and grim little mouth. Her short hair was all kinked up in a way that was fashionable just then, which made her somewhat resemble a dandelion, until you looked into her eyes and saw that she was awfully worried about something. You couldn't tell what it was, exactly, but it was clear that she was not at peace with her circumstances.

Tom stopped behind his son and next to the bar, and as he moved up to the bar, he reached out and absently tapped his son on the shoulder, and the boy turned around and smiled nicely. Tom didn't smile back, he didn't even look at Buddy. He looked across at Gary the bartender who also owned the place and ordered a bottle of beer.

"You're keeping your door locked now, Dad," Buddy said, as if Tom didn't realize it.

"I know." Tom turned around and faced him.

Buddy reached out and shook his father's hand. "This here's Donna," he said, nodding toward the girl. "Donna picked me up outside Portland on the Maine Pike, and we sorta got to be friends in a very short order, which is certainly nice for me because I'm nothing special and you can see that she is."

Donna gave Tom a thin smile, and she did not look like a person who was glad to find herself where she was finding herself, stopped in a dingy, mill town New Hampshire barroom to have a chat with her new boyfriend's father. Tom didn't give a damn about her, though, one way or the other. If she wanted to drive all over the countryside in her Japanese car just because she thought Buddy looked good beside her, it didn't matter to Tom, because women were always doing things like that, and so were men.

"How long you in town this time?" Tom asked his son. Gary the bartender delivered the bottle of beer, and Tom turned back to the bar and drank off half the bottle. He was feeling weighted and metallic inside, as if his stomach were filled with tangled stovepipe-wire, because even though Buddy was his son and he could recognize him in the darkness, he didn't like it when he saw him. Not anymore.

"So, Dad, you're keeping your door locked nowadays," he said again.

Tom was silent for a few seconds and did not look at the boy. "That's right. Ever since you left and took with you every damned thing of mine you could fit into that duffle of yours. My tape deck, tapes. You even took my cuff links. I must be stupid." He finished off the bottle of beer and Gary automatically slid a second over. Gary was a tall, skinny, dark-haired man with a toothpick in his mouth that made him look wiser than he probably was. He was the fourth owner of the bar in the last ten years.

Once again, Buddy smiled in that easy way he had, like a summer sun coming up, and Tom felt his stomach clank and tangle. "C'mon, Dad, I only *borrowed* that stuff. I only planned to be gone for the weekend, me and Bilodeau, that kid from Concord. It was a weekend, the weather suddenly got warm, you probably don't remember, but it did, and we were planning to chase some girls Bilodeau knew over on the coast near Kittery. But things just got screwed up, and before the weekend was over, we ended up going in different directions with different people. You know how it goes . . ." He showed Tom both his palms, as if to prove he wasn't hiding anything.

"That was last April." Tom knew his son was lying, and there was no damned sense trying to catch him out or somehow prove the boy was lying or get him to admit it, because he'd just go on lying, topping one lie with another, canceling one out with a new one, on and on, until you just gave up out of fatigue and boredom. He was one of those people who are always ready to go a step further than anyone else, and after a while you could see that about him, so you'd stop, and he'd be standing there just ahead of you, smiling back. It was almost as if he didn't know the difference between right and wrong.

"April?" the girl said. She lit a cigarette and looked at Buddy through the smoke. "So what's been happening since April? This is June," she observed, as if she had got a glimpse, from the conversation between the father and son, of what might be in store for her if she went ahead with her plans and hooked up for a while with this good-looking, smooth-talking, slender young man. It had probably started out as a whim, picking up and spending the weekend with a guy she'd seen hitchhiking in Maine. It would make a funny story she could tell on herself to her friends in Boston or Hartford or wherever she had originally been headed. But now things were starting to look a little off-center to her, not quite lined up, which is how it always was with Buddy, how it always had been. He was so damned good-looking, all white teeth and high cheekbones and quick-sloping narrow nose and deep blue eyes, the all-American boy, and he talked sweetly and in a strangely elaborate way, all in circles and curls that kept you listening, so that pretty soon you forgot what it was you were planning on doing and instead you plugged into his plans, but then someplace down along the line, things started to look a little bit off-center, as if a couple of basic pieces hadn't been cut right. And you couldn't tell which pieces were off, because the whole damned thing was off.

Buddy peered down at her as if he couldn't quite place her. "What's been happening since April?" he asked. "You really want to know?"

"No. Not really. It just seemed a funny thing, that's all . . ."

"Funny. What's funny?" Buddy asked. Tom watched the two carefully from the bar.

"Nothing," the girl said. "Forget it." She closed her eyes for a second, and when she opened them, her expression had changed, as if she had turned Buddy into a total stranger, as if she were seeing him for the first time all over again but this time with the knowledge of him that she had gained since morning, when she first saw him at the Portland exit with his thumb out and his duffle and suitcase on the road beside him.

"Forget funny?" Buddy said, smiling broadly. "Who can forget funny?" He turned away from the girl and faced his father and suddenly started talking to him. "Listen, Dad, that's why I stopped down at the trailer before I came up here. To give your stuff back, I mean. Hey, I couldn't do it way the hell up there in Maine among the trees and lakes, and then Donna here was nice enough to drive all this distance out of her way just to help me drop these things off at your place, before we resume our wanderings. Listen, Dad, since April I been way the hell out on a narrow neck of land in northern Maine, working on a lobster boat." He had laid a hand on his father's shoulder.

Tom didn't believe a word the boy said. He had decided long ago, as policy, not to believe anything his son told him. And that, he told himself, was one of the reasons he kept his trailer locked now, for the first time in his entire life. You're supposed to love your son and trust him and protect him, and while that would have been easy for Tom, it always had been, this new way of treating him was a burden, and he hated it. For years Tom had loved his son and trusted him and protected him, behaving precisely the way he knew the boy's mother, his ex-wife Maggie, would not have behaved. Maggie would have let the boy down. Maggie wouldn't have been home that night the state troopers brought him home all drunk and raving, and the boy would have ended up in jail. Maggie wouldn't have known how to handle it when he got his head bashed in by that guy with the baseball bat in Florida. She would have let him rot in that charity ward in the Florida hospital before she'd have brought him home, set him up on the living room couch in front of the TV, and then every night for six months taught the boy how to talk again, until finally he could make those looping, charming sentences of his again, and people would sit back in their chairs and listen with light smiles on their faces to see such a clever, good-looking young man perform for them. Maggie never would have borne up under the weight of Buddy, Tom knew. The proof of her weakness, if he'd ever needed proof, he'd obtained the summer Buddy turned twelve, when he had taken the boy by Greyhound all the way to Phoenix, Arizona, to visit his mother, at her request, while he, the father, took a two-week holiday alone farther west, visiting Disneyland, Knott's Berry Farm and Universal Studios and watching the surfers at Huntington Beach, the only time he had ever seen real live surfers. When the two weeks were up and Tom had called back at Phoenix for his son, things had changed, and he left the boy in Phoenix, at the boy's request, presumably for good (at least that was Maggie's and her husband's intention and Buddy's as well). Tom returned to New Hampshire, and didn't hear anything from his son until September, when the boy showed up at the trailer. She had put him alone on a Boston-bound bus in Phoenix connecting to another bus to Concord, New Hampshire, and the boy, more travelwise by then than he'd been in June, had hitchhiked the twenty-five remaining miles home. No, for Maggie it was the love and the trust and the protection that made the burden. For Tom, the burden was in withholding that love, trust and protection. That's what he believed.

For it wasn't simply Buddy's stealing his father's belongings that had turned the man against him, though of course that helped. And it wasn't that the boy seemed incapable of telling the truth about anything (he would lie when there was nothing to be gained by it, he lied for the sheer pleasure of lying, or so it seemed, and if you asked him was it raining outside, he'd look out the window, see that it was raining and say no, not yet, and when you stepped out the door into the rain, you'd turn around and look at Buddy, and he'd say with great delight that it must have started raining that very second). And it wasn't that the boy was reckless and troublesome, that he seemed incapable of avoiding the kind of person who happened at that moment to want to hurt someone, especially someone young and pretty and mouthy. Buddy would find himself in a bar, the Hawthorne House, say, next to a crossed-up truck driver or some hide-stacker from the tannery, and he would do everything he could think of to make himself look even younger, prettier and mouthier than he was, and of course he'd end up getting himself thrashed for it. And then somehow he'd get himself back to the trailerpark, and he'd drag himself to the door, swing open the door and fall into the living room, where his father would be sitting in front of the TV with a can of beer in his hand and the open newspaper on his lap.

"Buddy! What in hell's happened now?"

"Oh, Daddy, did I ever get myself into one this time! They got some mean and dirty-fighting rattle-snaking bad-ass cowboys hanging out nowadays at the Hawthorne House, and it's just not your family restaurant anymore."

No, it wasn't any of those actions and attitudes and incapacities that had turned Tom against his son, had made him lock his door against his boy. In fact, if anyone had asked him why, Tom, have you suddenly gone and turned against your boy after all those years of standing by him, Tom would not have been able to answer. All he knew was that it had begun for him about a week after Buddy left this last time, back in April.

Right off, Tom noticed that his son had taken with him his tape deck, tapes, a bottle of Canadian Club whiskey, his cuff links, two shirts, and probably a dozen more possessions that he wouldn't find out about until he needed them and went looking for them. He merely observed that once again his son had made off with everything of his that he could lay his hands on, and he was, once again, glad that none of it was irreplaceable. Nothing Tom owned was irreplaceable, even though that was not by intention. In recent years he had worked off and on as an escort driver for a mobile home manufacturer in Suncook, hiring out with his own pickup truck and CB radio, usually as the lead man, the one with the sign WIDE LOAD FOLLOWING on the front of his truck, and before that he had driven an oil delivery truck, so while he had always made enough to house and feed and clothe himself and his one child, he hadn't made much more than that. Certainly he had never made enough money to buy anything that was irreplaceable.

But about a week after Buddy left this time, Tom began to feel something he had never felt before—at least in regard to Buddy he had never felt it before. What he felt was relief, relief that the boy was gone from him, was not at home in front of the TV set or coming in late all drunk and bashed up or slamming cupboard doors in the morning in search of food. He was glad, for the first time he could remember, that he did not have to see the boy's face across the table from him, and he discovered that he enjoyed eating alone. And then, once he had admitted to himself that he was relieved to have the boy gone from him, it was as if he had released a flood of bad feelings about the boy, so that his face darkened every time Buddy's name was mentioned or every time he walked into some evidence of the boy's ever having lived with him, his dirty clothes in that final week's laundry, for example, or a letter that came to him three days after he'd left, a letter in a woman's handwriting, Tom could tell, because of the careful, large, rounded letters. And then even his memories of the boy's childhood began to turn sour and ugly, and he couldn't start to remember something he had once done with the boy without feeling his stomach tighten and grow heavy, so that he would turn away from the memory and think about something more immediate. For instance, he had taught Buddy to ice-skate when he was only four or five and had taught him to shoot a hockey puck into a makeshift goal he had set up on the lake behind the trailerpark not far from the shore and within sight of his own trailer. Buddy developed the basic skills quickly and soon was obsessed with practicing at the sport, especially the part that had him skating full-speed to a spot twelve or fifteen feet in front of the goal and firing the puck, a few inches off the ice, into the goal, then coasting forward, stick raised to celebrate the score, retrieving the puck and looping back out to make the run over again. For hours in the late afternoons that winter the boy would skate alone and shoot goals, and his father would look out the window of the trailer as it grew swiftly dark outside and he'd watch the tiny figure of his son move back and forth across the gray surface of the ice, until after a while it seemed the boy was floating in a dark haze, and the father would step outside to the frozen ground and holler for him to come in for supper. And the image of his son that he held in his mind as he called his name into the darkness was of his small, struggling figure afloat in a haze between the ice below and the sky above, as if sky and ice had merged and had become an ether, as if the firmament had been erased. Remembering this now, as he often did when, by accident, he happened to look out the window in the kitchen that showed him a wide expanse of the open lake, he winced and held on to the

edge of the counter as if to regain lost balance, and he
thought about getting some new asbestos tiles to replace
the half-dozen that were lifting from the floor in front of
the sink.

Tom didn't understand this shift in his feelings, this
great relief, as if a huge burden had been lifted from his
back. He was ashamed of it, which of course replaced
one burden with another. For it seemed wrong to him,
wrong to feel glad that his son was gone away, wrong to
hope that he would never come back, and it seemed
shameful to him that memories of his son made him
wince, that signs of his son's life made him look away
with irritation, that questions from friends about his
son's whereabouts and welfare made him grit his teeth
and answer abruptly and vaguely. But he couldn't help
himself. It was out of his control. Buddy had even
started entering his dreams in the same irritating way,
turning a pleasant dream sour, a peaceful dream turbu-
lent, a funny dream grim.

Of course he knew Buddy eventually would come
back, would show up in town again, probably down at
the trailer, and if not there, then up here at the Hawthorne House, where he knew his father could be found
almost every afternoon drinking three or four beers and
listening to Gary and the locals who stopped in after
work. And when Tom thought about that, his son's
coming back, he had taken to locking his door whenever
he left the trailer, something he had never done before,
not in all the years he had lived at the trailerpark. In
recent years most people in the park had taken to locking their doors, mainly because of rumors of theft (though
no one actually knew firsthand of any thievery), and
until now Tom had refused to go along with the trend,
saying that he had nothing worth stealing anyhow so
why try to protect it? Then one morning he had walked
out the door to his truck, about to leave for a two-day

job escorting a sixty-seven-foot Marlette from Suncook to just outside Syracuse, New York. He got into the truck, started the engine, then peered back at the powder-blue trailer and thought, The door. He got out, walked quickly across to the cinderblock steps, reached up and locked the door. That was that. And he had locked it, whenever he left the trailer, ever since.

THE GIRL DONNA WAS GONE. SHE HAD GOT UP AS IF GOING to the ladies' room, and she hadn't come back.

"Where's Donna, Dad?" Buddy asked, looking hurt and slightly bewildered. He sat down in the booth where the girl had been sitting earlier.

"Gone, maybe." Tom turned away from his son and faced the bar, standing between two barstools as if he were in too much of a hurry to sit down and relax.

Buddy sat in the booth looking half-dazed, but it was the wrong way to look, or so it seemed to Tom, so Tom said nothing, even though he thought about it, thought about how the boy should be acting at a time like this. After all, a new girlfriend had just got scared or spooked and had slipped out the door and had driven off in her car, and she might have taken all Buddy's belongings with her, even including his father's tape deck and tapes and cuff links. Why, then, wasn't the boy racing outside to see if the girl at least had tossed his bags out of her car before driving off? And why wasn't he cursing her? Or maybe even laughing, at himself, at the girl, at his fate? Instead, he sat in the booth, languid, head lolling back, eyes half-closed. Tom glanced down at the boy, then turned swiftly away again. The sight of his son sitting like that made him tighten inside and caused his shoulders and the small of his back to stiffen.

"You think she tossed your bags out before she took off?" he asked the boy in a low voice.

Gary looked across at Buddy and chuckled. He apparently didn't see anything wrong with the way the boy was acting. He craned his neck so he could see out the window to where the girl's car had been parked. "Nope, Buddy, you're in luck this time, she left your gear. It's sitting out there in the lot." He looked at Tom and grinned and winked.

Tom didn't respond. Instead he sighed and turned away from the bar and came and sat opposite his son in the booth, saying as he slid into the seat, "Well, Buddy, what are your plans now? Where you headed for this time?"

Buddy smiled warmly, as if noticing his father's presence for the first time. "I was thinking about staying here for the summer, you know, maybe get some work locally, drilling wells or as a carpenter's helper, and then in the fall see if I can't work something out down at the university, maybe get the government to help me pay for a couple of engineering drwing courses or something, you know, with the GI Bill, so I could get a better job next year and gradually work my way to the top, become a captain of industry, maybe even run for governor or open up a car dealership or start a tree farm . . ."

"Buddy, I'm serious."

"So'm I, Dad. I'm serious." And suddenly he looked it, his mouth drawn tightly forward, his blue eyes cold and grim, his hands clenched in fists in front of him on the table.

In a soft voice, Tom reminded the boy that the government wouldn't help him pay for anything, not with his kind of discharge from the army (he'd spent more than half his one year in the army locked up in the stockade, usually for trivial offenses, but offenses committed so compulsively and frequently that finally they had given up on him and sent him home to his father), and he told the boy, again, that he couldn't take courses down at the university until he first finished high school, and he told him, again, that with his reputation for trouble it was almost impossible for him to get work around here anymore, unless he was willing to work the night shift down at the tannery stacking hides, and he informed his son that he didn't want him to live with him in his trailer, not anymore, not ever.

Quickly, as if startled, Buddy looked directly into his father's eyes, and his blue eyes filmed over with tears. "You mean you're kicking me out?" His lip trembled. Tom saw that the boy was terrified and was about to cry, and he was shocked to see it.

He got up from the booth quickly. "C'mon, we'll talk about this outside," he said gruffly, and he hurried away from the booth, tossing Gary a pair of dollar bills as he passed the bar. Buddy followed silently along behind.

Outside, in the comparative brightness of the parking lot, they stood facing each other at the tailgate of Tom's pickup truck. Nearby, Buddy's duffle and battered brown canvas suitcase lay in a heap on the pavement.

"Dad, maybe I could just stay till I got on my feet, you know, saved a little money, enough to rent my own place . . . ?"

Tom looked at the boy steadily. They were the same height and build, though Tom, twenty years older, was slightly heavier and thicker through the shoulders and arms. Behind them a lumber truck changed gears, braked and slowed, passed through the town on its way south. Tom cleared his throat. "You got to take care of yourself now," he said slowly.

The boy walked to his bags and drew them toward the truck, lifted them and tossed them into the back of the pickup. He was smiling again. "C'mon, Dad, just a few days, I'll get hold of Donna, I got her number down in Boston, she gave it to me, and I'll call her and set something up with her . . . She just took off because she had to be in Boston by tonight and she could see I wanted to stay here awhile and visit alone with you, sort of to re-establish contact.''

Tom reached over the tailgate into the truck and pulled out the bags and dropped them onto the pavement behind Buddy. His face grew long and heavy with a deep sadness, and the boy stared down at the bags as if not understanding what they were doing there, and when his gaze came back Tom saw that the boy was about to weep again.

Another lumber truck approached the Hawthorne House, changed gears as it neared the curve and the slope from the bar to the tannery below. ''You could pick up a ride on one of them trucks this afternoon and be in Boston tonight, if you wanted to,'' Tom said, looking after the truck.

''Daddy . . .''

It had turned into a low, gray day, dark and heavy and cool, not sunny and warm as it had been an hour earlier. The streets of the town were nearly empty. No cars passed. Generally, in a mill town people don't move about much except early in the day and late.

''Daddy . . . I'm broke,'' Buddy said quietly, and his voice cracked and tears rolled down his cheeks, and he looked like a small boy standing there before his father, open-faced, weeping, his shoulders slanting toward the ground, his hands hanging uselessly down. ''I need some money . . . before I can take off on my own. Please help me, Daddy. I won't cause you any more trouble, I promise.''

Tom looked away from the sight of his son and up at the gray sky, and he could see that it would rain soon. Then he looked away from the sky and down the hill toward the dam and the red brick tannery and then finally down at the boy's duffle and suitcase. ''I've heard promises," he said. "And I've had to make up my mind regardless."

"I can't go off alone . . ."

"You just did, from last April."

"Yes," the boy cried, "but I thought I could come back! I didn't know you'd lock your door against me!"

Tom studied the boy's face carefully, as if seeing something there he had never seen before. When you love someone for years and years, you lose sight of how that person looks to the rest of the world. Then one day, even though it's painful, you push the person away and suddenly you can see him the way a stranger sees him. But because you know so much more about him than a stranger can ever know, you are frightened for him, as frightened as you would be for yourself if you could see in yourself, as you see in him, that you're not quite right, that you don't quite fit into the place the world has tried to make for you.

Tom stopped looking at his son and instead looked at the ground. Then he took a deliberate step past his son and picked up the two bags, turned and pitched them into the back of the truck. Slowly, as if exhausted, he walked around to the driver's side and got in. "C'mon," he said in a low voice and started the engine.

The boy suddenly brightened and, instantly transformed, ran around to the other side and slid in next to his father. "Oh, hey, listen, Dad," he said, "I promise I won't cause you any more trouble! I'll even pay you room and board, I'll get a job tomorrow down at the tannery, stacking hides, just like you said!" He stuck his right arm out the open window and slapped the side of the truck, making a loud noise, and repeated it with sudden, erratic exuberance. "I'll get a car, a good used car, and then I'll be able to rent my own place, Dad, maybe rent a trailer at the park near you, there's always a couple of vacancies . . .'' He went on banging the side of the truck.

Tom didn't answer. He dropped the truck into reverse, waited as another lumber truck passed, then backed into the street and turned left and headed downhill toward the tannery, following the lumber truck.

Buddy had ceased banging the door and was peering out the open window at the stores and houses and then the dam and old mill pond, with the tannery buildings on the left. ''Where we going, Dad? The trailerpark's the other way.''

Tom said nothing. He shifted down a gear as they came up close behind the lumber truck, which was laboriously making its way up the hill on the far side of the dam. At the top of the hill, the road straightened and widened, and Tom pulled out and passed the lumber truck, giving a toot and a wave to the driver as he passed. Driving rapidly, he soon was ahead of the truck by a quarter mile or more, and two miles down the road from the dam, with rolling green fields of new corn spreading away from the road, he came to the Turnpike, and he pulled over and stopped the pickup. The lumber truck was drawing slowly up behind him.

Buddy, suddenly understanding, looked at his father with terror, then anger. ''You sonofabitch.''

''You get out and stick your thumb out and that driver'll pick you up,'' Tom said in a low voice.

Buddy wrenched open the door and stepped out of the pickup and slammed the door shut behind him. Slinging his bags quickly to the ground, he waved up at the driver of the lumber truck hissing to a stop and showed him his thumb. The driver waved him up, and Buddy climbed aboard. Tom let the truck pass, then turned slowly around in the road and headed back to town.

Politics

Driving back through a cold October rain, somewhere near Rockingham Park racetrack and the New Hampshire state line, Nancy Hubner tried to decide to tell her husband Ronald that she wanted a divorce. But that's soap opera, she told herself, because what she really wanted was a separation—phrasing it carefully in a sentence, however, as if she could be heard by Moses. Moses was her doctor, her psychiatrist. His real name was Dr. Norman Moses, but Nancy, even when talking to him face to face, enjoyed referring to him as Moses. He wore a shovel-shaped beard, salt-and-pepper, was tall and broad-faced, had blue eyes and was in excellent physical shape. She'd had no difficulty mistaking him for Charlton Heston, especially in the liquid-eyed manner he used in listening to her every Thursday afternoon, and after six months of therapy, she had developed the habit of thinking in complete sentences that she felt would make sense to Moses, the way you do when you're first in love or when you have made a new, deep friendship with a person you admire very much.

She was not in love with Moses, of course, but she did admire him very much. Her problem, the one she had brought down to Boston with her six months ago, was that while she was in love with her husband Ronald, she did not admire him very much. As a matter of fact, she did not admire him at all. Moses apparently had no difficulty believing that part. Instead, what he seemed to question was the part about her being in love with Ronald in the first place. She had presented her problem to him, as if bearing a gift, smiling with her characteristic, slight self-effacement, and he had looked at her problem somewhat casually from several angles, and then had asked, "What makes you think you love your husband?" It was like asking the price of a gift.

Now, she said to herself, gratitude thickening the tone of her imagined voice, now, he was presenting *her* with a gift, for now her problem was solved. She not only did not admire her husband, she did not love him either.

She buzzed north on the Turnpike, and the rain slopped heavily down. It was dark, though still late afternoon, and traffic was thin, so she cruised at nearly eighty, driving the car without thoughts about the car or road, as if both could take care of themselves. She would like to tell Ronald tonight, just sit down at the kitchen table and tell him that she wanted a separation, and by next Thursday afternoon, when she saw Moses again, she would have told the children and her parents, would surely have told several of her friends. She may even have moved out by then. She would be the one to leave. She had been able to decide that much. It was only fair. Ronald loved the house—it was properly his. He ran his business, insurance, from the house. He had renovated and even decorated the place without much interest or special cooperation from her, converting it from a run-down, long-empty farmhouse on the edge of town into an attractive, modern dwelling fit for an attractive, modern family. It was her life that was changing, had changed, would go on changing—not his. And it was unfair of her to impose any more change on his life than was absolutely necessary for her survival. My emotional and spiritual well-being, she said to herself.

When a man and a woman have been married for two and one half decades and have raised or nearly raised three children together, they necessarily will have become different people at the end of those decades. Everyone knows that. Frequently, however, the single path they have been following together for so long, like Hansel's and Gretel's, does not come out at the same place for both Hansel and Gretel, and surprised, often confused, they find themselves standing in the clearing alone. Or so it seems to them. They can rejoin, but only if they go all the way back to the beginning, where they first entered the forest years ago. But that only happens in fairy tales. In real life, if you have not reached the clearing yet, you must go on. And if you have reached the clearing, you must live there.

Nancy believed that she had reached the clearing. She had become ''political,'' she said. She said it to everyone, to Moses, to Ronald, and to her daughter Noni, the only child still living at home, a fifteen-year-old, blond, self-absorbed child who gave the impression to strangers of being soulless. The other two children, her sons Chip and Ron, Jr., one in law school, the other working for a prestigious law firm in Washington, had such hidebound ideas of what ''political'' meant that Nancy did not try even to mention it to them, for they would have obliged her to explain it precisely, which she could not have done to their satisfaction, and they would have teased her about it then. To them, her "politics" would have seemed nothing more than the self-indulgent expression of middle-class taste refined by years of idleness. Naive, they would have called her. Sentimental. Woolly-headed.

But that was not true, she knew, for she had beliefs, she had principles and she had positions that she did not have when she was a younger woman and that she had acquired only after great thought and some reading and a considerable amount of conversation with people who shared those beliefs, principles and positions. She believed, for instance, that as a child of the 1940s and '50s she and her entire generation had suffered from the sexual restrictions imposed by her parents in particular and society in general, and further, that the guilt used to enforce those restrictions complicated and extended the suffering long after one's parents had died and society in general had changed its mind with regard to such crucial human activities as masturbation, foreplay and orgasm. On principle, then, she could say that a casual, sexual relationship between a man and a woman, so long as it was experienced without feelings of guilt, was a positive and enlarging event. And an example of a position Nancy held might be that society in general and individual citizens in particular have no right to judge in moral or legal terms the sexual activities, proclivities or technologies employed for pleasure between consenting adults.

She was, therefore, *for* vibrators. The sale of them, she meant. Just as she was for pornography, though she herself had never actually seen any. After all, as the middle-aged wife of a small-town insurance man, she did not find sexual paraphernalia and pornography easily available. On the other hand, as a direct result of her principles, she had enjoyed, really *enjoyed*, a casual sexual relationship with a man, an exceedingly attractive young man named Dino whose attentions to the details of her body had strengthened her beliefs concerning the injustices her generation had suffered at the hands of its parents. Dino was a carpenter who specialized in building houses the old way, without nails and with handhewn, mortised and pinioned beams. He abjured the use of power tools, and probably for that reason had taken from April to late November last year to build Nancy's solar greenhouse. Dino lived in the woods in a cabin with his wife Bliss, who wore gingham dresses that trailed along the ground. She had a tattoo of a rose above her right breast which she revealed fetchingly by leaving the top buttons of her dress undone at all times. Nancy's "relationship" with Dino had taken place over the summer, while Dino was building the greenhouse, and had ended in October (almost exactly a year ago today, Nancy said to herself) when she discovered that Bliss was five months pregnant. "It would only have complicated things," she had explained to Moses. "And ours wasn't the kind of love that could have endured complications and still provide us with pleasure."

Moses had listened, smiled, and then had asked, "Do you want happiness, Nancy, or pleasure? Or do you think they're the same thing?"

It was that question, Nancy realized afterward, that had started her movement toward the decision that she wanted to make today, this afternoon, driving back home to Catamount in the rain. Moses had made her think about the Basics, she said to herself. A sudden blast from the horn of a huge, eighteen-wheel truck cut into her silent monologue, showed her that she was out in the left lane and that an enormous, roaring vehicle, switching its headlights from low beams to high, wanted to pass her. The truck, seen in her rearview mirror, seemed almost close enough to touch the flimsy rear bumper of her Datsun coupe, and terrified, she wrenched the steering wheel to the right. The rear wheels of the Datsun let go of the road and the car started sliding. It happened too fast for her to hit the breaks, which, according to Ronald later, probably saved her life, because, as the nose of the low, silver-gray Datsun swung slowly to the right, the rear end followed, bringing the car into the right lane altogether and facing the opposite direction, while the truck roared past in the outside lane, its horn blasting one long wailing note into the rain and the dark.

She sat in the car, her entire body shaking, and after a few seconds realized that she was facing oncoming traffic, should there be any, so she backed the car around, turned it toward the north again, then drew it off the road onto the shoulder and shut off the motor and lights. She lit a cigarette and watched the rain slop down the windshield in skeins.

I could have been killed, she said to herself. I very nearly *was* killed! She pictured Ronald's round, reddish face, his small eyes, wet and blue behind horn-rimmed glasses, his calm, rational, nearly expressionless face that twenty-five years ago had seemed masculine and warmly protective to her—and suddenly she saw his face breaking into pieces, shattered by grief and loss, tears swarming over his cheeks. The children, too—she thought briefly of their faces, heard their groans, let their pain flicker past for a few seconds—but Ronald's face wouldn't go away. Her chest lifted and then settled beneath a great weight.

She rubbed out the cigarette butt, started the motor, switched on the lights and eased the car back onto the road. The rain was coming down more heavily now, and even had she wanted to, she could not drive over forty. She had to concentrate and squint to see farther than a hundred feet ahead, and she kept the car carefully in the right lane. Now and then a truck passed her on the left, splashing water and road-film over the tiny silver Datsun, shoving the car aside with its wake, so that she had to hold on to the steering wheel fiercely with both hands to keep the car from luffing off to the right.

Frequently, in her talks with Moses, she had described her life as a prisoner's. The walls of her prison were constructed of obligations to others—to the children, to Ronald, of course, even to the damned dog, and because of those obligations she was further obliged to please whoever was important to the children, Ronald and the dog, which meant behaving in a way that was acceptable to the families of the other small businessmen in town. In recent years she had let her dissatisfaction with the life of a prisoner reveal itself—bumper stickers against nuclear power plants and for the burning of wood, involvement with a dozen young couples in the formation of a cooperative nursery school and day-care center (which was where she had met Dino and Bliss), demonstrating outside the capitol in Concord during the ERA and, later, abortion hearings. These gestures and expressions of her discontent, she knew, were pathetic and, in the end, harmless, for she still entertained Ronald's local business associates in precisely the manner he had long ago grown accustomed to, she still cleaned up after and cooked for whichever members of her family slept and ate at home, she still kept her mouth shut and smiling in the face of conversations that she regarded as ignorant, narrow-minded, provincial, even cruel. And gradually, she had become a sullen, utterly self-centered, deeply pessimistic prisoner.

"Who's the warden in your prison?" Moses had asked her. She had thought about that one for a week, and then, the following Thursday, had begun their session by announcing her discovery that she herself was the warden.

"Ah," Moses said, clearly pleased. "Then you have the keys to unlock all the cells, don't you?" That remark had led her directly to the understanding that all of them were prisoners, not just she, but Ronald too, and

Noni. Even the dog. She could release them all, if she dared.

It would be a wonderful new life for them all. Ronald would be free to live and work just as he always had but without being obliged to deal with a surly, disapproving, somewhat embarrassing wife, and Noni would be free to choose which of her parents' lives seemed more coherent and honorable to her, choosing in that way the shape and direction of her own life, which, at fifteen, she was certainly eager to do. And the dog, well, the dog would receive a kind word now and then when it got fed, for Ronald was damned well going to have to take care of his beloved Irish setter himself now. And Nancy herself? Nancy at last would be free to live and work, to think and speak, to hate and love in all the ways she had wanted for years now. She would rent an apartment in town, or better yet, a small house or cabin in the woods, where she could grow her own vegetables, organic vegetables, maybe raise a dozen chickens, for eggs, not for meat, because as soon as she got settled, she meant to become a vegetarian. She would work, at first on a volunteer basis, then as a paid organizer, for the Clamshell Alliance against the construction and any further development of nuclear energy. Or maybe she could work for one of the small organizations interested in researching and publicizing the virtues and values of solar energy. She would live modestly, simply, honestly—alone, she assumed, but in time she would have a lover, a man younger than she but who nonetheless would be able to explore with her the intricacies of her wonderful new life, for he would have to be someone who shared with her the beliefs, principles and positions of her politics.

A few miles north of Manchester, she left the turnpike and continued on toward Catamount through Hooksett and Suncook on Route 28. The towns were smaller now, villages and old, decaying mill towns squatting alongside the rivers in the rain and cold darkness of October. North of Suncook, at the edge of a gray circle of fluorescent light cast by a filling station, she caught sight of a figure standing by the side of the road. It was a girl, she realized as she sped past, or a woman, and she was hitchhiking. On the ground next to her was a backpack, soaked through from the rain, and the girl was wearing an orange, stiff-looking, plastic poncho. Nancy slowed the car, feathering the brakes so as not to slide, and came almost to a stop several hundred yards beyond the girl. In the rearview mirror she saw the girl lift the backpack from the ground and start running in a clumsy, off-balance gait toward the car, which was still moving slowly ahead, a few miles an hour. The girl struggled along behind, splashing through deep puddles, until she had drawn to within a hundred yards of the car, and still Nancy kept the car moving forward. Finally, the girl stopped running. She dropped her pack onto the ground beside her and stood peering into the darkness at Nancy's car. In the mirror, as the car moved back into the roadway and increased speed, Nancy saw the girl jab her hand at her in a gesture of disgust and contempt, and then the car went around a long, slow bend in the road, and the girl was gone.

Nancy did not understand what she had done, because she did not know why she had done it. She drove the last twenty-five miles to Catamount puzzling over the event, replaying it and rephrasing her description of it as she drove, thinking, as if saying it to Moses, I stopped to pick up a hitchhiker in the rain but I didn't do it, but I don't know why I didn't do it. She tried several explanations—that she suddenly, inexplicably, had become frightened by the hitchhiker, since she might have made a mistake, the girl might actually have been a man; that she was still addled by the close call with the truck back on the Turnpike; that she had suddenly realized that the hitchhiker would break into her solitary thoughts, which at this time more than at any other she treasured and needed—but none of the explanations told her truly why she had tempted and then rejected the girl, why, by slowing almost to a stop, she had offered something she was not ready or willing actually to give.

She drove quickly along Main Street in Catamount, the tall elms and maples alongside the street shedding their last leaves in the rain, the stores and offices darkened and empty, except for the Copper Skillet, where, as she passed, she could see a few solitary diners at the counter. At the far side of town, she turned right toward home, uphill for a quarter mile, and there it suddenly was, the white Cape farmhouse and attached barn, the neatly trimmed lawn and flowerbeds, the bony, leafless oaks by the side of the road.

She turned into the drive and parked the car in front of the barn door. She would have to run no more than twenty feet to reach the breezeway and the kitchen door, but she knew she would be soaked through by the time she got there, so she sat for a few seconds, hesitating to leave the dry, smoky warmth of the car. She wished she had brought an umbrella. She decided that from now on she would bring an umbrella with her on Thursdays. Then she decided that she would not leave Ronald, and stepping from the car, she ran into the house.

The Right Way

THE BOY STEPPED OUT OF THE HOUSE TO THE PORCH AND from the porch into the glare of sunlight off the snow. The boy was fourteen years old, exactly, for it was his birthday. Tall and somewhat awkward, his height was coming early and in bits and pieces. First his hands and feet, then his legs, followed a few months later by his arms, so that his body seemed to be made of parts from several different-sized bodies, which made him look fragile and graceless, a long-legged bird walking on rocky ground.

He moved down the straight, wide, freshly cleared path in the snow, gazing at the path from different angles, as if admiring his work, for it was he who had shoveled the path earlier and then the driveway, from the barn all the way to the road, where he had diligently chopped away the hardpacked snowbank made by the town plow, tossing the huge, heavy chunks of snow over his shoulder, deliberately constructing with them neat, conical gateposts on either side of the driveway. Now he stood in the middle of the driveway and studied the crisp, dry snow, studied the way it smoothed the world, softened the fields and yard almost into abstraction, abruptly to break off where, with the shovel, he had cut cleanly into it, had carved out blocks of snow that got deposited in a rumpled row a few feet back from the cut, as if the snowfield had risen slightly into a rough wave before pitching over a low fault in the earth's crust.

The boy had his hands jammed into the pockets of his red plaid jacket and stood with feet apart, his wool hunter's cap pulled down over his ears. It was a cold day, despite the bright sunshine, and a stiff wind blowing through the tall pine trees at the edge of the yard became, on noticing it, a grieving kind of noise that made it difficult but not impossible for the boy to hear his father, inside the house, call his name, first from the front of the house, where the parlor was, then from the kitchen, until at last the door to the porch was flung open, and the man stood there, looking at the boy with a mixture of puzzlement and irritation.

The man was large, a few inches taller than the boy, but heavy through the shoulders and arms, with a large, full face and straight, dark brown hair. He was in his shirtsleeves, wearing brown twill trousers and green braces. "Dewey," the man said, as if making an announcement. He was silent for a moment, but the boy made no response. "What the hell you doing out here? I was calling all over."

"I'm all ready. I was only waiting for you out here."

"You ate breakfast."

"Sure."

The father turned and hollered to someone inside. "He's outside! He already ate, he says."

A woman, the boy's mother, answered indistinctly.

"I don't *know* when," the man said. He was pulling on a wool mackinaw and cap, still by the open door. When the man spoke to the woman he looked at the boy.

"Will you bring the others with you?" the woman asked.

"I don't know when I'll be back, maybe not till this afternoon. They'll get bored. It's just errands. Besides, Dewey's doing the driving."

"Oh," the woman said, as if the fact of the boy's driving was somehow significant.

The man was plainly irritated. He turned back to her and said, "It's his birthday, isn't it? Besides, he drives here at the farm all the time."

"Fine."

The man closed the door and stepped into the white glare beyond the porch. Moving ahead of him, the boy went quickly to the barn and pulled the wide door open. While the man walked around him and climbed into the passenger's seat of the Ford, the boy prepared to crank-start the sedan from the front.

"Set your spark?" the man asked.

"Oh, yeah," the boy said, and he rushed around to the driver's side and moved the spark lever. Then he hurried to the front again and commenced cranking, until the motor coughed and turned over, caught and was running.

"Let it warm up," the man said. He sat with his thick arms crossed over his chest, his head pulled low to his shoulders, and stared straight out the open barn door at the brilliant white world beyond. His freshly shaved face was gray and taut, and his pale blue eyes glistened wetly behind a film, as if he were peering at the world through a window. He was a sad-looking man, the kind of man who has given up trying to stop the dying going on around and inside him.

Behind the black sedan, in the warm darkness of the barn, there were animals and hay and grain, and the noises of the cows and the pair of draft horses as they ate, the cluck of the hens and the nervous snorts from the pigs mingled with the earthy smells of their confinement—a warm, crowded, utterly domestic place, like the inside of one's own body.

"All right," the father said, and the boy put the car in gear and drove out. When the sedan was clear of the barn, he stopped, and the father got out, walked back and closed the barn door.

Returning to the car, he said again, "All right," and they left the farm, turned right at the road and headed for town, tire-chains slapping loosely against the freshly plowed dirt road, the motor chirping warmly along, and the boy, for the first time, driving to town, driving skillfully, too, for he had driven for almost two years now, as his father had said, but only out at the farm, driving the tractor in the fields and the truck along old lumber trails in the woods, hauling wood back and trash out, bringing corn or hay or a load of potatoes in from the fields—never this, however, never along a public road and then along the streets of Catamount, where there would be other cars and where there would be people who would see him and wonder if that was Dewey Knox, Fred Knox's oldest boy, driving Fred's new Model A. That boy's growing up fast, they'd say. Before long he'll be as big as his father, they'd say.

AN HOUR LATER, THEY HAD FINISHED THEIR ERRANDS—THE purchase of a trap to keep a fox from the chicken coop, and at the hardware counter of the same store, nails, an ax handle, stove black, and a half-dozen carriage bolts;

they had stopped at the post office, and they had stopped at the farmers' exchange outlet to order seed; at Varney's Dry Goods Store the boy's father had purchased new boots for him, military-style boots the color of oak that laced almost to the knee. When the boy wore them out of the store he tried to walk as if he had always worn boots like these, but he stumbled at the threshold and almost fell through the doorway to the sidewalk, while behind him his father and George Varney laughed. But he drove well—skillfully and with increasing confidence, pulling into parking places and backing out to traffic, though of course in a town as small as Catamount, even on a Saturday when most people in the area were doing their weekly shopping, housewives at the A & P, husbands and fathers at the farmers' exchange or the hardware store, there was not much traffic.

Leaving town, they had turned left and had gone a few hundred yards past the Catamount River Bridge near Skitter Lake, when the man said to the boy, "You probably want a bite to eat."

"I do."

"Stop off at Daddy Emerson's, then."

The boy looked around at his father, who was staring straight out the windshield at the road.

"You can say you ate in town," the father said.

The boy didn't answer. They passed a small, run-down farmhouse, then took a left onto a narrow dirt road that looped through a pine woods and over a ridge. Here and there hundred-year-old farms with attached barns and outbuildings sat off the road, woodsmoke swirling from the big square chimneys while boys and sometimes men shoveled snow away.

"Okay?" the father said.

"What?"

"You'll say you ate in town."

"Yeah, fine. Sure."

Running alongside a rocky stream humped over with snow and ice and, except for the scrubby leafless brush that grew along the banks, almost indistinguishable from the fields that spread like bedsheets away from it, the road narrowed gradually, crossed the stream on a rickety wooden bridge and headed for a cleft in the ridge at the end of the valley.

At the bottom of the cleft there was a large old house, a colonial that had not been painted or repaired for a generation. Behind the house was a barn with a collapsed roof, the timbers showing through like bones, and beyond the barn the land rose swiftly up to the ridge. The house faced the road, which ran past it and through the cleft to a crossroads in another town. Beyond the road was a steep slope dotted with gnarled old apple trees and rocks shoving gray heads through the snow. Because of the ridge in back and the steep slope in front, the house at midday in winter was in shadow and looked cold, and despite the gray string of smoke curling from the chimney, the place looked uninhabited.

The boy drew the Ford off the road and followed tire tracks through the unplowed snow around to the back of the house, where there were two more vehicles, a Model T coupe and an open, wood-sided, pickup truck. He parked the Ford next to the truck, shut down the motor, and got out. His father was already out and was at the door, knocking on an old board panel that had been nailed over a pane of glass in the door. The boy came and stood behind his father and looked down at the color and precise definition of his new boots against the gray, trampled snow.

A man's gravelly voice called from behind the closed door. "Yeah?"

"Fred Knox."

"Who else you got there?"

"My boy."

"Okay," and the door opened to a dark hallway. Then the owner of the voice appeared, a burly man in his sixties wearing long underwear and floppy dark green trousers and on his feet loose, untied hunting boots. The man's red face was large and good-natured, sloppy and half-covered with a week's growth of white whiskers. "What say, Fred?" he said as he led the way along the dark hallway. He shuffled in his loose boots as he walked and bumped once or twice against one wall, as if his balance were off.

He opened a door at the end of the hallway and led the father and son into a warm, brightly lit kitchen. There was a long rectangular table in the center of the room with a few chairs scattered about and a Glenwood kitchen range near the stone sink crackling with a woodfire in its belly. There were two other men in the room, a tall, skinny man in a plaid wool shirt and wearing a hunting cap like the boy's and a shorter, more compact-looking man with a black beard and a thick shock of black hair that fell across his forehead. Both men were in their late twenties, and the boy knew them slightly— the tall, skinny one was Al Foy, a woodcutter, and the short, bearded one was Jimmy Sherman, a hide-stacker from the tannery. He was supposed to have been a prizefighter for a few years down in Boston, but apparently not a successful one, for he had returned to Catamount and now lived with his mother and father in their apartment above the paint store. The burly, older man who had let them in was called Daddy Emerson. He had lived alone in this house since the death of his wife, twenty or more years ago.

"H'lo, boys," Fred Knox said to the two men at the table. They had glasses in front of them, tumblers half-filled with a pale yellow liquid, and they were smoking cigarettes.

"Sit down, Fred," Al, the skinny one, said. "That your boy?"

"Yep. Dewey."

The boy took off his cap and crossed the room to a chair near the stove.

"Take off your coat, son. We'll sit and get warm." The father had taken a seat next to Al and across from Jimmy and had shed his mackinaw and hat. Emerson set a bottle and a glass on the table in front of the man, who quickly uncorked the bottle and filled the glass to the top, then drank off about an inch of the liquid. "Ahh! Now that warms a man up real quick!"

The other men laughed.

They drank and talked in low, relaxed voices. Emerson stood near the sink, resting his bulk against it, now and then lumbering across to the table to refill the glasses. At one point he turned to the boy and said, "Them're awful good-looking boots. Brand-new?"

Dewey looked down at his boots. "Yes, sir. This morning."

"Birthday present!" his father hollered.

The other men looked at the boy with interest. "Birthday?" Al said, smiling. "How old are you, kid?"

"Fourteen."

"I'll be damned! Fourteen! Happy birthday, kid," Al said and turned back to his drink.

"You oughta give him a birthday drink, Fred," Emerson said and, grinning, he reached for the bottle and a fresh glass.

"No," the father said.

"No? Hell, how old were you when you got started? I wasn't no older'n him, that's for sure."

"Go ahead, let the kid have a birthday drink," Al said.

"It won't hurt him none," the man with the beard added.

"No," said the father. "You got tonic, he can have some of that. But none of this stuff. This is too strong, you got to work up to it. You know that," he said to Emerson.

Emerson reached into the cupboard next to the sink, pulled out a bottle of orange liquid and poured a glassful for the boy.

"What's the proof of this stuff," the bearded one, Jimmy, asked.

"A hunnert, easy," Al said.

"Apple jack's got a kick like this, it's more than a hundred," Fred Knox said. "What d'you think?" he asked Emerson.

"Hunnert an' fifty, maybe," Emerson said.

"Hunnert an' fifty! Wow!" Al said, and he took another swallow from his glass. "Goes down like mother's milk!" He laughed with a wide-open mouth.

The others laughed with him and drank. At the suggestion of the boy's father, Emerson cut two thick slices of bread and made a cheese sandwich for the boy, then brought out a large jar of pickled pig's knuckles for the men at the table, and while the boy ate his sandwich and the men gnawed away at the knuckles and talked politics, the old man busied himself at the sink washing glasses and a few greasy plates. He asked the boy to go out in the shed by the barn and bring in an armload of stove wood and told the boy's father that the cheese sandwich was free. Quickly, the boy pulled on his coat and hat and went out.

When a few minutes later he returned with the wood, the men's voices were loud, and Al was shouting at Emerson, "You was crazy, man! It don't matter he was a Roman Catholic, he was gonna make it so we could sit in town and buy a damned drink of whiskey when we want!"

"Mattered to *me* he was Catholic," Jimmy said in a

loud, sullen voice. "You want the Pope runnin' the country? You want all them New York and Boston Irishers and Eye-talians takin' over everything we fought the damned war for? That what you want?" he shouted at Al. "Fish-eaters!" he sneered.

Emerson said to Al, "I never vote for a man who's gonna put me outa business. That's *my* politics. Period."

"Al Smith wouldn'a put you outa business," Fred Knox said. "Matter a fact, if it ever gets to be legal to drink, they's a hell of a lot of people will turn out to be drinkers. You'd be sellin' more of this stuff than you can make by now if Smith had won," he pronounced.

"The hell you say."

"The hell I do say. Smith wouldn'a put you outa business. But tell me this, Emerson, if Hoover was the Democrat an' Smith the Republican, instead of the other way around, which one would you have voted for then?" Fred lifted his glass woozily and snickered into it.

The other men looked steadily over at Emerson, and even the boy looked at him.

"What's it matter anyhow. People oughtn't to talk politics and religion when they're drinking," Emerson said, and he went back to wiping off the glasses in the sink.

"Religion an' politics is gettin' to be the same thing, you ask me," Jimmy said grumpily.

Fred signaled for more drinks, and Emerson refilled the glasses. For a while longer the men drifted in and out of several conversations concerning the subject of religion-and-politics, and then Al reached out and laid a long paw on Fred's wrist.

"*You* can do it!" he exclaimed, his face brightening.

"Do what?"

"You can take Jimmy here. Arm-wrestling. I tol' him this morning that they's all kinda farmers around town could beat his butt. *You* can do it!"

"He does it all the time," Fred said. "I don't know the tricks."

"There ain't any tricks," Jimmy said. He had sat up straight in his chair and was already poised, ready, his gaze fixed steadily on the boy's father.

"I don't know," Fred said.

"Sure you can. I got a dollar bill here says you can. You willin' to bet, Jimmy?"

"Sure." The bearded man reached into his pocket and drew out a wrinkled bill and tossed it casually onto the table.

"It ain't my money," Fred said, and he rolled up his right sleeve and hitched his chair closer to the table.

Jimmy squared off against him, and the men locked hands. The boy stood up, and he and Emerson came toward the pair and stood at the end of the table, facing them.

"All right," Al said, grinning broadly.

"Fine, fine. Call it," Fred said, his face taut and somber.

Jimmy was relaxed, his beefy shoulders loose, his left hand lying flat in his lap. He watched the other man's eyes.

"Ready?"

"Ready."

"Okay . . . wrestle!"

Fred strained, the veins and cords in his neck leaping forward as if he were lifting a great weight, but the other man's arm did not move. He tried to twist the man's wrist toward him, so he could pull his arm instead of push it, but the man's arm was like stone and would not be twisted or pulled. Then slowly, steadily, the man with the beard pushed Fred's hand back, inch by inch, in a slow, precise arc, all the way to the table. He let go of Fred's hand, smiled through his beard and extended his right hand, palm up, to Al. "You owe me."

Al shook his head and dug out a dollar bill. "I thought sure you could take him, Fred. You gotta lotta size on you."

"I guess it's in the wrong places," he said. "And I told you, I don't know the tricks." He stood up, wobbled a bit, and reached for his wallet. He handed two dollars over to Emerson, nodded toward his son, who put his hat and coat on, and headed toward the door.

As the boy passed his father's empty chair, he removed the man's mackinaw from the chairback and carried it out with him. "Here, Pa, you forgot your coat," he said in the hallway, but his father was already beyond the hallway and outside.

THE MAN AND THE BOY RODE HOME IN SILENCE, UNTIL THEY reached the driveway, where the man instructed his son to swing the car around so it could be backed into the barn. "I won't be going out again today," he explained. His voice was low and his words came slowly and thickly as if he were speaking through a cloth curtain.

The boy turned the car around at the road and proceeded to back into the driveway skillfully and without hesitation, as if he had been driving to town for years. At the barn, he stopped, drew the brake up and stepped down from the car to open the barn door. His father sat heavily in his seat, ignoring him, lost in thought or lost in feeling. When the boy returned to the car, the father turned to him and said, "You tell your mother we ate in town. You understand?"

The boy didn't look at him. He peered out the windshield across the square hood to the crisply shoveled driveway, along the path to the porch and house. There was a right way to do everything, even something as simple and unimportant as shoveling a path through snow to the kitchen. The boy's father believed that, he had said it, too, and now the boy believed it. The pleasure you got from looking at a job done the right way proved that there was such a thing as the right way. Not just the best way, not the easiest way, not even the logical way. You did things in life the right way, and then, afterward, you got to admire what you had done. You didn't have to avert your eyes from what you had done.

"You understand me, boy?"

"Yes, sir."

"All right, then," he said, and he got out of the car. He held the door open for a second, looking at the ground as if trying to remember something, then said to the boy, "Leave the trap out here in the barn, but bring the rest of the stuff inside to the shop. You set the trap tonight after supper. New snow'll make a fox foolish and hungry at the same time." Then he moved away, clumsily, wobbling slightly, with the door left wide open behind him.

The boy reached across his father's seat and drew the door closed. He let the brake off and backed the car into the darkness of the barn.

The Child Screams and Looks Back at You

WHEN YOUR CHILD SHOWS THE FIRST SIGNS OF ILLNESS—
fever, lassitude, aching joints and muscles—you fear
that he or she is dying. You may not admit it to anyone,
but the sight of your child lying flushed and feverish in
bed becomes for an instant the sight of your child in its
coffin. The nature of reality shifts, and it's suddenly not
clear to you whether you are beginning to dream or are
waking from a dream, for you watch the child's breath
stutter and stop, and you cry out and then struggle in
vain to blow life back into the tiny, inert body lying
below you. Or you see the child heave himself into
convulsions, thrash wildly in the bed and utter hoarse,
incoherent noises, as if he were possessed by a demon,
and horrified, helpless, you back to the door, hands to
mouth, crying, "Stop, stop, please, oh God, please stop!"
Or, suddenly, the bed is sopped with blood pouring from

the child's body, blood seeping into the mattress, over the sheets, through the child's tangled pajamas, and the child whitens, stares up pitifully and without understanding, for there is no wound to blame, there is only this blood emptying out of his body, and you cannot staunch its flow but must stand there and watch your child's miraculous, mysterious life disappear before you. For that is the key that unlocks these awful visions— your child's being simply alive is both miracle and mystery, and therefore it seems both natural and understandable that he should be dead.

MARCELLE CALLED HER BOYS FROM THE KITCHEN TO HURRY and get dressed for school. One of these mornings she was not going to keep after them like this and they would all be late for school and she would not write a note to the teacher to explain anything, she didn't give a damn if the teacher kept them after school, because it would teach them a lesson once and for all, and that lesson was when she woke them in the morning they had to hurry and get dressed and make their beds and get the hell out here to the kitchen and eat their breakfasts and brush their teeth and get the hell out the door to school so she could get dressed and eat her breakfast and go to work. There were four of them, the four sons of Marcelle and Richard Chagnon. Joel was the oldest at twelve, and then, separated by little more than nine months, came Raymond, Maurice, and Charles. The father had moved out, had been thrown out of the apartment by Marcelle's younger brother Steve and one of Steve's friends nearly nine years ago, when the youngest, Charles, was still an infant, and though for several years Richard had tried to convince Marcelle she should let him move back in with them and let him be her husband and the father of his four sons again, she had never allowed it, for his way of

being a husband and father was to get drunk and beat
her and the older boys and then to wake ashamed and
beg their forgiveness. For years she had forgiven him,
because to her when you forgive someone you make it
possible for that person to change, and the boys also
forgave him—they were, after all, her sons too, and she
had taught them, in their dealings with each other, to
forgive. If you don't forgive someone who has hurt you,
he can't change into a new person. He is stuck in his life
with you at the point where he hurt you. But her husband and their father Richard, after five years of it, had
come to seem incapable of using their forgiveness in any
way that allowed him to stop hurting them, so finally
one night she had sent her oldest boy, Joel, who was
then only four and a half years old, out the door and
down the dark stairs to the street, down the street to the
tenement where her brother Steve lived with his girlfriend,
and Joel had found Steve sitting at the kitchen table
drinking beer with a friend and had said to him, "Come
and keep my daddy from hitting my mommy!" That
night for Marcelle marked the end of the period of forgiveness, for she had permitted outsiders, her brother
and his friend, to see how badly her husband Richard
behaved. By that act she had ceased to protect her
husband, and you cannot forgive someone you will not
protect. Richard never perceived or understood that shift,
just as all those years he had never perceived or understood what it meant to be protected and forgiven. If you
don't know what you've got when you've got it, you
won't know what you've lost when you've lost it. Marcelle
was Catholic and even though she was not a diligent
Catholic she was a loyal one, and she never remarried,
which is not to say that over the years she did not now
and again fall in love, once even with a married man,
only briefly, however, until she became strong enough
to reveal her affair to Father Brautigan, after which she

had broken off with the man, to the relief of her sons, for they had not liked the way he had come sneaking around at odd hours to see their mother and talk with her in hushed tones in the kitchen until very late, when the lights would go off and an hour or two later he would leave. When in the morning the children got up and came out to the kitchen for breakfast, they would talk in low voices, as if the married man were still in the apartment and asleep in their mother's bed, and she would have deep circles under her eyes and would stir her coffee slowly and look out the window and now and then quietly remind them to hurry or they'd be late for school. They were more comfortable when she was hollering at them, standing at the door to their bedroom, her hands on her hips, her dressing gown flapping open as she whirled and stomped back to the kitchen, embarrassing her slightly, for beneath her dressing gown she wore men's long underwear, so that, by the time they got out to the kitchen themselves, her dressing gown would have been pulled back tightly around her and tied at the waist, and all they could see of the long underwear beneath it would be the top button at her throat, which she would try to cover casually with one hand while she set their breakfasts before them with the other. On this morning, however, only three of her sons appeared at the table, dressed for school, slumping grumpily into their chairs, for it was a gray, wintry day in early December, barely light outside. The oldest, Joel, had not come out with them, and she lost her temper, slammed three plates of scrambled eggs and toast down in front of the others and fairly jogged back to the bedroom, stalked to the narrow bed by the wall where the boy slept and yanked the covers away, to expose the boy, curled up on his side, eyes wide open, his face flushed and sweating, his hands clasped together as if in prayer. Horrified, she looked down at the gangly boy, and she saw him

dead and quickly lay the covers back over him, gently
straightening the blanket and top sheet. Then, slowly,
she sat down on the edge of the bed and stroked his hot
forehead, brushing his limp blond hair back, feeling beneath his jawbone as if for a pulse, touching his cheeks
with the smooth backside of her cool hand. "Tell me
how you feel, honey," she said to the boy. He didn't
answer her. His tongue came out and touched his dry
lips and went quickly back inside his mouth. "Don't
worry, honey," she said, and she got up from the bed.
"It's probably the flu, that's all. I'll take your temperature and maybe call Doctor Wickshaw, and he'll tell me
what to do. If you're too sick, I'll stay home from the
tannery today. All right?" she asked and took a tenta-
tive step away from the bed. "Okay," the boy said
weakly. The room was dark and cluttered with clothing
and toys, model airplanes and boats, weapons, costumes,
tools, hockey equipment, portable radios, photographs
of athletes and singers, like the prop room of a small
theater group. As she left the room, Marcelle stopped in
the doorway and looked back. The boy huddled in his
bed looked like one of the props, a ventriloquist's dummy,
perhaps, or a heap of clothes that, in this shadowy
half-light, only resembled a human child for a second or
two, and then, looked at from a second angle, came
clearly to be no more than an impatiently discarded
costume.

MOST PEOPLE, WHEN THEY CALL IN A PHYSICIAN, DEAL WITH
him as they would a priest. They say that what they
want is a medical opinion, a professional medical man's
professional opinion, when what they really want is his
blessing. Information is useful only insofar as it provides
peace of mind, release from the horrifying visions of
dead children, an end to this dream. Most physicians,

like most priests, recognize the need and attempt to satisfy it. This story takes place almost twenty years ago, in the early 1960s, in a small mill town in central New Hampshire, and it was especially true then and there that the physician responded before all other needs to the patient's need for peace of mind, and only when that need had been met would he respond to the patient's need for bodily health. In addition, because he usually knew all the members of the family and frequently treated them for injuries and diseases, he tended to regard an injured or ill person as one part of an injured or ill family. Thus it gradually became the physician's practice to minimize the danger or seriousness of a particular injury or illness, so that a broken bone was often called a probable sprain, until x rays proved otherwise, and a concussion was called, with a laugh, a bump on the head, until the symptoms—dizziness, nausea, sleepiness—persisted, when the bump on the head became a possible mild concussion, which eventually may have to be upgraded all the way to fractured skull. It was the same with diseases. A virus, the flu that's going around, a low-grade intestinal infection, and so on, often came to be identified a week or two later as strep throat, bronchial pneumonia, dysentery, without necessarily stopping there. There was an obvious, if limited, use for this practice, because it soothed and calmed both the patient and the family members, which made it easier for the physician to make an accurate diagnosis and to secure the aid of the family members in providing treatment. It was worse than useless, however, when an overoptimistic diagnosis of a disease or injury led to the patient's sudden, crazed descent into sickness, pain, paralysis, and death.

*   *   *

DOCTOR WICKSHAW. A MAN IN HIS MIDDLE-FORTIES. PORTLY but in good physical condition, with horn-rimmed glasses and a Vandyke beard, told Marcelle that her son Joel probably had the flu, it was going around, half the school was out with it. "Keep him in bed a few days and give him lots of liquids," he instructed her after examining the boy. He made housecalls, if the call for help came during morning hours or if it was truly an emergency. Afternoons he was at his office, and evenings he made rounds at the Concord Hospital, twenty-five miles away. Marcelle asked what she should do about the fever, one hundred four degrees, and he told her to give the boy three aspirins now and two more every three or four hours. She saw the man to the door, and as he passed her in the narrow hallway he placed one hand on her rump, and he said to the tall, broad-shouldered woman, "How are things with you, Marcelle? I saw you walking home from the tannery the other day, and I said to myself, 'Now that's a woman who shouldn't be alone in the world.'" He smiled into her bladelike face, the face of a large, powerful bird, and showed her his excellent teeth. His hand was still pressed against her rump and they stood face to face, for she was as tall as he. She was not alone in the world, she reminded him, mentioning her four sons. The doctor's hand slipped to her thigh. She did not move. "But you get lonely," he told her. She had gray eyes and her face was filled with fatigue, tiny lines that broke her smooth pale skin like the cracks in a ceramic jar that long ago had broken and had been glued back together again, as good as new, they say, and even stronger than before, but nevertheless fragile-looking now, and brittle perhaps, more likely to break a second time, it seemed, than when it had not been broken at all. "Yes," she said, "I get lonely," and with both hands, she reached up to her temples and pushed her dark hair back, and holding on to the sides of her own head she leaned it forward and kissed the man for several seconds, pushing at him with her mouth, until he pulled away, red-faced, his hand at his side now, and moved self-consciously sideways toward the door. "I'll come by tomorrow," he said in a low voice. "To see how Joel's doing." She smiled slightly and nodded. "If he's better," she said, "I'll be at work. But the door is always open." From the doorway, he asked if she came home for lunch. "Yes," she said, "when one of the boys is home sick, I do. Otherwise, no." He said that he might be here then, and she said, "Fine," and reached forward and closed the door on him.

SOMETIMES YOU DREAM THAT YOU ARE WALKING ACROSS A meadow under sunshine and a cloudless blue sky, hand in hand with your favorite child, and soon you notice that the meadow is sloping uphill slightly, and so walking becomes somewhat more difficult, although it remains a pleasure, for you are with your favorite child and he is beautiful and happy and confident that you will let nothing terrible happen to him. You cross the crest, a rounded, meandering ridge, and start downhill, walking faster and more easily. The sun is shining and there are wildflowers all around you, and the grass is golden and drifting in long waves in the breeze. Soon you find that the hill is steeper than before, the slope is falling away beneath your feet, as if the earth were curving in on itself, so you dig in your heels and try to slow your descent. Your child looks up at you and there is fear in his eyes, as he realizes he is falling away from you. "My hand!" you cry. "Hold tightly to my hand!" And you grasp the child's hand, who has started to fly away from you, as if over the edge of a crevice, while you dig your heels deeper into the ground and grab with your free hand at the long grasses behind you. The child screams and looks back at you with a pitiful gaze, and suddenly he grows so heavy that his weight is pulling you free of the ground also. You feel your feet leave the ground, and your body falls forward and down, behind your child's body, even though with one hand you still cling to the grasses. You weep, and you let go of your child's hand. The child flies away and you wake up, shuddering.

THAT NIGHT THE BOY'S FEVER WENT HIGHER, TO ONE HUN-dred five degrees, and Marcelle moved the younger boys into her own room, so that she could sleep in the bed next to the sick boy's. She bathed him in cool water with washcloths, coaxed him into swallowing aspirin with orange juice, and sat there on the edge of the bed next to his and watched him sleep, although she knew he was not truly sleeping, he was merely lying there on his side, his legs out straight now, silent and breathing rapidly, like an injured dog, stunned and silently healing itself. But the boy was not healing himself, he was hourly growing worse. She could tell that. She tried to move him so that she could straighten the sheets, but when she touched him, he cried out in pain, as if his back or neck were broken, and frightened, she drew back from him. She wanted to call Doctor Wickshaw, and several times she got up and walked out to the kitchen where the telephone hung on the wall like a large black insect, and each time she stood for a few seconds before the instrument, remembered the doctor in the hallway and what she had let him promise her with his eyes, remembered then what he had told her about her son's illness, and turned and walked back to the boy and tried again to cool him with damp cloths. Her three other sons slept peacefully through the night and knew nothing of what happened until morning came.

* * *

WHEN YOUR CHILD LIVES, HE CARRIES WITH HIM ALL HIS earlier selves, so that you cannot separate your individual memories of him from your view of him now, at this moment. When you recall a particular event in your and your child's shared past—a day at the beach, a Christmas morning, a sad, weary night of flight from the child's shouting father, a sweet, pathetic supper prepared by the child for your birthday—when you recall these events singly, you cannot see the child as a camera would have photographed him then. You see him simultaneously all the way from infancy to adolescence to adulthood and on, as if he has been moving through your life too rapidly for any camera to catch and still, so that the image is blurred, grayed out, a swatch of your own past pasted across the foreground of a studio photographer's carefully arranged backdrop.

WHEN HER SON WENT INTO CONVULSIONS, MARCELLE DID not at first know it, for his voice was clear and what he said made sense. Suddenly, he spoke loudly and in complete sentences. "Ma, I'm not alone. I know that, and it helps me not be scared. For a while I thought I was alone," he went on, and she sat upright and listened alertly to him in the darkness of the bedroom. "And then I started to see things and think maybe there was someone else in the room here with me, and then I was scared, Ma. Because I didn't know for sure whether I was alone or not. But now I know I'm not alone, and knowing it helps me not be scared." She said that she was glad, because she thought he was talking about her presence in the room, and she took his recognition of her presence as a sign that the fever had broken. But when she reached out in the darkness and touched his neck, it was burning, like an empty, black pot left over a fire, and she almost cried out in pain, and might have, had the child not commenced to shout at her, bellowing at her as if she were a large, ugly animal that he wished to send cowering into the far corner of his room.

MOST PEOPLE, WHEN THEY DO WHAT THE PHYSICIAN HAS told them will cure them, expect to be cured. When they are not cured, they at first believe it is because they have not done properly what they have been told to do. Sickness is the mystery, the miracle, and the physician understands such things, you say, whereas you, who are not a physician, all you understand is health. This is not so, of course, for health is the mystery and the miracle, not sickness. Sickness can be penetrated, understood, predicted. Health cannot. No, the analogy between the physician and the priest will not hold, for sickness and injury are not at all like divine protection and forgiveness. Sadly, most people and most physicians and most priests do not know this, or if they do, they do not act as if they know it. It's only in dealing with their children that people treat life as if it were indeed the miracle, as if life itself were the mystery of divine protection and forgiveness, and in that way, it is only in dealing with their children that most people are like priests serving God, making it possible for poor sinners to obtain grace.

DOCTOR WICKSHAW HURRIED INTO THE BOY'S BEDROOM AND this time knew that the boy had contracted meningitis, probably spinal meningitis, and he also knew that it was too late to save the boy, that if he did not die in the next few days, he would suffer irreparable damage to his central nervous system.

*   *   *

MARCELLE KNEW THAT BY HER SON'S DEATH SHE WAS NOW A
lost soul, and she did not weep. She went grimly about
her appointed rounds, she raised her three remaining
sons, and each of them, in his turn, forgave her and
protected her. The one that died, Joel, the oldest, never
forgave her, never shielded her from judgment, never let
grace fall on her. Late at night, when she lay in bed
alone, she knew this to the very bottom of her mind, and
the knowledge was the lamp that illuminated the mystery and the miracle of her remaining days.

The Fisherman

IF YOU HAVE AN ABSTRACT TURN OF MIND, YOU TEND TO measure the approach of winter by the sun, how in late October it starts slipping toward the southern horizon, spending less and less time each day in the sky and, because of that, seems to move across the sky at an accelerated rate, as if in a hurry to depart from this chilled part of the globe and move on to the southern hemisphere, there to languish slowly through the long, hot afternoons of the pampas, the outback and the transveldt. Or, on the other hand, you might measure the approach of winter by the ice, which seems a more direct, less abstract way of going about it. You wake up one morning toward the end of October, and when you glance out your window at the lake, you see off to your left, where a low headland protects a shallow cove from the wind, a thin, crackled, pink skin of ice that spreads as far as the point and then suddenly stops. There is no ice yet in the swamp, where the trickling movement of inlets to the lake and the pressure of tree stumps, brush and weeds forbid freezing this early, though by tomorrow morning or the next it will be covered there too; and there is no ice where the lake empties across the flat stones of the old Indian fishing weirs to form the Catamount River, though it too will gradually freeze solidly over; and there is no ice along the western shore, for here the ground drops down quickly from the tree-covered hills and the water is deep and black.

The man named Merle Ring, the old man whose trailer was the last one in the park and faced one end toward the weirs and the other toward the swamp, was what you might call an ice-man. When the ground froze, his walk took on a springing, almost sprightly look, as if he were happy to find the earth rock-hard, impenetrable and utterly unyielding. And when the air got cold enough for him to see his breath, he breathed with fond care, as if taking sensual pleasure from the sight of white clouds puffing out before his raggedy beard. And the morning of every October when he saw the first ice on Skitter Lake, he pulled on his mackinaw and trotted down to the shore as if to greet an old friend. He examined the ice, reading its depth, clarity, hardness and extension the way you'd examine a calendar, calculating how many days and weeks he'd have to wait before the entire lake was covered with ten or more inches of white ice, cracking and booming through subzero nights as new ice below expanded against the old ice above, and he could set up his bobhouse and chisel into the ice a half-dozen holes and commence his winter-time nights and days of fishing for pickerel, black bass, bluegills and perch.

For over a half-century Merle had been an ice-fisherman. Where most people in this region endure winter to get to summer, Merle endured summer to get to winter. Ice-fishing is not what you would ordinarily think of as a sport. You don't move around much, and you don't do it with anyone else. It's an ancient activity, though, and after thousands of years it's still done in basically the same way. You drop a line with a hook and piece of bait attached into the water and wait for an edible fish to take the bait and get hooked, and then you haul the thrashing fish through the hole and stash it with the others while you rebait your hook. If you are a serious ice-fisherman, and Merle was serious, you build a shanty and you drag it onto the lake, bank it around with snow and let it freeze into the ice. The shanty, or bobhouse, as it's called, has trap doors in the floor, and that's where you cut the holes through the ice, usually with a harpoon-like steel-tipped chisel called a spud or else with a long-handled steel auger. At some of the holes, depending on what kind of fish you are seeking and what kind of bait or lure you are using, you set traplines, or tip-ups, and at others you drop handlines. With live bait, minnows and such, you can use the traps, but if you're jigging with a spoon or using ice flies, you need to keep your hand on the line.

The bobhouse is only as large as need be, six feet by four feet is enough, and six feet high for a normal-sized person. At one end is a door with a high step-over sill to keep out the wind and at the other a homemade wood-stove. Along one of the long walls is a narrow bench that serves as a seat and also as a bed when you want to nap or sleep over the night. Your traps and lines are set up along the opposite wall. There is a small window opening, but it remains covered by a hinged, wooden panel, so that the bobhouse can be kept in total darkness, for, when no light enters the bobhouse from outside, you can peer through the holes in the ice and see clearly the world below. You see what the fish see, and you see them too. But they cannot see you. You see the muddy lake bottom, undulating weeds and decaying leaves, and in a cold green light, you see small schools of blue-gills drifting over the weed beds in search of food and oxygen, while lethargically along behind three or four pickerel glide into view, looking for stragglers. Here and there a batch of yellow perch cruise, and slowly, sleepily, a black bass. The light filtered through the ice is still, hard and cold, like an algebraic equation, and you can watch the world beneath pass through it with a clarity, objectivity and love that is usually thought to be the exclusive prerogative of gods.

Until one winter a few years ago, Merle Ring was not taken very seriously by the other residents of the trailerpark. He was viewed as peculiar and slightly troublesome, mainly because, while he had opinions on everything and about everyone, when he expressed those opinions, which he did frequently, he didn't make much sense to people and seemed almost to be making fun of them. For instance, he told Doreen Tiede, who was having difficulties with her ex-husband Buck, that the only way to make him cease behaving the same way he had behaved back when he was her husband, that is, as a drunken, brutal crybaby, was to get herself a new husband. "Who?" she asked him. They were in her car, and she was giving Merle a lift into town on her way to work at the tannery. Her little daughter Maureen, on her way to the babysitter for the day, was in the back, where she was unaccustomed to sitting. Doreen laughed lightly and said it again. "Really, Merle, *who* should I marry?"

"It don't matter. Just get yourself a new husband. That way you'll get rid of Buck. Because he won't believe you're not his wife until you're someone else's." He puffed on his cob pipe and looked out the window at the birches alongside the road, leafless and gold-tinted in the morning sun. "That's how I always did it," he said.

"What?" She was clasping and unclasping the steering wheel as if her fingers were stiff and cold. This business with her ex-husband really bothered her, and it was hurting Maureen.

"Whenever I wanted to get rid of a wife, I married another. Once you're over a certain age and have got yourself married, you stay married the rest of your life, unless the one you happened to be married to ups and dies. Then you can be single again."

"Maybe Buck'll up and die on me, then," she said with a quick grimace.

"Mommy!" the child said and stuck her thumb in her mouth.

"I was only joking, sweets." Doreen looked into the rearview mirror. "And stop sucking your thumb. You're too old for that." Then, to Merle: "Is that how you got to be single, after all those wives? How many, six, seven?"

"Numerous. Yup, the last one died. Just in time, too, because I was all set to get married again."

"To who?"

"Oh, I don't know. I didn't have anybody in particular in mind at the time. But I sure was eager to get that last one off my back."

"Jesus, Merle, isn't anything sacred to you?"

"Sure."

"For instance."

"Oh, marriage, for instance. But not husbands or wives," he quickly added.

"I can't take you seriously, Merle," she said, and they drove on in silence.

That was the form most of his conversations took. It didn't matter whom he was talking to, Merle's observations and opinions left you feeling puzzled, a little hurt and irritated. To avoid those feelings most people told themselves and each other that Merle wasn't all "there," that he didn't really understand how complicated life was, and that he really didn't like anyone anyhow. But because he was orderly and quiet and, like most small, neat, symmetrical men, physically attractive, and because his financial life was under control, he was accepted into the community. Also, he didn't seem to care whether you followed his advice or whether you took him seriously, and as a result, despite the fact that people took neither him nor his advice seriously, Merle was never a very agitated man, which, naturally, made him an attractive neighbor. No one thought of him as a particularly useful neighbor, however.

Until he won the state lottery, that is. That same October morning, the morning he saw the first ice on the lake and the morning he had the brief conversation with Doreen Tiede concerning her ex-husband, Buck, he bought as he did every month a one-dollar lottery ticket. It had been a habit for Merle, ever since the state had first introduced the lottery back in the '60s, to go into town the day after his social security check arrived in the mail, cash his check at the bank, and on the way home stop at the state liquor store and buy a fifth of Canadian Club and a single lottery ticket. There were several types available, but Merle preferred the Daily Numbers Game, in which you play a four-digit number for the day. The winning number would be printed the next morning in the *Manchester Union-Leader*. For your one-dollar bet, the payoff on four digits in the exact order was $4500. At that point, your number went into another lottery, the Grand Prize Drawing made later in the year, for $50,000. Merle won $4500, and here's how he did it. He bet his age, 7789—on October 30, 1978, he was seventy-seven years, eight months, nine days old. He had always bet his age, which of course meant that the number he played varied slightly but systematically from one month to the next. He claimed it was on principle, for he did not believe, on the one hand, in wholly giving over to chance or impulse or, on the other, in relying absolutely on a fixed number. It was a compromise, a realistic compromise, in Merle's mind, between randomness and control, two extremes that, he felt, led to the same place—superstition. There were, of course, three months a year when, because he was limited to selecting four single-digit numbers, he could not play his exact age, and in those months, December, January and February, he did not buy a ticket. But those were the months he spent ice-fishing anyhow, and it seemed somehow wrong to him, to gamble on numbers when you were ice-fishing. At least that's how he explained it.

Merle took his $4500, paid the tax on it, and spent about $250 refurbishing his bobhouse. It needed a new floor and roof and a paint job, and many interior fixtures had fallen into disrepair. The rest of the money he gave away, as loans, of course, but Merle once said that he never loaned money he couldn't afford to give away, and as a result of this attitude, no one felt especially obliged to pay him back. Throughout November, Merle hammered and sawed away at his bobhouse, while people from the trailerpark came and went, congratulating him on his good luck, explaining their great, sudden need of $300 or $400 or $500, then, while he counted out the bills, thanking him profusely for the loan. He kept his prize money inside a cigar box in his toolbox, a huge, locked, wooden crate far too heavy for fewer than four men to carry and located just inside the door to his trailer.

Meanwhile, the ice on the lake gradually thickened and spread out from the coves and shallows, creeping over the dark water like a pale shadow. Merle's bobhouse was a handsome, carefully fitted structure. The bottom sills had been cut to serve as runners, which made it possible for Merle to push the building out onto the ice alone. The interior was like a ship's cabin, with hinged shelves and lockers, hooks and drawers, a small wood-stove made from a twenty-five-gallon metal drum, a padded bunk that folded against the wall when not in use, and so on. The interior wood, white pine, had been left raw and over the years had darkened from woodsmoke and moisture to the color of old briar. The exterior, of lapstrake construction to stave off the wind, Merle cov-ered with a deep red stain. The pitched roof was of new, unstained, cedar shingles that would silver out by spring but that now were the color of golden palomino.

Clearly, the structure deserved admiration, and got it, especially from the denizens of the trailerpark, for, after all, the contrast between Merle's bobhouse and the cubes they all lived in was extraordinary. As November wore on and Merle completed refurbishing the bobhouse, peo-ple from the park daily came by and stood and studied it for a while, saying things and probably feeling things they had not said or felt before. Until Merle won the lottery, the people had more or less ignored the old man and his bobhouse, but when they started coming around to congratulate him and ask for loans, they noticed the tiny, reddish cabin sitting on its runners a few feet off the lake, noticed it in a way they never had before, for, after all, they usually found him working there and their attention got drawn to his work, and also they were curious as to how he was spending his money so as to determine whether there would be any left for them. And when they saw the bobhouse, really took a close look at its precision and logic and the utter usefulness of every detail, they were often moved in strange ways. It was as if they were deserted on an island together and suddenly had come upon a man from among them who was building a seaworthy boat, and not only that, a boat that could carry no more than a single person off the

island. They were moved by the sight of Merle's bobhouse, moved to hate the sight of their own rusting, tin
and plastic trailers, the cheap, manufactured clutter of
their shelters, and this unexpectedly disturbed them.
The disturbance moved them, unfortunately, quickly to
envy Merle's bobhouse.

"How come you making it so fancy?" Terry Constant
sneered.

Merle looked up from the floor where he was screw-
ing down the new two-by-eight-inch plank flooring and
saw the black man silhouetted darkly against a milk
white sky so that his features couldn't be seen. He wore
an orange parka and Navy watch cap and was chewing a
toothpick. Merle said nothing and went back to work.

"You win the numbers, like they said?"

"Yup."

"That's how come you're making it so fancy, then."

". . ."

"Luxury!"

". . ."

"Who's gonna see it, a little fish-house? I coulda
slapped this thing together in half the time for half the
cost outa plywood."

". . ."

"This thing'll last longer'n you will. You realize that?
You'll be dead a hundred years and this thing'll still be
sitting here by the lake."

Merle picked up a new plank and with a stubby plane
started shaving blond, sweet-smelling curls off the wood.
Then he lay the board against the first, cast his gaze
down its length, retrieved it and gave it another half-
dozen smooth strokes of the plane, until finally the plank
fit snugly, perfectly, into place.

"Well, it *looks* good, anyhow," Terry said. He shifted
his toothpick, and placing one foot onto the high sill,
dropped his right forearm onto his thigh and leaned

forward and into the close, dim, resin-smelling interior
of the bobhouse. "Say, Merle, I was wondering, see,
I'm outa work, ya know. Marcelle's all done winterizing
the park, so she don't need me any more until spring or
unless the pipes burst or something, and you know there
ain't no work in this damn town in winter, especially for
a black man, so I was wondering if you could help me
out a little, 'til I could get some more work."

"Sure."

As if he hadn't heard him, Terry went on. "I was
thinking of maybe heading south this winter, getting
some work in Florida. I got a cousin in Tampa, but it'll
take some bucks to do it. You know, for bus fare and
after I get there, 'til I get a job."

"What about your sister?" Merle asked without looking up. "She'd be pretty much alone here, without you.
Being black and all. Come spring you could get work
again, maybe for the highway department or something.
You don't want to leave her all alone up here."

"Well, yeah . . ." Terry let his glance fall across the
oak framing of the structure, noticing for the first time
how it had been notched and fitted together with pegs.
"But I can't take any more handouts from her. Maybe if
you could loan me enough to get through the next three
or four months . . ." He said. "I got problems, man."

"How much?"

"Five, six hundred, maybe?"

"Sure."

"Seven would be better."

"Sure."

"I'll pay you back." He stood up straight again and
stepped away from the door as Merle got slowly to his
feet and came out to the yard.

"Sure," he said. "Money's in the house."

"Okay," Terry said almost in a whisper, and the two
men crossed the yard to the trailer.

There were other loans: Bruce Severance, the long-haired kid in number 3 who sold dope, needed $300 fast, to get a very heavy dude off his back, he said; Noni Hubner, the college girl in number 7 who was then recuperating from her first nervous breakdown, wanted to do what her mother had so far refused to do, buy a proper gravestone for her father's grave, which, since his death two years ago, had gone unmarked; and Leon LaRoche, the bank teller in number 2, said he needed money to help pay his sick mother's hospital bills, but it came out (only as a rumor, however) that his mother was not ill and that he was spending money recklessly to support a young man supposedly going to college in Boston and whom Leon visited every weekend, practically; and Claudel Bing, who was no longer living at the trailerpark but still had friends there, and after having lost his job at the Public Service Company, needed money to pay for his divorce from Ginnie, who was living with Howie Leeke; Tom Smith was dead by then, but his son Buddy somehow heard about Merle's good luck and wrote from Albany asking Merle for $500 so he could pay off the debts he claimed his father's burial had left him with, and Merle mailed the money to him the next day; Nancy Hubner, Noni's mother, insisting that she did not want the money for herself, explained that she had got herself into an embarrassing situation by pledging $1000 to the Clamshell Alliance people and had only been able to raise $750; Captain Dewey Knox, in trailer number 6, who certainly seemed affluent enough not to need any of Merle's money, suddenly turned out to owe three years' back taxes on the last bit of land his father had owned in Catamount, a rocky hundred-acre plot on the northern edge of what had been the elder Knox's dairy farm, and to keep the Captain from losing that last connection to his sanctified past, Merle loaned him $638.44; and then, finally, there was Marcelle

Chagnon, the manager of the trailerpark, living in number 1, and needing money to protect her job, because the Granite State Realty Development Corporation was billing her personally for the cost of replacing all the frozen pipes in trailer number 11, then vacant, which Marcelle had neglected to drain last August when the previous tenants, a pair of plasterers from Massachusetts working on a new motel over in Epsom, had left. And then, well—then all the money was gone.

BY MID-NOVEMBER THE SUN WAS SETTING EARLY AND RISing late, and the daily temperatures rarely got above freezing, the nights often falling to zero and below. Except for where the water rushed across the weirs, the lake was frozen over entirely. The bobhouse was ready, and Merle's tip-ups, lines, jigs and chisels were repaired, cleaned, oiled and packed neatly into the bobhouse. First thing every morning Merle pulled on his cap and mackinaw and trotted from his trailer down to the shore to read the ice. It was going to be a good winter for ice—no snow so far, very little wind, and lots of steady, unbroken cold. A Canadian high had moved southeast in late October and had hunkered over northern New England for two weeks straight, so that, with clear nighttime skies, the ice had formed, spread and thickened several weeks ahead of schedule.

So far as fishing went, winter or summer, Skitter Lake was Merle's. Three sides of the lake adjoined the Skitter Lake State Forest, which made it fairly inaccessible from the road, except through the trailerpark, and people, strangers especially, were reluctant to drive through the trailerpark and stop their cars before the short, sandy beach at the end of the peninsula, get out their gear, launch their boats, canoes or bobhouses and commence fishing. It was a little too public, and also a little too private, as if the trailerpark were actually a kind of boarding house with all the tenants watching you cross their shared front yard to get to their shared fishing place. The same went for ice-skating and swimming. The residents of the trailerpark skated on and swam in Skitter Lake, but other people went elsewhere, which wasn't much of an inconvenience anyway, since in town there was the mill pond, and throughout the surrounding countryside there were dozens of small, accessible ponds and lakes where the fishing was as good as, if not better than, the fishing at Skitter Lake.

As a result, when at the end of the first week in December Merle decided that the ice was thick enough to support the weight of his bobhouse, he made the decision alone. He couldn't wait until someone less cautious or patient than he had dragged his bobhouse safely out to the middle of the lake. He couldn't even wait until schoolboys from town, eager to play hockey, had crossed and crisscrossed the lake a dozen times the way they did down at the mill pond, whacking the ice with hockey sticks and listening to the cracks and fault lines race away from the blow rather than down, revealing in that way that the ice was now thick enough to support the weight of large human beings.

Merle took his long-handled chisel in hand, and tapping lightly in front of him as he walked, moved like a blind man carefully onto the ice. He walked twenty or so feet from the shore and parallel to the shore toward the marshy area west of the park, where the hermit they called the Guinea Pig Lady would build her shack. Here, he knew, the water was late to freeze, because of the several trickling inlets and the marsh grass and bushes, and here, too, the water was not very deep, so that if indeed it was not safe and he fell through, he would not be in any danger. It was late in the day and the sky was peach-colored near the horizon and blue-gray where thin clouds scudded in from the northeast. Merle, in his dark green mackinaw and plaid trooper's cap with the fur earflaps tied down, tapped his way away from the trailerpark toward the swamp, then past the swamp and out along the point, crossing the cove, and then beyond the point, until he was over deep water. Below him, the lake was a hundred feet deep, and the ice was black and smooth, like polished obsidian. This first solitary walk on the ice is almost like flying, for you have left the safe and solid earth and are moving over what you know and can see is an ether, supported by a membrane that you can feel but cannot quite see, as if the difference between the ice below and the air above were merely a difference in atmospheric pressures. Later, your mind will accept the information coming from your body, and then there will be no difference between ice with a hundred feet of water below it and the frozen ground itself, so that when you cut a hole in the ice and it fills with water, you will be surprised but no more frightened than if you had dug a hole in sand at the beach and watched it fill with seawater.

Confident now that he could safely put his bobhouse onto the ice, Merle spent the following day picking through the brushy overgrown fields out by Old Road, collecting galls from dried stalks of goldenrod. Inside each gall slept a small, white grub, excellent bait for bluegills, and it wasn't long before Merle had collected in his mackinaw pockets half a hundred of the woody containers. Then, on returning to the trailerpark, he was hailed on the roadway just opposite Marcelle Chagnon's trailer by Bruce Severance. Bruce had driven his black Chevy van with the Rocky Mountain sunsets on the sides up behind the old man—it was midafternoon but almost dark, and he probably hadn't seen Merle until he was almost upon him. He stopped a few feet away, raced his motor until Merle turned, then waved him over to the driver's side and cranked down the window.

"Hey, man, what's happening?" The sweet smell of marijuana exhaled from the vehicle, and the kid took a last hit, knocked the lit end off the roach and popped it into his mouth.

"Temperature's dropping," Merle said with a slight smile. As he peered up at the boy his blue, crinkly-lidded eyes filled and glistened in the wind.

"Yeah. Wow. Temperature's dropping. That's what's happening, all right." He swallowed the roach.

"Yep." Merle turned to walk on.

"Say, I've been meaning to ask you, I saw you this morning when I came in from Boston. You were in those old fields out by the road. Then later I came back out, and you were still there. And now here you are again, this time coming in from the fields. What's going on out there?"

"Nothing. Temperature's dropping there too. That's all."

"No, man. I'm curious. I *know* you know things, about herbs and things, I mean."

Merle said, "You want to know what I was out there for? Is that what you're wondering, boy?"

"Yeah."

The old man reached into his mackinaw pocket and drew out one of the goldenrod galls. "These."

"What's that?"

"Goldenrod gall."

"What's it for?"

"I'll show you. But you'll have to spend awhile first helping me move my bobhouse out on the ice tonight."

"Tonight? In the dark?"

"Yep. Got to bait the camp with chum tonight so's I can start to fish tomorrow."

With a slow and maybe reluctant nod, the kid agreed

to help him. Merle walked around and climbed into the van, and the two drove through the park to Merle's trailer.

When an old man and a young man work together, it can make an ugly sight or a pretty one, depending on who's in charge. If the young man's in charge or won't let the old man take over, the young man's brute strength becomes destructive and inefficient, and the old man's intelligence, out of frustration, grows cruel, and inefficient also. Sometimes the old man forgets that he is old and tries to compete with the young man's strength, and then it's a sad sight. Or the young man forgets that he is young and argues with the old man about how to do the work, and that's a sad sight too.

In this case, however, the young man and the old man worked well together. Merle told Bruce where to place his pole so he could lift the front of the bobhouse while Merle slid a second pole underneath. Then the same at the back, until practically on its own the bobhouse started to roll down the slope toward the ice. As each roller emerged from the back, Merle told Bruce to grab it and run around to the front and lay it down, which the young man did, quickly and without stumbling, until in a few moments, the structure was sliding onto the ice, and then it was free of the ground altogether. It slid a few feet from the bank, and the momentum left it, and then it stopped, silent, solid, dark in the wind off the lake.

"Incredible!" the kid said.

"Everything's inside except firewood," Merle said. "Put them poles in, we'll cut them up out on the lake."

The kid did as he was told.

Merle walked around to the front of the bobhouse, away from the land, and took up a length of rope attached to and looped around a quarter-inch-thick U-bolt. "I'll steer, you push," he called to the kid.

"Don't you have a flashlight?" Bruce yelled nervously.

The wind was building and shoved noisily against the bobhouse.

"Nothing out there but ice, and it's flat all the way across."

"How'll I get back?"

"There's lights on here at the park. You just aim for them. You don't need a light to see light. You need dark. C'mon, stop gabbing and start pushing," he said.

The kid leaned against the bobhouse, grunted, and the building started to move. It slid easily over the ice on its waxed runners, at times seeming to carry itself forward on its own, even though against the wind. As if he were leading a large, dumb animal, Merle steered the bobhouse straight out from the shore for about a quarter mile, then abruptly turned to the right and headed east, until he had come to about two hundred yards from the weirs, where the lake narrowed and where, Merle knew, there were in one place a gathering current, thirty to forty feet of water and a weedy, fertile bottom. It was a good spot, and he spun the bobhouse slowly on it until the side with the door faced away from the prevailing wind.

"Let it sit," he said to the kid. "Its weight'll burn the ice and keep it from moving." He went inside and soon returned with a small bucksaw and his long chisel. "You cut the wood into stove lengths, and I'll dig us in," he said, handing the saw to the kid.

"This is really fucking incredible," Bruce said.

Merle looked at him silently for a second, then went quickly to work chipping the ice around the runners and stamping the chips back with his feet, moving swiftly up one side and down the other, until the sills of the house were packed in ice. By then Bruce had cut two of the four poles into firewood. "Finish up, and I'll get us a fire going," Merle told him, and the kid went energetically back to work.

In a short time, a fire was crackling inside the round

belly of the stove, the kerosene lantern was lit, and the bobhouse was warmed sufficiently for Merle to pull off his mackinaw and gloves and hang them on pegs behind the bunk. Bruce laid in the wood carefully below the bunk, then looked up at Merle as if for approval, but Merle ignored him.

"Now," the kid said, shaking off his blue parka and, following Merle's example, placing it on a peg, "show me what you got there, those whachacallits from the fields." He sat down next to Merle and started to roll a joint. "Smoke?" he said, holding out the cigarette.

"No, thanks, I got whiskey."

"You oughta smoke grass instead," the kid said, lighting up.

"That so. You oughta drink whiskey. 'Course, you got to be smarter to handle whiskey than you do that stuff." He was silent and watched Bruce sucking on the joint.

The kid started to argue with the old man. Grass never did to you what whiskey surely did, made you depressed and angry, ruined your liver, destroyed your brain cells, and so on.

"What does grass do to you?" Merle asked.

"Gets you high, man." He grinned.

Merle grunted and stood up. "If it can't hurt you, I don't see how it can get you high." He opened the trap doors in the floor, exposing the white ice below, and with his chisel went to work cutting holes. With the lip of the steel, he flaked ice neatly away, making a circle eight or nine inches across, then dug deeper, until suddenly the hole filled with water. Moving efficiently and quickly, he soon had a half-dozen holes cut, their tops and bottoms carefully beveled so as not to cut the line, and then with a smaller strainer he scooped the floating ice chips away, until there was only clear, pale blue water in the holes.

On a lapboard he proceeded to chop hunks of flesh off several hand-sized minnows he'd plucked from a bait pail. This done, he placed the chum into a tin cone that had a line attached to the top through a lever that released the hinged bottom of the cone when the line was jerked. Then he let the cone slowly down the center hole, slightly larger than the others, and hand over hand let out about thirty feet of line, until he felt the cone touch bottom. He jerked the line once, then retrieved it and brought the cone back into the bobhouse, dripping and empty.

Bruce watched with obvious admiration as the old man moved about the confines of the bobhouse, adjusting the draft of the stove, taking out, using and then wiping dry and putting back his tools and equipment, drawing his bottle of Canadian Club from under the bunk, loosening his boots, when suddenly the old man leaned down and blew out the lantern, and the bobhouse went black.

"What? What'd you do *that* for?" His voice was high and thin.

"Don't need it now." From the darkness came the sound of Merle unscrewing the cap of the whiskey bottle. Then silence.

"How long you plan to stay out here tonight?" The kid sounded a little frightened.

"Till morning," came the answer. "Then for as long as the fishing's any good and the ice holds."

"Days and nights both?"

"Sure. I only hafta come in when I run outa whiskey. There's lotsa wood along the banks, I'll hafta step out now and then for that, and of course you hafta piss and shit once in a while. Otherwise . . ."

They sat in darkness and silence a while longer, when finally the kid stood up and groped behind him for his coat. "I . . . I gotta go back in."

"Suit yourself."

He took a step toward the door, and Merle said to him, "Those goldenrod galls you was asking about?"

"Oh, yeah," the kid said.

Merle struck a match, and suddenly his face was visible, red in the glow of the match as he sucked the flame into the barrel of his pipe, his bearded face seeming to lurch ominously in and out of the light when the flame brightened and then dimmed. When he had his pipe lit, he snuffed out the match, and all the kid could see was the red glow of the smoldering tobacco. "Bait. That's all."

"*Bait?*"

"Yep. Old Indian trick."

The kid was silent for a few seconds. "Bait. You mean, that's how you got me to push this thing way the hell out here tonight?"

"Old Indian trick."

"Yeah," Bruce said coldly. "And I fell for it. Jesus." He drew open the door and stepped quickly out to the ice and wind, looked into the darkness for the lights of the trailerpark, found them way off and dimly in the west, and started the walk back.

No one brought Merle any Christmas gifts or invited him to any of the several small parties at the park. The reasons may have been complicated and may have had to do with the "loans" they all had received from him, but more likely the residents of the trailerpark, as usual, simply forgot about him. Once in a while someone mentioned having seen him walk through the park on his way to town and return later carrying a bag of groceries and a state liquor store bag, but otherwise it was almost as if the old man had moved away, had gone west to Albany like Buddy Smith or south to Florida like

Captain Knox's mother and father or into town to the Hawthorne House like Claudel Bing. Nobody thought to send them Christmas gifts or invite them back to the trailerpark for a Christmas party.

Then, the week before Christmas, there was a snowstorm that left a foot and a half of snow on the ground and on the lake, followed by a day and a night of high, cold winds that scraped the snow into shoulder-high drifts along the shore, and that further isolated Merle from the community. Now it was almost as if he had died, and when in the morning you happened to look out at the lake and saw way out there in the brilliant white plain a red cube with a string of woodsmoke unraveling from the stovepipe chimney on top, you studied it the way you would the distant gravestone of a stranger reddening in the light of the rising sun.

A week later, just after Christmas and before the turn of the year, Noni Hubner's mother was reading the *Manchester Union-Leader* at breakfast, when she started up excitedly, grabbed the paper off the table and hurried back through the trailer to her daughter's bedroom.

"Noni! Noni, wake up!" She shook the girl's shoulder roughly.

Slowly Noni came to. She lay in the bed on her back, blinking like a seal on a rock. "What?"

"The Grand Prize Drawing! They're going to have the Grand Prize Drawing, dear! Think of it! What if he won! Wouldn't that be wonderful for him? The poor old man."

"Who? What the hell are you talking about?"

"Don't curse, dear. Merle Ring, the old fellow out on the lake. He won the lottery back in October, and now they're going to hold the Grand Prize Drawing on January fifteenth. Apparently, they put all the winning numbers for the year into a basket or something, and the governor or somebody draws out one number, and whoever holds that number wins fifty thousand dollars! Wouldn't that be wonderful?''

"Yeah," the girl said, and rolled over, yanking the covers over her head.

"No, you can't go back to sleep. You've got to go out there and tell him. He hasn't been out of that cabin of his for days, so he can't know yet. You can ski out there with the news. Won't that be *fun*, dear?"

"Let someone else do it," Noni mumbled from under the covers. "It's too cold."

"You're the only one who has skis, dear," the mother said.

"Most of the snow is off the ice."

"Then you can skate out!"

"Oh, God," Noni groaned. "Can't you leave people alone?"

"He's such a sweet old man, and he's been *very* generous. It's the least we can do."

"He's a grumpy pain in the ass, if you ask me. And he's weird, not generous. If you ask me." She got out of bed and looked at her reflection in the mirror.

"Well, no one asked you. You just do as I say. You have to involve yourself more in the fates of others, dear. You can't always be thinking only of yourself."

"Yeah, I know."

It took her an hour to prepare for the journey—first breakfast, then dressing herself in three layers of clothing, bickering with her mother, as she ate and dressed, about the necessity for the trip in the first place—and then another hour for the trip itself. It was a white world out there, white sky, white earth beneath, and a thin, gray horizon all around, the whole of it centered on the red cubicle where the old man fished through the ice.

At the bobhouse, sweating from the work of skating against the wind, and having come to rest, suddenly chilled, Noni leaned for a few seconds against the leeward wall, then knocked at the door, and without waiting for an answer, entered. The door closed behind her, and instantly she was enveloped by darkness and warmth, as if she had been swallowed whole by an enormous mammal.

"Oh!" she cried. "I can't see!"

"Seat's to your right," came the old man's gravelly voice. The interior space was so small that you couldn't tell where in the darkness the voice was coming from, whether from the farthest corner of the bobhouse or right up next to your ear.

Noni groped to her right, found the bench and sat down. A moment of silence passed. Gradually, her eyes grew accustomed to the darkness, and she was able at last to see the six holes in the ice, and in the green light that emerged from the holes she saw the hooked shape of the old man seated at the other end of the bunk next to the stove. He held a dropline in one hand and was jiggling it with the other, and he seemed to be staring into the space directly in front of him, as if he were a blind man.

"Why is it so dark in here?" she asked timidly.

"Window's shut."

"No, I mean, how come?"

"So I can see the fish and they can't see me," he said slowly.

More silence passed. Finally, in a low voice, Noni spoke. "How very strange you are."

Merle didn't respond.

"I have some news for you, Mr. Ring."

Still nothing.

"You know the lottery you won back in October?"

Merle jiggled his handline and continued staring straight ahead. It was almost as if he'd entered a state of suspended animation, as if his systems had been banked down to their minimal operating capacity, with his heart and lungs, all his vital organs, working at one-fourth their normal rate, so that he could survive and even thrive in the deprivation caused by the cold and the ice and the darkness.

"It seems ridiculous," the girl said, almost to herself. "You don't care about things like lotteries and Grand Prize Drawings and all."

A few seconds passed, and Merle said, "I bought the ticket. I cared."

"Of course. I'm sorry," Noni said. "I just meant . . . well, no matter. My mother saw in the paper this morning that they're holding the Grand Prize Drawing in Concord on January fifteenth at noon, and you ought to be there. In case you win."

Merle said nothing.

"It's a lot of money. Fifty thousand dollars. You have a good chance to win it, you know." He didn't respond, so she went on, chattering nervously now. "Think of what that would mean. Fifty thousand dollars! You could have a wonderful old age. I mean, retirement. Retirement, I mean. You could go to Florida in the winter months. You could go deep-sea fishing in Florida . . . maybe buy one of those condominiums, and play shuffleboard, and have lots of friends . . ." She trailed off. "God, I sound like my mother." She stood up and moved toward the door. Tenderly, she said, "I'm sorry I bothered you, Mr. Ring. My mother . . . my mother wanted you to know about the drawing, that's why I came out here. She thought you'd be . . . excited, I guess."

"I haven't won yet."

"But you have a good chance of winning."

"Good chance of dying, too. Better."

"Not by January fifteenth, Mr. Ring."

"About the same. I'm old. Not much left to do but think, and then, in the middle of a thought, die."

"Oh, no," she said heartily. "There's *lots* left for you to do."

"Like what?"

"Well . . . fishing, for instance. And spending all that lottery money you're going to win."

"Yes," he said. "Yes, I suppose there's that." Then he lapsed back into silence again.

The girl opened the door and slipped out, and the bobhouse was filled again with darkness and solitude.

THE DOOR TO THE BOBHOUSE WAS FLUNG OPEN, AND A BLINDing light entered, bringing with it a blast of cold air and the hulking shape of a man in a hooded parka. The man splashed the light from his flashlight around the chamber, located Merle stretched out in his blanket roll on the bunk and then let the beam droop deferentially to the floor. The man closed the door behind him.

"Mr. Ring?"

"Yep."

"I'm . . . I'm Leon LaRoche. You know, from the trailerpark?"

Merle swung his body into a sitting position. "You can shut out that light."

Leon apologized and snapped off the flashlight. "May I sit down and get warm? It's mighty cold out there tonight." He chuckled. "Yes, sir, mighty cold."

"Suit yourself."

They were silent for a moment. Merle opened the stove front, throwing sudden shadows and sheets of dancing red and yellow light into the room; then he tossed a chunk of wood onto the crimson coals and closed the firedoor again.

The young man nervously cleared his throat. "Well, Mr. Ring, how's the fishing?"

"Slow."

"I've been hearing a lot about you lately, from folks at the park, I mean . . . how you stay out here night and day, only coming in now and then for supplies . . ."

"Whiskey," Merle said, and he went under the bench with one hand and drew out his bottle. "Drink?"

"No. No, thank you."

Merle took a slow pull from the bottle.

"Anyhow, it's all very interesting to me. Yes, maybe I will have a drink," he said, and Merle fetched the bottle again and passed it over. "So tell me, Mr. Ring, what do you eat out here? How do you cook and all?"

"Fish, mostly. A man can live a long time in this climate on fish and whiskey."

"Very interesting. And you use lake water for washing, I suppose?"

Merle grunted.

"How long do you plan on staying out here, Mr. Ring?" Leon took another drink from the bottle and passed it back.

Merle said nothing.

As if his question had been answered, Leon went on. "And do you do this every winter, Mr. Ring? I mean, stay out on the ice, isolated like this, living off fish and whiskey and solitude?" He chuckled again. "I'm relatively new to the park," he explained.

"I know."

"Yes, of course. Well." He wrestled himself free of his parka and flexed his shoulders and hands. "Say, it's really comfortable in here, isn't it? Smells a bit of whiskey and fried fish, though," he said with a light laugh. "You wouldn't mind if I had another sip of that, would you? What *is* it, by the way? It's quite good! Really warms a man's insides, doesn't it?"

Merle handed him the bottle. "Canadian Club."

Leon unscrewed the cap and took a long swallow,

then slowly screwed the cap back on. "Yes. So, yes, I was saying, do you do this every year?"

"Man and boy."

"But *why?*"

"It makes the rest of the year more interesting," Merle said wearily.

Leon was silent for a moment. "I wonder. Yes, I'll bet it does. I couldn't stand it, though. The isolation. And the cold, and the darkness."

"It's a good idea to get used to the idea. Like I said, it makes the rest of the year more interesting."

Leon's voice was tight and frightened. "Are you talking about dying?"

"I'm talking about living," Merle said with quiet emphasis.

"Speaking of living," Leon said, suddenly hearty again, "you are probably wondering why I came all the way out here this evening."

"Not particularly."

"Yes. Well, anyhow, it has to do with the Grand Prize Drawing next week. You know, the state lottery?"

"Yep."

"Folks in the park have been wondering, Mr. Ring, if you plan on attending that drawing over in Concord, and if not, assuming you win, for you just might win, you know, folks are wondering how you plan to pick up the prize money. You have to be there in person to pick up the prize money, you see . . ." He trailed off, as if waiting to be interrupted.

Merle said nothing.

"Well. It occurred to some of us that you might not care to take the time off from your fishing to go all the way in to Concord and deal with all those state officials and the reporters and so forth, seeing as how you enjoy your privacy and like to spend your winters alone out here on the lake, and we thought you might be able to empower someone else to do that chore for you. So I did a little checking around at the bank, and sure enough, you *can* empower someone else to pick up your prize money for you!" He waited a few seconds, but nothing more than the crackle and spit of the fire came out of the darkness, so he went on. "Anticipating your reluctance to leave your fishing at this time of year, I went ahead and took the liberty of having the necessary document drawn up by the bank attorney." He went into his shirt pocket and brought forth a crisp, white envelope. "This document empowers me to act as your agent, should you win the Grand Prize Drawing," he said, handing the envelope to Merle.

The old man took out the paper folded inside, and at the sound, Leon snapped on his flashlight. "Where do I sign it?" Merle asked. His voice was suddenly, strangely woeful and riddled with fatigue.

Leon directed him to a line at the bottom of the paper and handed him a pen.

Slowly, the old man placed the paper against his knee and scrawled his name on it. "There," he said, and he handed the paper, envelope and pen back to the bank clerk, who doused the light. "It's your problem, now," the old man said.

"No problem at all, Mr. Ring. None at all," he said, as he stood and pulled his parka on. "I assume," he went on, "that if you win, you'll want your check deposited in a savings account down at the bank."

"No."

"No?"

"Bring the money here."

"Here?"

"In cash."

"Cash?"

"Cash. No point letting some bank make money off my money. The government owns all the money anyhow. They just let us use it for a while. It's the banks that foul everything up by getting in the middle. You bring me anything I win in hundred dollars bills. You might use one of them to buy me a case of Canadian Club. I've always wanted a case of Canadian Club," he said wistfully.

Leon seemed to have been struck dumb. He moved toward the door in the darkness, groping for the latch and finally finding it. Then he let himself out.

FROM HERE ON OUT, IT WAS AS IF EVERYONE WHO KNEW Merle knew that he was going to win the lottery. Consequently, his solitude rarely went a day without its being broken by a visit from someone wanting to congratulate him and talk about the money. Also, the weather broke into what's called the January Thaw and people found the half-mile walk over ice and long floes of crusted snow less formidable than before. The wind died, the skies cleared to a deep blue, and daytime temperatures nudged the freezing mark, so at one time or another during the week following the visit from the bank teller, practically everyone else in the park found an occasion to visit the old man. Even Claudel Bing (though he had not lived at the trailerpark for several years, he was still paying for a trailer there and, in his fashion, was courting Doreen Tiede, and as a result had kept up his links with the park) came out to Merle's bobhouse early one sunny afternoon.

He was already drunk when he arrived, a not uncommon occurrence that year, and therefore he wanted to talk about luck. In particular, his own bad luck, as compared to Merle's good luck. Luck was Claudel's obsession that year. It was the only way he could understand or even think about his life.

"You, you sonofabitch, you got *all* the luck," he told

Merle, who silently arranged his lines in the tip-ups and
scooped ice chips away from the holes. "And that means
there's none left over for people like me! That's the
trouble with this goddamn country." Claudel had brought
his own bottle of whiskey, which he held between his
legs and every now and then swigged at. "Now you take
them fucking Commie bastards, like that Castro and
them Russians, their idea is to get rid of luck completely, so *nobody* gets any. That's as bad as what we
got here. Worse, actually. What I'd like to see is a
system that lets everybody have a little luck. That's
what this country needs. Nobody gets a lot, and nobody
gets none. Everybody gets a little."

"How about the bad luck?" Merle asked him. "Everybody get a little bit of that, too?" His beard and face
and hands were pale green in the light from the holes,
and as he moved slowly, smoothly over his traps and
lines, checking bait and making sure the lines were laid
precisely in the spools, he resembled a ghost.

"Sure! Why the hell not? When you got a little good
luck, you can handle a little bad luck. It won't break
you. If I had money, for instance, it wouldn't bother me
that Ginnie run off with that goddamn sonofabitchin'
Howie Leeke. It's *like* that, Merle," he said earnestly.
"But you wouldn't understand. Not with your kind of
luck. Shit," he said, and took a long drink from his
bottle. "You ever lose a woman you loved, Merle?" he
asked suddenly. "No, of course not. You've had all
them wives, got wives and kids scattered all over the
country, but none of them ever left *you*. No, you left
them. Right? Am I right?"

"Can't say exactly that I intended to leave them,
though," Merle said. "I guess I just willed it. You can
will what you actually do, but what you intend is all you
accomplish in the end."

"You preaching to me, Merle, goddammit?"

"Nope. Just thinking out loud. Not used to company, I guess."

"Hey, that's all right, I understand. Shit, it must get awful lonely out here. I'd go nuts. It's good for thinking, though. Probably. Is that the kinda stuff you think about out here, Merle, all that stuff about will and intending?"

"Yep." A red flag on one of the tip-ups suddenly sprung free, and in a single, swift motion Merle was off the bench and huddled over the line, watching it run off the spool and then stop, when he jerked it, set the hook and started retrieving the fish. "Black bass," he said to no one in particular. It was a small one, not two pounds. Merle drew it through the hole, removed the hook from its lip and deposited the fish in the bucket of ice chips scooped from the holes.

"If I was you, I'd be thinking all the time about how I was going to spend all that money," Claudel went on. "You talk about will and intentions!" he laughed. "How do you intend to spend the money, Merle? Fifty thousand bucks! Jesus H. Christ."

"Can't say." He had rebaited the hook and was winding the line back onto the spool.

"You mean you don't know?"

"What d'you think my intentions toward that much money ought to be? Can't spend it, not the way I live. 'Course, I haven't got it yet, so it ain't like we're talking about reality."

"No, we're talking about money!" Claudel said, leering.

"All I know is death and taxes. That's reality. I intend to pay my taxes, and I intend to die."

"Merle, you are fucking crazy," Claudel said. "Crazy. But smart. You're smart, all right. You coulda been a lot of things if you'd wanted to. Big. A businessman."

"I always did what I wanted to do," Merle said gloomily. Then, as if writing a letter, he said, "I was a carpenter, and I was married, and I fathered some children.

Then I got old. Everyone gets old, though, whether he wants to or not."

They were silent in the darkness for a moment.

"Yeah," Claudel said, "but then you got lucky. Then you won the lottery!"

"It don't matter."

"Of course it matters, you *asshole!*"

"Not to me."

"Well, it matters to me, goddammit!"

Merle remained silent this time, and after a while, Claudel's bottle was empty. Without leaving his seat, he reached over, opened the door and pitched the bottle out. "It'll sink in spring," he mumbled. Then slowly, awkwardly, he pulled his coat on and stumbled out the door, not bothering even to say good-bye.

DAILY, WITH AND WITHOUT CEREMONY, THEY CAME OUT TO the bobhouse. The younger ones, Terry Constant, Noni Hubner, Bruce Severance, Leon LaRoche, Doreen Tiede, and poor Claudel Bing, could pretend they just happened to be in the neighborhood, ice-skating, skiing, walking or, as in Claudel's case, bored and lonely and thought to drop in for a visit. The older ones, however, found it difficult to be casual about their visits. As Merle had said, you expect the actions of adults to have intention behind them and therefore meaning. The adults tend to expect it of themselves, too. Carol, Terry Constant's older sister, claimed she walked all the way out to the middle of the lake against a cold wind because she had never seen anyone ice-fishing before and wanted to learn how it was done. While there, the only question she asked Merle directly was how would he spend the money if he won on the fifteenth. He said he didn't know. Nancy Hubner baked Merle a minced meat pie (she said it was his favorite) and insisted on carrying it to him herself. While he ate a piece of the pie she told him how excited she was at the prospect of his becoming a wealthy, carefree man, something she said *everyone* deserved. He agreed. Captain Dewey Knox appeared one morning at the bobhouse to confirm Leon LaRoche's claim that Merle had signed a document authorizing Leon to act as his agent at the Grand Prize Drawing. Merle said yes, he had signed such a document. "Without coercion?" the Captain asked. Merle said he couldn't be sure because he didn't know how a person went about coercing someone to sign something. "But you understood fully the meaning and consequences of your act?" the Captain asked. Merle said he wasn't drunk or crazy at the time. "And is it true," the Captain went on, "that you requested young LaRoche bring your winnings out here in cash? Hundred dollar bills?" Merle said it was true. The Captain thought that extremely foolish and told Merle, at great length, why. Merle went about his business of fishing and said nothing. After a while, when the Captain had finished telling Merle why he should have Leon LaRoche deposit the money in a savings account at the bank where he was employed, he departed from the bobhouse. The last person from the trailerpark to visit Merle's bobhouse came out the day of the drawing, January fifteenth. It was Marcelle Chagnon, and as the manager of the trailerpark, she felt it was as much her duty as her privilege to announce to Merle that on that day at twelve o'clock noon he had won the $50,000 Grand Prize Drawing.

THE WINTER CONTINUED TO BEAR DOWN, QUITE AS IF MERLE had not won the lottery. There were snowstorms and cruel northeast winds out of Nova Scotia and days and nights, whole weeks, of subzero temperatures. Merle's money, the five hundred one-hundred-dollar bills delivered by Leon LaRoche, remained untouched in Merle's cigar box under the bunk in the bobhouse. The brand new bills, banded into thousand dollar packets, filled the cigar box exactly, and the box, with an elastic band around it, sat in the darkness of the bobhouse and the minds of everyone who lived in the trailerpark. Everyone carried the image of that box around in his or her head all day and all night. Some even dreamed about it. Leon LaRoche told Captain Knox that when he delivered the money the old man in stony silence, as if angry at being interrupted, had taken the money from the bank pouch and without counting it had stacked it neatly into the cigar box and tossed, literally tossed, the box under his bunk. The Captain, as if disgusted, told Marcelle Chagnon, who, worriedly, told Doreen Tiede, who told Claudel Bing that night after making mild, dispassionate love, and Claudel, stirred to anger, told Carol Constant the next morning when, on her way to work, she gave him a lift into town because he hadn't got out of bed in time to go in with Doreen and her daughter. Then, that evening, Carol told her brother Terry, because she thought Merle would listen to Terry, but Terry knew better: "That man listens to everyone and no one," he said to Bruce when telling him about the cigar box that contained $50,000, and Bruce, full of wonder and admiration, agreed with Terry and tried to explain the pure wisdom of the act to Noni Hubner, but she didn't quite understand how it could be wise, so she asked her mother, Nancy, who thought it was senile, not wise.

In that way, within twenty-four hours of Leon's having delivered the money to the bobhouse, everyone in the trailerpark shared an obsession with the image of the cigar box full of hundred dollar bills. They could think of little else. Merle's earlier winnings had not achieved anything like this status, but their experience with that considerably lesser amount had gone a long way toward determining how they looked at this new money. The October lottery had dropped $4500 into Merle's lap, and the residents of the trailerpark each had gone to him and asked for some of it and directly had received what he or she had asked for. This new amount, however, was so incomprehensibly large that no one could apply it to his or her individual needs. Consequently, they applied it to what they saw as the needs of the community as a whole. It was not Merle who had won the $50,000; the trailerpark had won it. Merle had merely represented them in that magical cosmos where anything, absolutely anything, can happen. Of course, it's probably true that if, on the other hand, what had happened to Merle through no effort on his part had been as colossally, abstractly *bad* as the $50,000 was *good,* the residents of the trailerpark would not have felt that it had happened to the community as a whole. If, for example, Merle had been shot in the head by an errant bullet from the gun of a careless deer hunter out of sight in the tamaracks on the far side of the lake, the people in the park would have blamed Merle for having been out there wandering around on the ice during hunting season in the first place. They would have mourned for him, naturally, but his death would be seen forever after as a warning, an admonition. Anyone can be a cause of his or her own destruction, but no one can claim individual responsibility for having created a great good. At least that's how the people in the trailerpark felt. Which is why they believed that Merle's winnings belonged not to Merle alone, but to the entire community of which he was a part. And, of course, there was their earlier experience with the $4500. That sort of proved the rightness of their feeling, gave them something like a logic.

The days went by, and Merle showed no sign of recognizing that something extraordinary had occurred in his life and the lives of everyone else at the park as well. Every morning they peered out their windows and saw again the red bobhouse in the distance, a horizontal strip of smoke trailing from the stovepipe chimney if the wind was blowing, a vertical thread if the wind had let up. In the afternoon, as it grew dark, they looked toward the lake again and saw that nothing had changed. Because Merle refused to act any differently than he had in the weeks before he won the lottery, no one else could act any differently, either, and so it almost came to seem that they had imagined it, which is one reason why they were eager, whenever possible, to talk about the money with one another. It *was* true, wasn't it? I didn't just *dream* that Merle Ring won the lottery, did I? And then, as time passed, with the continuous discussions having satisfactorily proved that Merle did in fact win the Grand Prize Drawing, they began to take and present to one another their respective positions on what Merle ought to do with the money he had won. It was the natural consequence of Merle's apparent refusal to deal with the reality of the situation.

"The man's obviously incapable of behaving responsibly toward money," Captain Knox explained to Leon LaRoche. "Money demands to be taken care of in a responsible manner. You can't treat it like some sort of waif, you have to take *care* of it," he said.

Leon agreed. Wholeheartedly. They were sitting in the living room of the Captain's trailer, Leon on the sofa, the Captain slumped back into his red leather easychair. Behind him on the wall hung a map of the world. In the center of each of a large number of countries, mostly central European and southeast Asian countries, the Captain had pinned a small Russian flag. Earlier in the evening, having delivered to Leon a fairly lengthy oration on the subject of the insidious workings of what he called Castroism in the very corridors of the United States State Department, he had ceremoniously pinned a red flag to Panama. That had led him to a discussion of the responsibilities that go with power, which in turn had led him naturally to a discussion of the responsibilities that go with wealth, and that was how they had come around to talking about Merle again.

And now that people were taking positions on what should be done—with Merle, with the money, or, in certain cases, with Merle and the money—they had begun quarreling with one another. For while the Captain and Leon, for example, both believed that one had a moral obligation to take care of money in a responsible manner, they were not in anything like clear agreement as to what, in the case of Merle's lottery winnings, constituted a responsible manner. Nor did either of them agree with what Carol or Marcelle or Claudel or anyone else thought ought to be done with Merle and the $50,000 that, through no particular effort or even intent of his own, he had so recently come to possess. And since everyone had a stake in what was done with the money, the feelings ran pretty high, and it didn't take long for the residents of the trailerpark to think that everyone else in the trailerpark was stupid, greedy, or both stupid and greedy, while he himself, or she herself, was neither. Here, then, are the ways the people in the park thought the situation should be handled.

Doreen Tiede: There are some of us here who have children to support, who work for a living, who don't get any help from ex-husbands or dead husbands or big government pensions. I think we know who we're talking about. There are some of us here who won't take welfare, who don't have fancy jobs in fancy doctors' offices, who don't stay home and collect other people's rent while other people are out working their asses off at the tannery. There are some of us who would like a normal American life. And who deserve it, too. I think we know who we are.

Terry Constant: We could form a corporation and buy out the trailerpark, develop the beach, fill in the swamp and put up a restaurant and bar. We have to think for ourselves and take over control of our destinies. Enough of this business of making somebody else rich while we get poorer for it. Make a summer resort out of this place. Swimming, fishing, water-skiing. Or maybe a summer camp for city kids. Nature walks, arts and crafts, sports. Put up cabins for the kids, while the rest of us live in the trailers. I'd get number 9, where that guy who shot himself lived with his kid. We could run the place in winter as a lodge for snowmobilers. Maybe, if you promoted it right, ice-fishing would catch on. The point is, we all work together for the common good. You don't just spend the money, you use the money, because it doesn't matter how hard you work, it takes money to make money. Not work. Not time. Money. Leon could be Treasurer, old Captain Knox could be Chairman of the Board. I could be the Executive Director. We'd make Merle President of the Corporation or something honorary like that. I'd get a good salary. Marcelle could run the restaurant, Carol the infirmary.

Bruce Severance: When you got money, unless you're stupid, the first thing you do is eliminate the middle man. That way you control the entire operation, like Henry Ford did. What do you think pissed off the Arabs? All those American oil companies, man, they controlled the entire operation. I got connections in Jamaica like Shell had in Saudi Arabia, man. You could bring a plane in here in winter and land it on the lake. Simple. Easy Street. How the hell do you think the Kennedy family got started? Running booze from Canada during Prohibition, man. It's not like we're the Mafia or something. I mean, *everybody* smokes grass!

Noni Hubner: It's important to be fair. That's what I believe in. Fairness. Right?

Leon LaRoche: In a savings account at the Catamount Trust, Merle's money will earn enough for him to live without financial anxiety for the rest of his natural life. The stock market goes up and down, government and municipal bonds, though they offer a distinct tax advantage, are a young man's game, and there's no need to speculate on the risky commodities market. After all, Merle only wants to live in a modest way, free of worry or risk, that's obvious and natural, and with his social security plus interest on his lottery winnings, he certainly ought to be able to do so. What kind of selfishness would prompt a person to deny him that opportunity? The bank would be happy to take care of Merle's funds for him. He'd be the single largest depositor, and I myself would handle his account for him. I'd probably become an officer of the bank, maybe eventually a vice president. It's not every teller can bring in a $50,000 savings account. The publicity would be good for the bank, too. We could have a picture-taking session, Merle signing the deposit slip, me taking the cigar box out of his hands. We'd need an extra guard. I don't care what the Captain says, I know money.

Carol Constant: With that much money he could do something useful for a change. He could help others. The whole thing makes me sick. He sits out there on top of fifty thousand dollars, while back here people are struggling to survive. If he doesn't want the damn money, let him give it to the town so it can help the poor, for Christ's sake. I see people from this town every day so poor and sick they die before they're supposed to, people whose houses burn down, people who've been out of work for years. I see kids with nutritional diseases, birth defects, kids who need glasses to read but can't afford them so they do lousy at school. While that old man, that senile jerk, sits out there fishing through a hole in the ice. It makes me sick. I'm sure he's senile. Those are always the ones who end up with money to burn, the ones who are too feeble-minded to know what to do with it. He doesn't even know how to use it for himself. I wouldn't mind so much if he just took off for Florida and spent it on some old lady and a condominium on the Gulf. I hope someone steals it off him. I just hope it's not Terry. Though, God knows, Terry could make better use of it than that old man is. Terry might at least pay me back a little of what I've spent taking care of him these last few years.

Claudel Bing: You hear all the time about an old geezer dying and then they find a million bucks or something stashed under his mattress. All those years the sonofabitch has been cashing welfare checks and living like a fucking rat in a hole, and meanwhile he's sitting on top of a fucking million bucks or something. Then the government goes and takes it all for taxes or something. I think we oughta just go on out there, get the bastard drunk, and take that goddamn cigar box off his hands. He'd never know the difference anyway. Sonofabitch. If I do it, no one's gonna know about it. I'll be long gone from here. California. No reason why his dumb luck can't be my good luck. Nothing wrong with that. I earned it, for Christ's sake.

Buddy Smith: You probably remember the tragic death of my father by his own hand. He was very fond of you, Mr. Ring, and often spoke highly of you to me, telling me himself what a kind and generous man you are. I will soon be returning to N.H. on business of a personal nature and was thinking of dropping by the trailerpark, where I have so many fond but also sad memories of my childhood. I thought, if you had the room, because my father was so very fond of you, I could perhaps visit with you a few days and we could talk about the old times. I'm a young man, alone in the cold world now, and without the kind of wise counsel that an older man like yourself can provide . . .

Nancy Hubner: The man is obviously depressed. You people amaze me. He's depressed. It happens often to elderly people who live alone and don't feel needed anymore. We simply have to take better care of our senior citizens. The man needs company, he needs to feel wanted, and especially he needs to feel needed. We ought to make up an excuse to have a party, a Valentine's Day party, say, and march out there and say to him, "Merle, if you won't come to our party, then we'll bring the party right out here on the ice, we'll bring the party to *you!*" We'll all have a lovely time. We've got to bring him back into our circle, a man like that should not be allowed to be alone in life. The money has nothing to do with it.

Dewey Knox: The man's obviously incapable of taking care of himself, so it shouldn't be difficult to have him declared incompetent to handle his own affairs. The money can then go into a blind trust, which clever and aggressive management ought to be able to double in a matter of a few years. Imagine, if you'd bought gold five years ago, as I did, when it was going for $112 an ounce, you'd now have a nice little nest egg. I myself, if pressed to it, would certainly be willing to put together a management team to handle the trust. Other than taking for myself a nominal fee for services provided, the capital accrued would of course go directly into the trust and ultimately to Merle Ring's heirs. It could be arranged so that Merle himself received a modest monthly stipend. People like Merle need looking after. Not vice versa, the way some of you would have it.

Marcelle Chagnon: Am I crazy, or is everybody trying to figure out how to get Merle's money for themselves? It's his money, and I don't care what in hell he does with it. He can wipe his butt with it, for all I care, if you'll excuse my English. So what if he's got lots of money he don't need and you don't have enough. So what else is new? That's life. Do I expect my sons all grown up and making good money to send me money just because they got lots of it now and I don't have enough? No, I do not. That's life, is all I got to say. All I care now is that Merle does *something* with that money, spends it or gives it away or loses it, something, anything, just so life can return to normal around here. I wish to hell he'd never got it in the first place. Thinking about it, all this talk and argument about it, gives me a goddamned headache. I hate thinking about money, and here I've been doing it all my life. I get the same damned headache every time one of my sons writes and tells me he just bought a new dishwasher for his wife or a color TV or just got back from Bermuda or someplace. What do I care what he just bought or where the hell he went on vacation? What the hell do I care about money? There's lots more important things in life than money. I just want to forget it exists. I'm tired.

IT'S HARD TO KNOW MORE ABOUT A PERSON'S LIFE THAN WHAT that person wants you to know, and few people know even that much. Beyond what you can see and are told (both of which are controlled pretty easily by the person seen and told about), what you come to believe is true of who a person is and was and will be comes straight from your imaginings. For instance, you know that a man like Merle Ring had a mother and a father, probably brothers and sisters, too, and that for most of his life he was a working man and that he was married and had children. He said as much himself, and besides, these things are true of almost any man you might choose to read about or speak of. That he was married numerous times (you might imagine four or five or even more, but "numerous" was all he ever said) and fathered numerous children explains only why in his old age he was as alone in the wide world as a man who had never married at all and had fathered no one. Whether he meant to or not, Merle had avoided the middle ground and in that way had located himself alone in the center of his life, sharing it with no one. In fact, you could say the same of everyone at the trailerpark. It's true of trailerparks that the people who live there are generally alone at the center of their lives. They are widows and widowers, divorcées and bachelors and retired army officers, a black man in a white society, a black woman there too, a drug dealer, a solitary child of a broken home, a drunk, a homosexual in a heterosexual society—all of them, man and woman, adult and child, basically alone in the world. When you share the center of your life with someone else, you create a third person who is neither you nor the person you have cleaved to. No such third person resided at the Granite State Trailerpark.

In any event, to return to Merle Ring, though you knew all these things about Merle's inner and outer lives, you could know little more about them than that, unless he himself were to provide you with more information than he had already provided, more actions and reactions, more words. And, unfortunately, as the winter wore on he seemed less and less inclined to say or do anything new. People's imaginings, therefore, as to who he really was, came to dominate their impressions of him.

This, of course, was especially true after he won the money. By then most of the people at the park were frightened of him. The money gave him power, and the longer he neither acted on nor reacted to the presence of that money, the greater grew his power. For the most part, though they argued among themselves as to how

Merle should exercise his immense power, no one dared approach him on the subject. They spoke of it, naturally, and made plans and commitments to send one or another of the group or several in a delegation out onto the plain of ice to ask Merle what he was going to do with the money, but by morning the plans and commitments got broken, ignored or forgotten altogether—until the next time a group of them got to bickering, accusing one another of selfishness and greed and downright stupidity, when a new agreement would be made as to who should make the trip. The trouble was, they no longer trusted anyone or any group from among their number to return with accurate information as to Merle's behavior, and for that reason they could not be relieved of their imaginings. Finally someone, possibly Marcelle Chagnon and probably as a bitter joke, suggested they send a child, the only true child who lived at the trailerpark, Doreen Tiede's five-year-old daughter Maureen.

Her mother dressed the child warmly in a dark blue hooded snowsuit, mittens and overshoes. It was an overcast Sunday afternoon, the low sky promising snow, when the residents of the trailerpark walked Maureen down to where the land ended and the ice began. Smiling and talking cheerfully together for the first time in weeks, they called advice to their tiny emissary:

"Don't forget, ask him about his fishing first! *Then* ask him about the money."

"Just say we all miss him here and wonder when he's coming back in!"

"No, no, just ask if we can *do* anything for him! Can we bring him any supplies, wood for his fire, tools—anything!"

The child looked about in bewilderment, and when she got to the edge of the ice, she stopped and faced the crowd.

"All right, honey," her mother said. "Go ahead. Go

on and visit Uncle Merle, honey. He's out there waiting for you."

They could trust the child. Merle, they knew, would tell her the truth, and she in turn would tell them the truth.

"Go on, sweets," Doreen coaxed.

The little girl looked up at the adults.

"Merle's probably lonely," Nancy Hubner said. "He'll love you for visiting with him."

"It's not very far, you'll have fun walking on the ice," Terry assured her.

"She doesn't wanta go, man," Bruce said to Terry in a low voice.

"For Christ's sake, make the kid go!" Claudel told Doreen. "I'm getting cold standing out here in my shirtsleeves."

"Shut up, Claudel, she's just a little nervous."

Marcelle snorted. "First time *I've* seen her nervous about playing on the ice. Usually you can't get her to come in off it."

"Go on," Doreen said, waving good-bye.

The child took a backward step and stopped.

"G'wan, honey, Uncle Merle's waiting for you," Carol said with obvious impatience. "Whose idea *was* this anyway?"

"You're the child's mother," Captain Knox reminded Doreen. "You tell her what you want her to do, and if she doesn't do it, punish her. It's her choice." He turned and stepped from the group, as if all this fuss had nothing to do with him.

"If you don't march out there and visit Merle Ring right now, young lady, I'll . . . I'll . . . take away TV for a month!"

The little girl looked angrily up at her mother. "No," she said.

"I will too! Now get out there! He's *expecting* you, dammit!"

"You come, too," Maureen said to her mother.

"I can't . . . I . . . have to do the laundry."

"He only likes kids," Terry said. "Grownups like us just bug him. You'll see. He'll be real glad to see you come all the way out there to visit him."

"He might have some candy for you," Bruce said.

The child turned and started waddling away.

"Don't forget about the money!" Noni Hubner called.

The child turned back. "What?"

"The *money!*" several of them bellowed at once, and the child, as if frightened, whirled away.

The adults stood for a moment, watching the blue hooded figure get smaller and smaller in the distance. The ice was white and smooth and, because of the constant wind, scraped free of snow, so that the blue figure of the child and the red bobhouse way beyond stood out sharply. The sky, the color of a dirty sheet, stretched over the lake, and lumpy gray hills lay like a rumpled blanket between the ice below and sky above. Slowly, the people drifted back to their trailers, until only the child's mother and her friend Marcelle remained at the shore. Once, the child stopped and turned back, and the mother waved, and the little girl went back to trudging toward the bobhouse. Then the mother and her friend walked to the mother's trailer together.

"Kid's got a mind of her own," Marcelle said, lighting a cigarette off Doreen's gas stove. "Just like my kids used to be."

"Why do you think I let her go all the way out there alone?" Doreen asked.

"You can only protect them so much."

"I know," Doreen said sighing. "Otherwise you got 'em clinging to you the rest of your life."

"Yeah."

*   *   *

THE CHILD MAUREEN TIEDE PUSHED THE DOOR OF THE
bobhouse open an inch and peeked inside. The wind had
come up sharply and the snow was beginning to fall in
hard, dry flecks. Maureen's face was red and wet from
tears. Outside, a rag of smoke trailed from the chimney,
but inside the bobhouse it was as dark as inside a hole in
the ground and, except for the howl of the wind, silent.
The little girl let the door close again and backed
away from it as if there were no one there. For a few
moments she stood outside, looking first across the ice
to the trailerpark, then at the closed door of the bobhouse.
At the trailerpark, the frozen beach was deserted. The
trailers, their pastel colors washed to shades of gray in
the dim light, sat like two parallel rows of matchboxes.
Finally, Maureen moved toward the door and pushed it
open once again, wider this time, so that a swatch of
light fell into the bobhouse and revealed the hooked
shape of the old man seated at the end of the bunk. He
was squinting out of his darkness at the open door and
the child beyond.

"Come inside," Merle said.

The girl stepped carefully over the high threshold and,
on closing the door behind her, realized that, while she
could no longer make out the old man, the place was not
entirely dark, for an eerie green light drifting from circles cut in the ice was bright enough to cast shadows
against the ceiling and walls. Immediately, Maureen
backed up to the bunk, and holding to it with both hands
stared down at the holes in the ice, looked through the
ice and saw the fluid, moving world there—tall, slender
weeds and broadleaf plants drifting languorously back
and forth, schools of minnows and bluegills gathering,
swirling skittishly away from one another, then, as if at
a prearranged signal, quickly regathering. The little girl

was mesmerized by the sight, possibly even reassured or comforted by it, for she seemed to relax. She pulled off her mittens and stuffed them into the pockets of her snowsuit, then untied and pushed back her hood, all the while keeping her gaze fixed on the world beneath the ice, the world that moved beneath the cold, granitic, wind-blown world here above.

"All by yourself today?" Merle asked quietly from his corner by the stove.

Maureen nodded her head and said nothing.

Merle queried the child for a few moments, discovered that she was not lost, that her momma knew where she was, and that she had never seen anyone fish through the ice before. "Well, you just sit still with me," he told her, "and before long your momma or somebody else from the park will be out here looking for you. It's snowing here and ought to be there, too. That'll bring 'em out to get you."

By now she had her snowsuit off and was seated cross-legged on the bunk. She had said very little, answering Merle's questions with yes or no and nothing more.

Her silence seemed to please him. "You're a nice kid," he said, and for the first time in months, he smiled.

After a while, Maureen lay back on the bunk against the old man's blanket roll and fell asleep. Outside, the wind moaned and drove the snow against the ice and across the ice, piling it in long, soft drifts along the shore. The sky had closed in, and even though it was still early in the afternoon, it seemed like evening. Every now and then, Merle tossed a chunk of wood into the stove, lit his pipe, took a sip of whiskey, and checked his lines.

*   *   *

IT WAS DARK OUTSIDE AND SNOWING HEAVILY, WHEN THE door was suddenly shoved open, and Maureen's mother, her boyfriend Claudel right behind her, stepped into the tiny chamber, filling the crowded space to overflowing, so that Claudel had to retreat quickly. There were others outside, their heads bobbing and craning behind Doreen for a look the instant Claudel could be got out of the way.

Merle had lit the kerosene lantern and had prepared a supper of fried bass filets, boiled greens pulled from the lake bottom, and tea in his only cup for the child, whiskey from the bottle for himself.

Doreen, in her hooded parka crusted with snow, embraced her child. "Thank God you're all right!" The little girl pulled away. "I don't know what got into me!" Doreen cried. "Letting you out of my sight for a minute on a day like this!"

Maureen stared down at the holes in the ice, which were dark now.

"She insisted on coming out here to visit you, Mr. Ring, and I said no, but the second my back was turned so I could do the laundry, she was gone. It never occurred to us that she'd come out *here*, till later this afternoon, when the snow started building up. I thought she was just playing around the park somewhere . . ."

Merle went on eating, quite as if the woman weren't there.

"She's probably been telling you all *kinds* of stories!"

Merle said nothing.

"Did you, honey?" she asked her daughter. "Have you been telling Mr. Ring here all kinds of stories about us?"

The child pouted and shook her head from side to side. "No," she said. "I just wanted to watch him fish. I fell asleep," she added, as if to reassure her mother.

The door swung open, letting in a blast of cold air and

blowing snow. It was Terry's face this time, and he said in a rush, "Listen, we're freezing out here, we got to get moving or we're gonna freeze to death. Everything okay?" he asked, peering at Doreen, at the child and then at Merle. "You know," he said to Doreen, winking. "Everything okay?"

Behind him, Bruce's pale face bobbed up and down as he tried to get a glimpse of the interior, and behind Bruce, several more figures moved about impatiently.

"Yes, yes, Terry, for Chrissakes!" Doreen hissed. "Just give me a minute, will ya?" She pushed against the door to close it, but another hand from the other side shoved back.

It was Captain Knox, his square face in the gentle light cast by the lantern scarlet and angry, clenched like a fist inside the fur-lined hood of his parka. "Ring!" he barked. "This time you've gone too far! Kidnapping! A federal offense, Ring."

"Get the hell outa here!" Doreen shouted. Merle, wide-eyed and silent, watched from the far corner. Someone grabbed the captain from behind and pulled him away, and Doreen slammed the door shut again. The sound of bodies bumping violently against the outside walls of the bobhouse, shouts, cries—all got caught in the steady roar of the wind and borne away.

"The goddamn old fool!"

"Let me talk to him, let *me!*"

"Get off! Get off my legs, goddammit!"

The door was flung open yet again, and this time it was Marcelle who was shouting, her voice high and full of fear and anger. "Doreen, get the kid dressed and get the hell out of here so I can talk sense to this crazy old man!" She pushed her way through the doorway, her bulk jamming Doreen against the wall. Maureen had started to cry, then to shriek, and now to wail. Leon LaRoche called to her, "Little girl, little girl, don't cry!"

and he pushed his way in behind Marcelle, only to have Terry throw an arm around his neck and drag him backward onto the ice.

"Asshole!" Terry snarled.

"Get off my legs, young man!" It was the Captain shouting at Bruce.

Noni Hubner started screeching. "This is insane! You're all insane!" while her mother Nancy pulled Terry away from Leon and cried, "That's all you people know, violence!"

"Get your hands off him!" Carol warned. "And what the hell do you mean, 'you people'?" she sneered, bringing her face up close to Nancy's.

Nancy slapped the woman's face, then started to bawl and, tears freezing on her cheeks, collapsed to the ice, moaning, "Oh, my God, I'm sorry. I'm so sorry."

The door to the bobhouse, held back by the press of the people inside, was wide open now, and the light from inside cast a flickering, orange glow over the ice. Claudel, a pint bottle in his hand, clearly drunk, sat a ways from the others with his legs splayed as if he had been thrown there from above. He got himself up on his feet, wobbled for a second and made for the bobhouse, holding his bottle out before him. "Hey! Merle! Lemme talk to 'im! Let's have a drink, Merle, an' we'll git this whole fuckin' thing all straightened out! Lemme talk to 'im. Me 'n' him unnerstan' each other," he said, pawing at Marcelle's shoulder.

Marcelle turned and shoved the man back, and he careened into the darkness. "You just wanta get on his good side, you leech!" she shrieked at the man. Bruce was trying to slide through the doorway past the woman's large body, but she bumped him against the jamb with her chest. "Hold it, pal."

"No, man, just let me cool things out, just give me a few minutes . . ." he whined.

"Keep the hippy away from him!" bellowed Captain Knox.

". . . safe-keeping . . ." came a wail from Nancy Hubner. "Just for safe-keeping!"

"Mother's right! Listen to my mother!"

"Get the cigar box!" Leon LaRoche shouted. "It's in the cigar box!"

Terry was on his hands and knees squeezing between Bruce's and Marcelle's legs, one long arm snaking behind Doreen, and then he had it, the cigar box, the money.

Doreen saw him. "Gimme that thing!" She reached for the box.

"I'll take it!" Marcelle cried. "I'm the manager, I'm the one who's responsible for everything!"

Bruce made a grab at the box, grimly and silently. Behind him, Leon had reached in, and the Captain had his hand stuck out, while the others, Nancy, her daughter Noni, the nurse Carol and poor, drunk Claudel, tugged at people's shoulders and backs, trying to pull them away from the door. The wind howled, and the people shouted and swore, and the child wept, and Merle watched, wide-eyed and in silence, while the cigar box went from hand to hand, like a sacred relic, until, as it passed through the doorway, it flapped open and spilled its contents into the wind, scattering the suddenly loose bills into the darkness. People screamed and grabbed at the bills that in a second were gone, driven instantly into the darkness by the wind. Scrambling after the money, the people quickly slipped on the ice and fell over one another and cursed one another, and then were suddenly silent. The box lay open and empty in the circle of light outside the door. The people all lay sprawled on the ice in the darkness just beyond. At the door, holding it open, stood Merle and the little girl. The child was confused, but Merle was weeping.

*   *   *

HERE IS WHAT HAPPENED AFTERWARD. ALL THE RESIDENTS of the trailerpark, except Merle, went back to their trailers that night. By dawn, of course, they all, except for Merle, were out on the ice again, searching for the money. They worked alone and as far from one another as possible, poking through snowdrifts along the shore, checking among the leafless bushes and old dead weeds, the bits of driftwood frozen into the lake, rocks and other obstructions, all the likely places. No doubt many or even all the residents of the trailerpark found money that day, and the next and the next, until one morning, as if by pre-arrangement, no one showed up on the ice. The people who had jobs went back to them; those who ordinarily stayed home did so. No one ever told anyone else whether he or she had been lucky enough to find some of the lost, wind-blown hundred dollar bills, so it's possible that no one, in fact, had been that lucky. More likely, some were and some weren't, but all were ashamed of having tried to acquire it. Besides, everyone had seen up close what happens when your neighbors find out that you have been luckier, even by a little, than they have been.

Merle, naturally, stayed on at the bobhouse for the few weeks of winter that remained. In early March, the ice began to soften and turn mushy in places. Gauzy fogs hung over the wet, pearlescent surface of the lake, obscuring the bobhouse from the trailerpark and erasing the opposite shore altogether. Before long, V's of Canada geese were passing northward overhead, and then, at the weirs, a narrow wedge of open water appeared. Long, shallow pools of water lay resting on top of the ice, swelling and spreading in the sunlight, while beneath the ice deep, dark, slowly warming water chewed its way patiently toward the surface, which gradually got blotchy- and pale green and then actually broke away from itself in places, making fissures and wide, tipping plates.

No one knew the exact day Merle left the bobhouse, but one morning there was a sheet of open water where the bobhouse had been, dark water sparkling under the morning sun, and Merle himself was seen by several people that same day outside his trailer somberly scraping the bottom of his old dark green rowboat.

He built another bobhouse the following winter, and as usual spent most of the winter inside it. He never spoke of the lottery money, and you can be sure that no one else ever mentioned it to him, either. Until now, that is, when Merle seems to have gotten over his despair and the others their shame.

About the Author

Russell Banks is the author of THE BOOK OF JAMAICA; FAMILY LIFE; SEARCHING FOR SURVIVORS; THE NEW WORLD; HAMILTON STARK; and THE RELATION OF MY IMPRISONMENT. He has won Guggenheim and National Endowment for the Arts fellowships, the St. Lawrence Award for Fiction, and Fels, O. Henry, and Best American Short Story awards. He lives in Brooklyn, New York.

NEVIL SHUTE...
At His Best